I0760871

A Brief, Interminable Peace

Alexis Carew
Book 7

J.A. Sutherland

Darkspace Press

A BRIEF, INTERMINABLE PEACE
Alexis Carew #7

by J.A. Sutherland

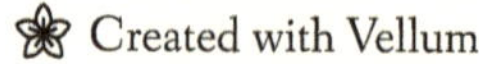

For my Patreon supporters
You guys stuck with me through a hard time and I can never repay your encouragement, understanding, and support.
I'll try to make the rest of my writing career worthy of you.

Chapter One

Alexis Arleen Carew eyed her enemy with only the slightest narrowing of her eyes to show her displeasure.

She remained still, patient, for a moment, then exploded into movement.

Her right hand went to the ancient revolver at her side, drawing and raising it, her left coming up close behind to cup and steady the butt of the heavy gun's grip.

Her eyes narrowed more, vainly attempting to squint away the bit of a blur that plagued the vision in her right eye.

The tendons in her right hand twinged at her grip on the pistol and from the added stress of having to use her thumb to pull back the hammer.

The sights aligned and her trigger finger tightened.

She didn't consciously hear the sound of the shot, concentrating instead on the muscles in her forearm, which stabbed with pain as she fought the heavy, bucking pistol down, thumb to hammer, for a second shot.

Third, fourth, and fifth followed shortly after, each with its own stab of pain from her ring finger, along the back of her hand, and up her forearm, but she bulled through, ignoring the discomfort.

One bullet left of six, a ridiculously small number by modern standards, but all this thing would hold, given the massive size of the black-powder cartridges it required.

"Buggering, Dark-damned, cunny-thumbed, cack-handed, *bastard*," she muttered, striding forward to approach her target, keeping the pistol raised and thumbing the hammer back for her one remaining shot.

She placed the pistol's barrel directly against the still-intact melon, taken from a nearby wild patch, that sat atop the chest-high stump of a lightning blasted tree. The damned stump itself was still mostly intact as well — or as intact as it had been before she started.

She'd not only missed the bloody melon, but everything around it, sending all five shots across the bit of empty space between this clearing and the tree-covered slope she'd chosen as a backstop for her shooting.

Alexis pulled the trigger, shattering the melon into a quite satisfying number of pieces, even if it was from point-blank range.

"Satisfied, *ma petite*?" Delaine Theibaud asked from his place on a blanket near their tent and fire, several meters away.

She couldn't tell, given his accent, whether his tone was amusement or if he was simply being French.

"I used to be able to strike such a target five times out of six with this pistol — since I was ten years old, mind you. Not so quickly, I'll admit, but my aim was true." She thumbed open the cylinder to dump the still-hot brass casings into her hand, juggling them a bit to cool them, making certain she didn't drop one as the grass here was high and there was a dry undergrowth, then made her way toward Delaine.

"You have done well with your flechettes," Delaine reminded her. "That ... *antique* —"

Alexis hid a smile, knowing he'd deliberately pronounced the word as French, even though it had been stolen all entire into English, to deliberately tweak her.

"— is nearly a full kilogram, is it not?"

"A bit more when fully loaded," Alexis allowed.

She reached the blanket where he reclined. Their horses were a few dozen meters away, doing their very best to ensure that no one would need to worry about the long grass here for some time — saddles off and draped over a convenient rock *far* away from where Alexis had spent the morning shooting.

"And it pulls up like a horse who's scented a bearcat nearby."

Alexis suppressed a smile. While Delaine's horse had pulled up quite a bit on their way here, it was more a matter of an inexperienced rider than any fear on the horse's part.

"A modern pistol will weigh a third that — a laser less, and your flechette less still," Delaine said. "You strain yourself to no end — when will you ever have use for such a thing? The cartridges are not even fully sealed for vacuum, so you will not use it aboard ship, *non*?"

Alexis dumped her empty casings into a sack with the others and glanced at the rounds remaining in the box she'd started the morning with — enough for one more reload, but ... she holstered the ancient revolver and flexed her hand. More pain from hand to elbow — perhaps she'd overdone things as it was — fatigue would surely explain how poorly her last attempt had gone.

"No, but I won't always have the choice of weapons," Alexis said, "and a boarding cutlass has this weight and more if I'm to turn an enemy's blow." She shrugged. "The doctors say the surgeries have done as much as may be done, and both arm and eye should return to normal, but it's been *months*." She sighed, flexing her fingers.

"I can't yet tell if it's all the arm or the eye," she muttered, blinking again.

Both her right arm and eye had been injured in an explosion on Penduli Station. Ostensibly a bomb attack by Gaelic separatists, though that group's efforts to divorce themselves from the kingdom of New London had been merely political for decades. She'd come to believe the nearly unstated theory of Malcome Eades, the Foreign Office spy who'd got her into her last predicament in the first place —

And more than one before that, she thought. *Perhaps it might be best to avoid the man in future.*

— that the Gaelics were a poor subterfuge by the real culprits, the Marchant Company, and their effort to hide involvement with piracy and slavery in the Barbary worlds, something Alexis had discovered in her adventures there.

Or that Captain Skanes discovered.

That Skanes, a former Marchant captain who'd been about to testify to that very thing before an Admiralty board of inquiry, had perished in the bomb blast did seem to lend credence to Eades' theory.

For her own part, though the doctors had said she'd "fully recover" from her own injuries, those reassurances were now months in the past and she still couldn't shoot a bloody melon off a bloody stump.

"It's not enough I be adequate with a tiny flechette pistol," she said, though she'd done well enough with that weapon a time or two in the past. "If I'm going to recover, I want to bloody *recover*, do you understand?"

"*Oui, ma colombe*, but also you do push yourself."

Alexis sighed, but he did have a point. She'd shot a rather large number of rounds that morning — and the morning before, and before. Nearly any time she might do so safely on this trip, in addition to every day while she'd been back at her grandfather's farm. Her work with everything but the heavy, antique revolver had improved, though she wasn't quite ready to admit she was back in her previous form — there was still a tremor in her hand and a blur to her vision.

"Perhaps you're right," she allowed, "though my sword work does have much of a way to go still."

"*Non*," Delaine said, standing and holding out his hands palm up. "I will not spar with you again this morning. The day is warming, and I wish to swim."

His hands went to his shirt fasteners and half opened them, exposing sun-browned skin that spoke to just how much time he'd spent without that shirt while visiting her here on her home world of Dalthus IV.

Her own skin had browned as well, giving up the paleness spacers took on.

Delaine turned and strode toward the stream-fed pond at the opposite end of the clearing. Denim trousers soon followed shirt, and drawers after that, which made Alexis grin at the evidence of how much else of Delaine had been exposed to Dalthus' sun. She rose and followed after him, though not so quickly as to catch up and spoil the view.

Delaine strode into the water until it reached his thighs, then dove forward to reach deeper water and make his way toward the pool's middle.

It was nearly a hundred meters across at the widest, and twice that long, fed by a waterfall from the hills and cliffs upslope, and then draining by a long, meandering stream that ran down into the valley, side by side with the trail leading there.

Alexis stripped her own clothes off, though she draped hers carefully over a rock instead of haphazardly tossing them about as Delaine had done. The French captain didn't have a judgmental steward and clerk who'd sniff and roll his eyes at every bit of dirt or grass stain Alexis returned home with — or, worse, a rip to mend.

She wasn't about to wade in, either. Despite the hot sun overhead, that water coming down off the mountains was bloody cold.

No, some things are best done quickly, she thought, climbing up a larger rock near where she'd set her clothes — this one had a ledge that overlooked deeper water, and the sun-warmed stone was almost hot against her bare feet as she climbed.

At its edge, she was three meters above the water and able to look down on Delaine as he swam, his body perfectly visible through the clear water.

She gripped the stone's edge with her toes, bent her knees, and dove, arching her back and spreading her arms before her leap stalled and she began to fall. She bent and tucked, bringing her arms to meet above her head and split the cold water an instant before the rest of her entered it.

And it was *cold*, tightening every bit of her skin and nearly driving the breath from her.

She dove deep until she was at the bottom, all gravel, rocks, and bits of weeds there. The occasional dim, scurrying form of a fish fled at her approach, then swam toward where Delaine had been.

The cold and effort made her right forearm ache, but this was more the strain of decent work than the hurt she'd felt firing the pistol.

Lungs near bursting, she tucked her legs up, felt the rocky bottom beneath her feet and drove herself toward the surface, popping free of the water with a loud exhale and gulp of air before she put her head down and swam along the surface toward Delaine.

Chapter Two

Later, after swimming, some other activities brought on by swimming in their particular state, taking advantage of their isolation, and a bit of a second dip to refresh themselves from the other activities, Alexis found herself nestled against Delaine's side, his back resting against the side of the rock Alexis had climbed. One of their heavy saddle pads cushioned his back and he cushioned much of Alexis, which, all things considered, she thought an equitable distribution of such comforts.

The sun was warm on those parts of her not warmed by Delaine, but an intermittent, cool breeze played around them, sometimes raising goosebumps before disappearing for a time.

Forest sounds returned slowly as they remained still, only just audible over the sound of the waterfall. One of their horses nickered softly, then the other answered.

They were close enough to the waterfall that it scented the air, along with nearby patches of wildflowers and the rough, comfortable smell of horse from the pad Delaine rested against. Underneath all that was the slightly acrid, but still homey, trace of their campfire —

banked to coals for the day, but sitting ready for new life with their evening meal.

All in all, Alexis considered it a well-spent afternoon.

"This blanket smells of horse," Delaine said.

Alexis caught her lower lip between her teeth to keep from giggling.

Delaine had ridden little before coming home with her to Dalthus, and had yet to develop any real fondness for the animals.

Their ride up to this spot from the Arundel estates, her mother's family lands, had been a chore for him, even at the slow, meandering pace she'd set. Though the aches in unused muscles had provided her with opportunities to alleviate those as well.

"After a week, I imagine we do as well," she murmured.

"*Non*, we, at least, may wash." He sniffed. "A thing which will do this no good, I think."

Alexis sniffed as well. "I rather like the smell."

Delaine sighed. "You would, *ma chérie*." He scratched at his leg with the hand that wasn't wrapped around Alexis. "All of outdoors, it seems."

Now she did giggle. "One can't spend all of one's life aboard ship, despite your having been born on a station."

"One may aspire," Delaine said, "to a place that does not bite."

Alexis latched her teeth onto the nearest bit of flesh. "Really?" she asked.

Delaine drew in a sharp breath. "That is ... *très différent*."

"*Vive la différence*," Alexis whispered, releasing him with her teeth, then running fingers lightly over the spot.

Delaine brought the hand he'd scratched himself with back to its proper place around her, something Alexis thought quite overdue, given their current state.

"*Oui*."

Dinner, when they got around to it, was roast rabbit, taken from the thick brush at the top of the waterfall that morning and now on a spit over the fire. More than one of the things had gotten loose from some settler's farm since the founding of Dalthus, and they'd managed to find each other to then breed like ... well, rabbits, despite the native predator or two that cared naught for being unable to properly digest them.

Whatever of the native plants the rabbits themselves found to eat had never been determined, but there must be something for the population to have spread so far from human farms they might raid.

Potatoes, thrust into the coals at the edge of the fire, made up the other half of the meal.

"You must admit," Alexis said, continuing the conversation which had been rightly interrupted earlier, "that this smells better than shipboard fare."

Delaine nodded, or she assumed so from the feel of his head moving next to hers. She was in his lap, with the fire warming her front and him warming her back, and quite cozy.

He took a hand from around her to grasp his cup of wine and sip, something she'd forgive him for, provided he returned the hand to its proper place once he'd drunk.

"*Oui*," Delaine said. "I do not miss the vat-grown meats when I am ... ah, *en anglais*, in atmosphere, *oui*? But a ship, she has other things to her credit."

Alexis sighed. "*Oui*," she agreed.

She supposed, aside from teasing Delaine, which was quite enjoyable, the back and forth had more to do with her own growing desire to be back aboard a ship — and her growing certainty that she'd not be allowed that by New London's Admiralty.

After returning from Erzurum, the pirate world in the Barbary where she'd done everything she could to rescue the enslaved spacers of Admiral Chipley's lost fleet, the boards of inquiry assembled at Penduli Station had punted the whole mess up to Admiralty itself and there'd been no word yet of their decisions.

It had been a right mess, she allowed.

First there'd been the dubious nature of her own commission, coming from status as a privateer to Royal Navy command by virtue of the ostensible senior captain on station, himself one of the newly freed captives, ordering her recalled to service. Then disobeying ... or, at best, questioning his orders they sail immediately for New London space, abandoning the tens of thousands of spacers still captive on the planet.

That she'd got around that by virtue of Lieutenant Deckard's self-sacrifice in holding Captain Ellender at gunpoint until his ship was safely away in *darkspace* could, in an uncharitable light, be cast as conspiracy to mutiny.

She'd then — through a tortuous legal justification thought up by her former legal clerk turned captain's steward, Isom — named herself returned to service and now senior in system herself.

That should have been enough for Admiralty to hang her, even without the subsequent pardoning of thousands of pirates *and* paying them bounties on the released naval spacers from three different starnations — her own New London, the French Republic, and their oft-times enemy, the Republic of Hanover.

Thousands of murdering, raping, pillaging pirates pardoned and released, with notes-in-hand drawn on Admiralty funds and totaling, if Isom's maths were to be believed ... well, an amount she'd rather not think about.

All under her signature as senior officer in-system ... and in the Queen's name.

If there'd ever been a more singular stretch of an officer's power in New London's history, Lieutenant Alexis Arleen Carew couldn't fathom how she'd not heard about it.

Well, I suppose they might have dropped the poor bastard down a privy somewhere and sealed things up behind him ... or set him to some escort for an indenture convoy the rest of his career so there'd be no further excitement.

The captains and admirals at Penduli Station — no few of them and none, at least in this, fools — having sent the mess to New London itself and told her someone would, surely, be in touch about the consequences once they found a way to hang such an overstepping officer the proper number of times ... Alexis had taken the opportunity to travel home to Dalthus.

And here she'd sat, for near six months, even after the time to reach home from Penduli, with no word at all.

No news is good news, I warrant, she thought, *when the news is the sort I'm expecting.*

At least she had Delaine here — the French captain being, as it were, at loose ends himself, what with his former fleet, from the Berry March in Hanover, not having been properly brought in to either the New London fold or the French Republic's after the ill-fated attempt at freeing those worlds.

After all she'd done, though, she expected the best she should hope for would be to have her commission withdrawn and her naval career over, without, her being a lieutenant and not a captain, even the dubious benefit of being Yellow Squadroned off to some shore posting.

That would be hard to accept. She'd never felt so alive as when in command of a ship in action, setting herself and her crew against some foe, sails and shot flashing light across the blacker-than-black background of *darkspace*.

She could, she supposed, go for a merchantman's berth if the navy dismissed her, though the thought didn't appeal so very much.

Much as she loved a ship, she didn't think she could take to the merchant service at all. Blandly plying the space between worlds, carrying goods and passengers, simply didn't compare to the thrill of battle — even despite the costs.

She'd much resigned herself that her career in the navy was over and thought she might — only just — be satisfied with managing the family lands here on Dalthus, provided she had Delaine with her. That had much to do with her questioning, she allowed — that he'd receive a renewed commission *somewhere* was almost certain. If New

London didn't make the offer, then surely the French Republic would, as it would be foolish to leave an officer of his caliber without a ship.

Soon he'd be made the offer and she'd face losing him for a time to the love of a ship, command, and the Dark — while she was left behind to deal with the lands and, seemingly, all of the planet's problems.

Since she'd been home, it seemed everyone wanted her assistance with some issue — her cousin, Lauryn Arundel, inexplicably in agreement with Edmon Coalson on the matter, wished her to throw her support behind a campaign to grant voting rights to former indentures, and the planet's chandler, Doakes, was not above calling her out at odd hours to assist with some matter in Port Arthur regarding rowdy gallenium miners in from the system's belt.

She could pass the latter along to Villars, her erstwhile midshipman, who was also at loose ends with no ship himself.

And, she had to admit, the occasional run into Dalthus' largest port town for a rousing dustup with drunken miners did tend to break the monotony.

"The rabbit is ready, I think, *ma colombe*," Delaine whispered.

Chapter Three

Morning brought an early light, the sun rising away from the cliffs and lower plains, along with birdsong — if one particularly off-note native species' call could be termed song.

Fire stoked again and a pot of oatmeal left to simmer, Alexis and Delaine took to the waters to be wakened by the chill.

Mid-pool, Alexis wrapped arms and legs around Delaine, letting him tread water for the both of them.

"I'm told my parents came here often," Alexis said, looking around to admire the place in the clear, morning air.

"It is *très beau*, I will allow," Delaine said. "You did not know them, *oui*?"

Alexis shook her head. "No more than as an infant. I was but three when they..." She paused. For most of her life she'd thought her parents died in an accident — until Daviel Coalson had confessed that he'd used one of the colony's antigrav haulers to spook their buggy's horse and drive them off the road. She was still not used to the thought of what he'd done — or of what she'd done to him in return, sending him out a ship's airlock in *darkspace*, hands bound so that he could not even dump his own air to end the suffering, to die the death most feared by spacers everywhere. "Were killed," she finished finally.

Delaine wrapped an arm around her tightly.

"In any case," Alexis said, "I'm told this was their favorite place. My father somehow got himself invited along on a bearcat hunt with mother's family and they were separated from the main party on the ride up. They stumbled upon this place ... it's where they first kissed, first..." She cleared her throat. "Did many things." A nip at Delaine's neck. "It's likely even where I was conceived."

Delaine cleared his throat. "Ah, *ma gazelle*, I —"

"I'm *not* suggesting a thing, silly goose," Alexis said, laughing. "It's only that this is a special place for me. I always feel ... closer to them, somehow, when I'm here." She looked around again. "These are Crown lands, I think, only abutting the Arundels', but I may speak to Uncle Sebastian about a trade of some sort for a bit of theirs that adjoins these — now I'm properly Grandfather's heir, I'd rather like to see this place protected."

"You do not trust the Arundels to do so?"

Alexis shrugged. "I don't know them well, truth be told. We had so little contact growing up and I've been away so very much on ships. Lauryn is a good sort — though misguided, I think, in her political efforts. Uncle Sebastian has no plans to develop the area, he says, but one never knows. It's ... I prefer to be certain of things."

"Much in life is uncertain, *Alexis*," Delaine said.

Alexis shivered. Say what you will about French pet names — which were many, varied, and, she must admit, did have a great deal to be said for them — there was something about her own name, spoken in Delaine's accent, that quite undid her.

"All the more reason to control what one may," she said after a time. "All my life, there've been others dictating my world — as a child, I suppose that's as it must be, but then, with our inheritance laws here such as they were, it seemed the whole planet was telling me what I must do. I *must* marry, you see? And in order to do so, I *must* be of a certain, proper sort — I *must* be a certain way, must speak a certain way, must even dress a certain way. Sweet Dark —" She laughed. "— you should have seen the awful dress Grandfather bought for me to wear while courting. It was sickeningly pink and, I swear, had more layers than the grandest wedding cake you might imagine."

"I am certain you were still beautiful," Delaine said, "even in pink layers."

"Pink is *not* my color," Alexis said sternly, "should you ever need to know such things. It clashes horribly with my eyes and isn't suited for my coloring. Deep jewel tones are far better. See? I do *know* a thing or two, even if my preference is for denim trousers and homespun. Regardless, I set that nonsense aside by joining the bloody navy — which, when one thinks about it, might not have been the best choice for someone who didn't want to be told what to do."

Delaine laughed.

"It's not that I object to orders," Alexis said, "so long as they aren't foolish ... or wrong ... or outright harmful."

That brought another laugh from Delaine. "When you are *Amiral de la Flotte*, you may forbid such things. Until then, you will find many *capitaines* who are unable to order else."

"If I'm ever made Admiral of the Fleet, I imagine a general signal will go out disbanding the whole bloody kingdom for having gone irredeemably mad. Captains everywhere ordering their midshipmen to the signals boards — *Carew is in charge. Imperative. Run away.*" She sighed. "No, even captain is likely out of reach now. It would have been a fine thing, though, to have a proper command."

Delaine chuckled. "Even *les capitaines* have *les amiraux*. Orders from fools are the way of the world."

"Well, I'm likely done with the wider range of fools and have only those here on Dalthus to worry about."

A sound drew Alexis' attention, and she looked up. It was a distant rumble, growing closer, and she quickly spotted the growing dot of an air vehicle of some sort. At first, she thought it one of the colony's still-few antigrav haulers — a newer one, larger than those she'd grown up around, but still a relative native to Dalthus.

Then it grew closer, weaving in its course like a hound searching for a scent, before circling their clearing and pool, and she could see that it was a ship's boat — an odd sight so far from any port city or farmstead.

The growing roar of the engines cut off abruptly and the craft drew closer, descending silently on its antigrav field, coasting the final bit to come overhead.

Before she and Delaine could even come to terms with this intrusion, the boat passed low over their pool, pivoted in midair with a rush of thrusters, then came to rest in the sky with a skillful, if loud, *blat* from the main engines to kill its last bit of momentum.

"Damn all pilots," Alexis muttered as the whinnies of their horses reached them.

The animals were used to haulers and ship's boats coming and going, but the sound of the main engines, rather than the quieter thrusters, must have startled them, coming so close overhead and after so many days in the more peaceful wilderness.

The boat settled to one side of their clearing — away from their camp, but taking up much of the available space. Its bulk pressed the vegetation flat and crushed several saplings at the forest's edge.

"We should see what's so bloody important," Alexis muttered, reluctantly releasing Delaine so that they might both swim toward shore.

A figure exited the boat, and, between strokes, Alexis could see he wore a uniform, though different to a naval one.

Delaine's longer arms and legs soon outpaced her, and he neared shore just as the arriving figure did. Alexis slowed her own pace, so that she could lift her head from the water and hear.

"I'm looking for a Lieutenant Carew!" the figure called. Now Alexis could make out the man's uniform in more detail — it was a lighter shade of blue than a naval uniform, but still dark, and with only a bit of gilt at the lapels, with a sort of peaked hat instead of the naval beret. "Alexis Arleen Carew, Royal Navy — if there's more than one of them about and you need to know the distinguishing bits!"

"*Oui*, you have found us," Delaine called back.

"What? Both of you? I only just need the one, as I said!"

Alexis had reached near enough to the shore that she could set her feet to the bottom, provided she stretched them out and used only her toes. She worked her way shoreward that way so that she could hear better.

"I'm Lieutenant Carew," she called.

The figure pointed at Delaine. "Why'd he say 'we', then?"

"He's French," Alexis said, nearly even with Delaine now, though, she noted, the water which covered her to the neck still only reached his chest.

The figure frowned. "Heard about them."

Alexis paused near Delaine, any further and both of them would be showing the intruder more than he'd come for.

"What is it you require of me, sir?" she asked.

The figure cleared his throat. "Sorry, lieutenant. Captain Kayser, RMS *Carpathia*. You're Lieutenant Alexis Arleen Carew, Royal Navy, are you?"

"I am, Captain Kayser."

Kayser pulled a tablet from his coat. "I've messages for you to sign for ... and a bloody visitor."

Alexis frowned. The Royal Mail ships were fast cutters, set to designated routes and carrying the vast correspondence which kept the kingdom running.

Most everyday messages might be carried by any ship — merchant, navy, or private — heading in a particular direction, loaded aboard its electronic systems and streamed to the planet at the proper stop. One could never be sure, though, if a merchant captain might change his plans, so a single ship was never trusted — the mails were uploaded to nearly every ship heading toward the destination, over and over, until a response returned that each had been received at the proper system. It made for a great deal of duplication — and Alexis sometimes wondered what the oldest message floating around the universe might be, buried deep within some ancient ship's systems and awaiting an arrival that would never come.

More reliable — and more costly — were the Royal Mail routes, where each ship had set destinations and could veritably guarantee, hazards of the Dark aside, delivery in a timely manner.

She hadn't heard that Dalthus had got a stop on some route before this, though. Most ended at Zariah and the final bits toward the farther, fringeward, colony worlds were left to what merchant traffic there was.

Still, if they had been added to a route, which she supposed was reasonable given the new importance of the system and their gallenium resources, she'd still never heard of signing for a message before. The things were usually just downloaded to planet and distributed to the recipient's tablet as soon as the ship carrying them could transmit — often, in her experience, at the most inconvenient time for the tablet's owner.

"Can you just transmit it to my tablet?" Alexis asked. "It's just there in our saddlebags —"

Kayser drew his shoulders up and lifted his chin. "This is a guaranteed, Lieutenant," he said. "Signature and thumb required." He waved his own tablet about. "And I've other work to be about, if you please."

"Captain Kayser," Alexis said, patiently as she might. "We're a bit..." She waggled her fingers just under the surface so as to send up spray. "Indisposed, if you take my meaning."

Kayser rolled his eyes. "Ah, well, pardon me, Lieutenant, for interrupting your morning splish, but someone's gone to the trouble of sending you a guaranteed, and I've need of a signature and thumbprint. Already flitted about this planet more than I should have to in finding you."

"Perhaps you wouldn't mind returning to your ship's boat for a moment, then?" Alexis asked.

She couldn't get to her tablet or thumb the captain's without leaving the water, and, clear though it might be, it did mask her lack of clothing. Alexis wasn't particularly body-conscious — the homestead village's swimming hole saw people bathing in all sorts of states, and aboard ship one couldn't remain too very modest for long when the wardroom's tiny shower meant a towel-wrapped walk through the common area both ways — but neither did she wish Captain Kayser to think she was brazenly strutting about.

Kayser glanced back at his boat. "I'm right here now, aren't I?"

"Captain Kayser, it's only that, you see —"

"I'm the bloody Royal Mail, Lieutenant, I've a schedule to keep and between haring off to find you and your visitor refusing —"

Delaine strode forward a few steps until water churned white at mid-thigh. He cocked his head at Kayser and gave one of his very Gallic shrugs.

Kayser's eyes grew wide and Alexis could see the red rise up from neck to face even at a distance.

"Oh." He looked from Delaine to Alexis, still neck deep in the pool, though the water, she supposed, was quite clear enough if one concentrated. Kayser's eyes grew wider and face redder. "It's, uh, that way is it? Oh."

He spun about.

"I'll just speak to my pilot for a moment, shall I?"

"Thumb here," Kayser said, holding his tablet out to Alexis. "And here." He swiped at the screen himself. "Here and here." Another swipe. "Here."

Alexis pressed her thumb to his screen each time he indicated. "Is the receipt longer than the message, do you suppose?"

"There're reasons, let me tell you," Kayser said. "You'd be surprised what folks try to put past the mail service." He paused. "Here and here, if you please, Lieutenant."

Alexis pressed the screen again.

"That's all then," Kayser said. He tapped his screen a few more times and Alexis' tablet pinged with receipt of a message.

"You said I had a visitor, as well, Captain Kayser?"

Kayser's mouth twisted in a grimace. "*That* one. Wouldn't come looking past your home, Lieutenant. Said he'd had enough of ships and boats both, and he'd spend some time on proper ground." He snorted. "And who was it asked him to board my ship in the first place? Not me, it wasn't."

"So he's awaiting me at home?" Alexis asked. "Who is he?"

Kayser shrugged. "I haven't a clue — only that he showed up at the Zariah quay when we docked and said he's 'commandeering' my ship to come here after you. Had the proper authorizations to do that, not that I've ever seen the like before. So comes aboard and wouldn't say another word about it — but he had plenty to say about my ship, and ships in general, let me tell you. If it weren't for that guaranteed already being aboard and having to come this far anyway, I'd have tossed him back on the quay — authorizations or no authorizations."

Alexis started to ask the visitor's name, then sighed. It was quite unnecessary to do so, as she could suspect who might take great pleasure in commandeering a service's ship to his own ends, with a juvenile delight at hacking into whatever systems might generate the necessary authorizations. "Malcome Bloody Eades," she muttered.

"What's that?" Kayser asked.

Alexis shook her head. "It's no matter what name he gave you, Captain Kayser, I can imagine who it is now that you've described his manner. The kingdom can't be so large as for there to be two like him, I'm certain."

"I'd hope not," Kayser said. "Well, if you know the man then you know what to expect, and that he's not like to be kept waiting. Strap in and we'll lift."

Alexis raised an eyebrow. "We'll have to pack up our camp first, Captain Kayser — and load the horses."

Kayser's face froze. "Horses?"

Alexis nodded. "Those large beasts just there. The ones eyeing your boat with a certain amount of distrust."

"Now, look, Lieutenant – this is a Royal Mail boat and while your visitor might have said to fetch you back, he didn't say a thing about horses." He waved a hand at Delaine. "Have your Frenchman here bring the horses back however you'd planned to and let's be on the go."

Alexis took Delaine's arm. She supposed it wasn't fair to Kayser – the Royal Mail captain clearly hadn't chosen to work with Eades toward the end of interrupting her time with Delaine, but neither was she willing to simply leave him. Not least because she couldn't imagine him managing to wrangle two horses and their gear out of the wilderness on his own.

"Then you may inform the guest you've brought me that we'll be along at our own pace, Captain Kayser."

Kayser's jaw hardened, then his shoulders slumped. Alexis felt a bit of sympathy for him, Eades and his demands had affected her similarly more than once.

"Trouble," Kayser muttered. "No one gets a guaranteed if they're anything but trouble." He turned to the cockpit and his pilot. "Open the cargo – we've bloody beasts to load if you can fathom it."

Under Captain Kayser's impatient eye, Alexis managed the fire and horses while Delaine packed the rest of their things.

The oatmeal breakfast, not quite done, went into the brush, where, no doubt, the rabbits rustling about in there would find it to their liking – and possibly a suitable offering in return for the brethren they'd given up. Fire well-doused, then covered in a layer of sand and mixed about until there were no embers left to come to life after they were gone, Alexis moved on to the horses.

Those had settled since the boat's engines fired overhead and were used to being loaded aboard such things. They went into the cargo box up the rear ramp with some enthusiasm, for they'd long ago learned that such a thing, coming when they were far from home, usually meant they were now bound for their own stalls and lazier days.

Neither Kayser nor his pilot helped with the loading of gear, leaving the saddles, packs, and other bags — none repacked with the precision Alexis might prefer, for they were in a hurry — to Alexis and Delaine.

Kayser's stern, hurried looks, though, did keep her from taking the time to check her tablet for the content of Kayser's "guaranteed" — time enough for that once they were in the air, though she suspected it would be related to whatever scheme Eades had in mind.

Once the boat was in the air, however, she had time to wonder at her certainty the visitor was Eades.

If it is *Malcome Bloody Eades whose drawn me away from time with Delaine I'll gut the man*, Alexis thought, staring at the boat's bulkhead at the front of the passenger compartment. *It would be just his nature to show up with some new, hare-brained scheme.*

Upon reflection, though, perhaps not — Eades, she suspected, would not have landed at her home. The Foreign Service man would have found it all too fine a show of his cleverness to track Alexis down in the wilderness and come directly to her, so that he might display his smug little smile at her reaction.

Neither was it likely to be Avrel Dansby, the roguish merchant, former, by his own accounts, pirate, but certainly still smuggler. That man would have arrived aboard one of his own ships, not taken passage with the mails.

The boat settled onto its course toward the Carew homestead and Alexis pulled her tablet from its pocket. Whatever the mystery of the visitor Captain Kayser'd brought her, she could find out what the bloody "guaranteed" contained.

She made to tap the screen, then stopped, finger poised, and an involuntary shiver ran through her.

Her grandfather joked about her grandmother having the Sight and, for a moment, Alexis didn't see a tablet in her hands, instead it seemed she reached toward a doorway, behind which she felt certain something lurked.

"*Mon cœur?*"

Alexis sat still, eyes still on her tablet, message unopened.

"*Alexis?*"

"We had such peace, for a time," she whispered, unable to shake the certainty that was about to change.

Chapter Four

"Two thousand forty-eight pounds, nineteen shillings, ten pence," Alexis murmured.

"And a half a farthing," Delaine added, reading over her shoulder.

Alexis shot him a look. "Don't you start."

"But what is this, *Alexis*?" he asked.

"I'm sued, or rather judged already, by the prize court at Zariah," she said, rereading the message, Kayser's "guaranteed," and trying to make some other sense of it. "They demand repayment."

Delaine's brow furrowed as he tried to make sense of the copy she'd sent to his tablet. "They are making no sense, talking of these two ships with the same name."

"It was one ship," Alexis said with a sigh. "My first voyage, on *Merlin*, saw us capture a pirate vessel called *Grapple*. I was sent aboard with a prize crew and set to following *Merlin* back to Zariah. It should have been a simple task, but there was a storm, and the pirates were locked in *Grapple's* hold where they had some sort of secret passage through the hold to the quarterdeck. They retook the ship during the storm and evaded *Merlin*, taking us, the prize crew, captive.

"We sailed about for some time — rather lost, as I'd rekeyed the ship's navigation systems and the pirates had no observations to work with for even estimating their position." She paused, silent for a long time. "We took the ship back," she said finally — no need to get into the details of how she'd seen, then, her first close look at the violent, intentional death of another when the spacer Robert Alan had taken the bullet meant for her and she'd shot the pirate captain in turn.

The details of that scene played out for her often enough in her dreams, no need at all to share them with Delaine and add to his own burdens.

Alexis shrugged. "We rejoined *Merlin* and thought no more of it, until the prize court's notice came." She sighed. "They'd gotten it all so mixed up — perhaps my own report was less than clear, I don't know. It was my first such thing to write, after all. In any case, they set about insisting that I'd been in command of a ship which captured *Grapple* — also named *Grapple*, you see, which added to the confusion. So they awarded the worth of one prize to the prize crew who already had her — *Merlin's* sailing master, a pair of spacers, and myself as the only survivors of the prize crew still aboard."

"Did you not correct them?"

Alexis gave Delaine a sharp look. "Give some thought to your own experiences with New London's worthies and ask yourself if you'd try."

"*Merde*," Delaine muttered after a moment.

"Indeed. Captain Grantham — everyone aboard *Merlin*, really — nearly fell apoplectic when I suggested we try to correct the mistake. Said we'd be tied up in the prize court for years trying to sort it out — including the awards on several other prizes taken by *Merlin*. Not a one of the crew objected — seemed to think they'd come out ahead in free drink by having the story in their pocket. '*Grapple*, the ship what took herself', so they said."

"And now this prize court wishes you to repay?" Delaine said.

Alexis nodded. "So it seems. I had an ... encounter some time ago with a member of the prize court there on Zariah when I commanded *Nightingale*, and we took a bit of a dislike to each other. He looked into my past and did say he'd see me punished in some way, so I expect he dug about in the records and found this."

Delaine scanned his tablet for a moment. Alexis closed hers — she'd read enough, and they were nearing home.

"I am sorry, *Alexis*, this is a grand sum."

Alexis waved that away. "I'm not concerned with the funds — I suppose I have enough for that set aside. I'll have to ask Isom."

"You do not know?"

"Isom handles the prize money for me, but there's been far more since I was aboard *Merlin*. Some few prizes from my time on *Hermione*, with whatever they gave me for that tub I brought the lads home in. I think some head and gun money was awarded for them, as well — the officers, at least. Can't imagine Captain Neals would have brought more than another quarter-farthing at auction, but they may have put some value on the bastard." She sighed. "Privateering prizes from the Barbary, though Dansby got the larger cut of those as *Elizabeth's* owner." She frowned. "I suppose there might be similar head monies for the prisoners kept on Erzurum ... no, I expect they would have kept that to offset the bounties I authorized." She shrugged again. "Isom will know for certain."

She caught Delaine looking at her, eyebrows raised.

"Oh, don't look at me like that — I've not had need to follow such things, have I? It's not as though I can bring a suite of luxuries aboard ship. My needs aren't so great that I'd have spent all of it — in fact, I doubt I've spent my pay most cruises. So long as there's a bit of cheese and fresh meat in the pantry, I let Isom deal with the settling of the funds. He's far cleverer than I'd be at such things, I'm sure." She turned her gaze forward. "No, there's more than enough to pay that back, I have no doubt, and since it'd be redistributed to *Merlin's* crew as the proper takers of *Grapple*, I've no cause to be upset about the underlying idea. I'd have given it to them at the time if they hadn't refused it."

"Then what bothers you so?"

Alexis' jaw clenched. "The same thing that kept me from questioning the court at the time — it's not just my award they've gone after, it's the others' as well." She held up her tablet. "The sailing master, Mister Gorbett, was to use his share to buy a pub somewhere and settle down, do you suppose he's four hundred pounds set aside to repay this now? And what about Peters? He was but an able spacer with a full eighth dropped in his lap. Whatever he's done with the funds, he's got one of these bloody judgments coming to his hand too, and likely no way to pay the amount. They're even — cack-brained idiots that they are — going against Robert Alan's share, and he's bloody dead!"

"Who has those funds?"

"The crew of *Merlin*." Alexis clenched her fists at the absurdity of what had been written in that message. "The court must have called up *Merlin's* log and seen the report of the disbursements and seen who it went to in the end, so they've named every bloody member of the ship's crew in this judgment, demanding that —" She ripped her tablet from its pocket and quickly scrolled to the proper bit, wanting to get the idiocy exactly right.

"'The recipients of Robert Alan's four hundred nine pounds, fifteen shillings, eleven and a half-pence, one-half farthing, the crew of HMS *Merlin*, herein named individually, shall repay said sums in the amounts indicated below, forthwith, and with calculated penalties and interests, so that this court may properly distribute the awards to their deserving recipients and takers of the prize *Grapple* —'" Alexis paused, unable to believe she was voicing what was written there. "'— to the proper takers of that prize, the crew of HMS *Merlin*.'"

Alexis glanced up from her tablet to find Captain Kayser turned about in his cockpit seat to stare at her, brow furrowed and mouth part open.

"Yes, that look exactly," she agreed. "They've gone and done it again, confusing one ship for two, so are demanding the lads give back the prize money they've already got, so it can be divided up and given back to them. All with a bit sticking to the prize court's fingers, no doubt — certainly to their allies who're prize agents, as they'll insist on good, hard coin from my lads, then they'll issue their bloody certificates back and demand the lads collect on Zariah itself, no matter where the bloody fleet's sent them now, or sell at a discount to some agent." She shoved her tablet back into its pocket. "If this is the sort of ruling the prize courts can make, I shudder at what must happen in the criminals."

Alexis frowned. With the idiocy of this missive, she began to wonder if her mysterious visitor might not be Eades at all, but might be a representative of the Zariahn Prize Court, come to demand payment in person.

Well, if it is, she thought, *it's more than payment I'll give him.*

Chapter Five

Kayser's boat landed and Alexis found herself being quite rude to the captain, but unable to contain herself.

Even as the boat jostled to its landing struts, Alexis was out of her seat and tapping at the hatch controls in violation of the long-held tradition that a ship's captain is to be first-on and first-off his own boat. She didn't even have the thin argument of him being a Royal Mail captain, for she knew full well the right of it — yet she could not contain herself.

Somewhere past that hatch was someone she could vent her anger over the Zariahn Prize Court's actions on — whether Eades or Dansby, they'd do well enough, for she had her own reasons to be angry at both men, and felt they could do with a bit of being vented on. If it were truly a representative of the prize court who'd come along with their bloody "guaranteed," then all the better, for the Dark knew she had some words for that worthy.

The hatch cycled and she was down the ramp, ignoring both Delaine's call and Kayser's annoyed sniff.

The landing pad was only a hundred meters or so from the farmhouse — separated just enough by surrounding trees from the farmyard that there'd be no annoyed geese or chickens to contend with after an arrival — and she took those steps, if not at a dash, then at a respectable pace.

I've quite a lot to say, she thought, slowing her pace as she neared the house, *and I'll not want to be all gasping and sucking at the air as I say it.*

She did have to detour around a mound of dirt from a bit of construction her grandfather'd ordered, adding an addition to the old house in light of more crowded conditions. With Alexis at home and Delaine along with her, as well as Marie Autin, a French refugee from Giron that Alexis'd offered a place to, along with her young son, Ferrau, the place was growing quite crowded. Though there was some talk between Marie and Villars, Alexis' midshipman since she'd commanded HMS *Nightingale* in the space around Dalthus, of a more official union than their current courting — a thing Alexis wished the French girl luck with. Villars had been on half-pay as Alexis had also been since that command, officially at least, with no chance of a commission to lieutenant in that time, and he'd taken to the old adage of *a lieutenant may not marry, a commander might marry, a captain should marry, and an admiral must marry* — which left Villars, as a midshipman, right out.

Alexis burst through the farmhouse's kitchen door, ready to have her say against whomever'd come, and found herself facing an empty room.

There were voices from the drawing room, though, and that made her all the angrier, for it told her who the visitor was. Her grandfather and Julia knew both Dansby and Eades, so would have kept those rascals in the kitchen where much of the farm's gatherings were — or, if Julia was feeling particularly irritable toward such as they, they'd have been sent out to wait in the yard with the chickens.

That the voices came from the drawing room said the visitor was a stranger they felt was owed some greater courtesy — which meant the prize court.

"Maybe even — what was the man's name? Bramble? No, Bramley," Alexis muttered, heading toward the drawing room door — yes, she'd very much like to give the prize court's man himself a bit of her mind.

She burst through and found a crowded scene, not unusual for the drawing room in such a full household, but this was no evening gathering. Her grandfather had his usual seat in a comfortable, overstuffed chair. Across from him, on a long sofa sat Marie along with Villars, and her son, Ferrau, in her lap. Julia, her grandfather's housekeeper, and Alexis' own steward, Isom, were standing — the one hovering about with a tea pot and the other an open bottle of wine, as though the two were fighting for the territory of who to serve. And last, sat on the smaller sofa set facing the unlit fireplace down the aisle made by her grandfather's seat and the others, was a stranger to her. A stranger with both a teacup and wineglass set before him, as though he were the very territory Julia and Isom fought over.

So not Bramley himself, but he'll do, Alexis thought, then glanced at Isom and saw the bottle. One of her finer vintages, at no little cost, which set her fuming more. Her family'd not known the bastard's business and so were treating him far better than he deserved.

"Ah, Alexis, you're home —" her grandfather started at the same time the stranger gave her a bland look and said, "Lieutenant Carew?"

"Here for your bloody two thousand pounds, are you?" Alexis demanded. "Well, you'll get none of it today and see none of it from my lads, neither!"

The stranger sat back on the sofa, eyes widening.

"You and your conniving, thieving, ill-got brethren," she went on. "You cheat the lads at every turn. Delay their awards, send decent ships to the breakers instead of buying them in because you've an interest there —"

"Lexi-girl, what are —"

"— send off naught but your worthless 'certificates' instead of good, decent coin, when you know the recipients are moved on, six systems away by the time of your ruling and on a ship bound farther so there's no —"

"Alexis —"

"— bloody way they can return to redeem the things! But you've got that all settled, don't you?" Alexis nodded knowingly and stalked toward the stranger. "With your fingers in the settlement agents' pockets, as well, so you can slice off your own piece of the few pence some able spacer gets for the time and risk and effort of working those guns you'd never lower yourself to!"

"Sir, he's —"

"*Belay that, Isom, for I'm not finished with him yet!*"

Thankfully the drawing room's sofa was low-sat, as Alexis' next two strides brought her close to the man and he was set low enough that she felt she could be described as looming over him, despite her scant meter-and-a-half stature.

"You give no thought to what it took to bring that prize in. The days at the sails, the hours at the guns, the danger and toil of the action itself — have you ever seen a gundeck in action, sir?" She didn't give the man time to answer. "Of course not, you've been safe on Zariah all your life, likely, and never set your back to heaving a gun back from its shot. Never had to trust a mate to check the barrel for cracks, so that your next shot doesn't splinter and slice you into bits. Never heaved a nine-pounder out and sighted down its length, knowing there's some bugger on the other side looking at you down his own barrel and it's the one of you gets the better shot off faster who'll see the next watch with all his bits still attached!"

"*Alexis* —"

She felt Delaine take her arm, but shrugged him off. It felt too good to finally vent her feelings — and, truth told, she'd been feeling a bit hemmed in here on Dalthus these last months. Villars'd taken the lads on most of the calls to corral too-enthusiastic miners in the Port Arthur bars, so she'd not even had a decent dustup in ages. A good rant at someone richly deserving of it eased some of the pressure.

"Never in life gone over the side, already tired from heaving the guns and hauling shot, sweat stinging your eyes and no way to wipe it away through your vacsuit helm, cutlass in hand to turn the other's blade if you can or take his life with yours! All for your mates, your ship, and your bloody Queen who'd not even know your name if she were called to speak it! Never in life, sir, I'm sure, have you *even thought on the matter!*"

Alexis cast her tablet down to the table with a clatter, nearly upsetting the agent's still-full teacup and certainly the wineglass if Isom hadn't dashed forward to lift it to safety.

"But you'll send this off to them, won't you? Demand what little reward they've been allowed back and take a slice again? Well, I'll not have it, sir, I'll not have it! I'll appeal your judgment — your judgment made with no notice and no defense, of course! Straight up to the courts on New London itself, if I must, but you'll not collect from these lads and steal from them more than you have, sir, not even if we lose.

"You'll get no four hundred pounds from Master Gorbett and take his pub, nor four hundred pounds from Peters and ruin what life he's made, nor your petty few pounds from my lads who were on *Merlin* and see them borrowing their future for you to clip each coin — *not a bloody pence from them, sir! Not a farthing!*

"I will fight you to the last, sir, and pay you from my own purse, though it may break me, but you will take one answer back to your masters on Zariah, sir, and it is *leave my lads be!*"

The man stared at her for a moment, as did everyone in the room, then slowly reached forward to take up his cup of tea and sip — he then set his cup down, pulled a paper — real paper, for a wonder — from his vest pocket and held it out to her.

"Lieutenant Carew," he said calmly, "I am afraid I do not, in fact, represent the Zariahn Prize Court."

"Well, then who are you bloody here for?" Alexis demanded. "If you're working with that bastard Eades, it'll go worse for you than if the prize court. Who?"

"Work for?" the man repeated. "That would be Queen Annalise, Lieutenant. I am a Queen's Herald, after all."

Chapter Six

BY THE QUEEN
A Proclamation
Annalise r.

WHEREAS, We have taken into Our Royal Consideration the Extensive and Valuable Services provided to Our Crown, Our Kingdom, Our Royal Navy, and Our People, of recent and of late, and in Consultation with Our Lords of Admiralty and Our Privy Council and Diverse Others, We do declare, with the advice of our said Lords of Admiralty and Our Privy Council, as follows; viz.

WHEREAS, For action in the recent Bloody War with the Republic of Hanover, where, at Great Peril to Self, and in Opposition to a Far Superior Foe, in the region known as La Bae Marche, *she did place herself, her ship, and her crew in stalwart Canterbury of said Foe, allowing, at no little cost to herself, for the escape and recovery of diverse forces of Our Armies and civilians of* La Bae Marche, *many of whom have now become and shown themselves to be Our Loyal Subjects.*

WHEREAS, For action in the worlds of the Barbary, not in state of War, but of recently recalled to Service, she did locate, engage, and make harmless a Force of Pirates which has plagued said region, preying upon Our Merchant Fleets to the eternal detriment of Our Kingdom and Our People.

WHEREAS, For this same action in the worlds of the Barbary, she did locate and free from Durance Vile and Enslavement, diverse elements of Our Royal Navy and the naval forces of our Grand Ally La Grande République de France Parmi les Étoiles.

RESOLVED, For these Services and Acts, We do Request and Require the presence, At Court, of one Lieutenant Alexis Arleen Carew RN, subject of New London, citizen of Dalthus, at her Earliest Convenience, for the purpose of Recognition and Investment into the Most Noble Order of the Founding, thereafter to be known as Knight, Most Favored of Our Subjects, and Dame Carew.

On This Date It Is So Ordered

Annalise r.

(By Her ***Own*** *Hand)*

Chapter Seven

Alexis' feet dangled from the highest rafter of the hay barn – up where the roof was so close overhead that even she, even sitting, had to duck her head so that it didn't rub against the rough, unfinished underside of the roofing boards.

"There's no use talking to me about it, Grandfather," she called down. "I'm jumping."

"Wouldn't be the first time," Denholm called up to her.

Her grandfather, she noted, had stopped following her at the loft level and now stood amongst the piles and bales of hay and straw.

"I'm not eight anymore," she said, "adults have more mass. It could do for me."

"Not so much more than when you were eight, really." Denholm shrugged. "Hay'll break your fall, as always, but you go ahead and jump if you feel you must, Lexi-girl."

Alexis thought he might take her situation and intent a bit more seriously than that.

"There's a bare bit of floor just there," she pointed out. "I could aim for that."

"Might crack a leg, but no worse," her grandfather said, though she noted he did take a step and kick half a pile of straw to cover the bare boards she'd pointed out. "Plenty of time for it to heal on your way to New London."

"I can't go to New London, Grandfather, I screeched like a harridan at a Queen's Herald."

Denholm nodded. "Aye, you did."

Alexis sniffed, thinking a truly supportive person might have told her she hadn't been quite that bad — even if she had been. "And then I ran."

Another nod. "Aye, you did. Surprised me, that."

"I've never run from anything in my life."

"Why it surprised me."

"I — did I really yell, 'bugger me' when I ran off?"

Yet another nod, which, Alexis thought, a *truly* supportive person wouldn't feel the need to be on about quite so much just then. "You did that."

Alexis swallowed, throat tight. "Do you suppose he might have thought I said 'bother', instead?"

Denholm shook his head, which, Alexis thought quite a cruel twist to the pattern they'd been working on. "No — no, you were rather clear about it. As well as the bit before. No mistaking it."

"Bugger," Alexis muttered.

"Do you think you might come down, Lexi-girl? My neck's getting a crick in it, staring up at you."

Alexis sighed. She might as well, she supposed, as her grandfather was likely right. There wasn't a structure on the farm high enough to put a proper end to her embarrassment anyway.

She scooted forward and left the rafter, feeling, for too short a time, the freedom and thrill of falling. It was less than she remembered from her childhood — less free, less thrilling, and less time falling, all — and she wondered at that. She'd not grown so very much larger than she'd been then, and the barn certainly hadn't shrunk. Why, then, should it be so lessened?

Landing in the hay was much as she remembered, but also

somehow lessened. It was still soft and, thankfully, not as sticky as a straw pile might have been. It gave under her, and she sank in, the edges of the hole she made coming over to partially cover her. The smell covered her too — new-mown meadows and fields, as though the hay pile stored up all the bits of summer it could and then released them only to those who knew its secrets.

She lay still for a moment, then felt the pile shift as her grandfather lay down beside her.

"This was a wise choice, Lexi-girl. There's little in life that a good lay-down in a hay pile won't help you work your way through."

Alexis was silent for a long time. "They want to make me a knight, Grandfather."

"So I gathered."

Alexis couldn't say what it was about that she was so bothered by. She only knew that when she thought about it, her eyes burned and her throat swelled shut. She rolled toward her grandfather to wrap an arm around him and rest her face on his chest as she had so many times as a little girl.

"Pop-pop, the Queen's said ... she said I did well."

The tears came as she felt his arm go around her and hold her tight.

"Aye, Lexi-girl."

Alexis paused, afraid to say the next words that came to her. "Only I've never thought that I had, particularly." His arm tightened. "I've done my duty as I saw it, and, I think, as well as any who was there in my place might have, but..." She sniffed. "There's been so much death, Grandfather, and so many lost, I must think I should have done more."

Her grandfather was silent for a time. "Do you remember Dog?"

Alexis sniffed, wondering what her first real pet had to do with things now. "Of course I do, and if you're going to tease me about his name, I'll remind you that I was rather young to be naming things."

"Aye, you were just a young one. Do you remember how you got him?"

Alexis thought for a moment. "No — it was just after mother and father died, and he seemed to then be there whenever I was sad, wasn't he? I assumed you must have gotten him for me?"

Dogs were still rare on Dalthus, the original colonists having concentrated more on bringing along animals they could eat.

"No, Lexi-girl, you picked that dog on your own — or fate or some such did. Not surprised you don't remember, being so young." He took a deep breath. "It was some time after Harlyn and Katlynne died. I took you into the village and I was in the store when I heard this great shouting and goings on out back. The storekeep, Slauson, and I were out the door in a shot, thinking someone was being skinned alive with all the caterwauling.

"Back in the alleyway behind his shop we came across a sight.

"Three of the village boys, one of them bent over and grasping himself while he made the most appalling screech I've heard outside of a tomcat on the prowl, another sitting back in a mud puddle with blood pouring from his nose like a fountain, and the third gibbering terror and backing away as though he faced some guardian of Hell itself."

Denholm laughed.

"You, Lexi-girl, with a bit of board in your hand, waving it at that last boy like a sword — like Excalibur itself, if we're on about knights — all of half their size, but you backed them off.

"They ran off at the sight of Slauson and me and, I'll tell you, I was terrified at the why of it, thinking they'd attacked you and wondering why — then you stood aside and I saw the pup.

"Dog was not an attractive sight, I'll tell you — not much in the way of spare food was tossed away on Dalthus even then, so he was a skinny stray, all ribs and joints and angles. The boys had been at him for a time, poking and striking with some sticks and stones, so he was a bloody mess. But he stood by you like he knew you were his savior.

"You dropped your wooden sword, Lexi-girl, planted your fists on your hips, and looked at me to say one word. 'Mine.'" Her grandfather sighed. "Alexis Arlene. Julia always said your naming'd be a burden, with the one meaning defender and the other oath-keeper, and I don't take much with that nonsense — but I felt it then, girl, that my people here'd be kept well by you one day ... after your father, I thought, not knowing what was to come."

"I wasn't able to keep Dog safe later, though."

"No, but he kept you and the others safe, did he not?"

Alexis nodded, images of that day still seeming fresh in her mind, and still able to make her eyes well with tears.

Denholm sighed. "Never had a bearcat come that close to town before and never since, but you, and every other child at the swimming hole, made it home safely. Dog did his duty that day, no matter the cost — and if there was a bloody knighthood for it, I'd have given him one myself." He tightened his grip on her. "What I'm on about, Lexi-girl, and you know it yourself, though it's a hard thought to reach your heart, is you do your duty and your best at it, and that's done well, girl, in any book that matters."

"Aye, pop-pop."

"Of course, if I'd really thought about Dog and all the other strays you took in over the years, I'd have built the village up a bit when you went navy."

Alexis flushed.

"I will say your sense of who's yours to care for might have become a bit ... overdeveloped."

"I'm sorry, Grandfather."

Now she thought about it, she had played rather freely with her grandfather's hospitality, and wondered at how he must have felt over the years, with first the families of *Hermione's* mutinous spacers arriving, then Marie and her babe, who'd gone not to the village, but the homestead itself. Her furloughed crew from *Nightingale* had mostly found places on ships or elsewhere on Dalthus by now, but there were a few, mostly from her boat crew, who seemed content to hang about.

Denholm chuckled. "There's room, Lexi-girl, and they're good folk, for the most part ... though I will say when I heard the news of your last adventure and how many you'd led out of bondage, so to speak, I was gladder than I can say when only the Isliki's showed up."

Alexis giggled at the image of her leading the thousands of spacers she'd helped free on Erzerum back to Dalthus and presenting them to her grandfather for places.

"I'll try to restrain the urge in future, Grandfather."

"No, you'll not — even if you said so now and I agreed — and you wouldn't be true to yourself if you tried it." He held her tighter. "There's room here for any you feel you owe especial care to, and I'll trust your judgment on it. The Dark knows you've shown your own worth."

Alexis giggled again, noting how her lads' presence on the farm had influenced even her grandfather's language, their spacers' curse creeping into his words.

"That's better, now," Denholm said. "Are you ready to go back in?"

Alexis took a deep breath. "I suppose so — I should apologize to the herald, at least."

Denholm grunted. "Aye. Not too much, though — he's been a proper prat since he got here."

Chapter Eight

The Herald — Lord Braithwaite, the Right Honorable Earl of Southby March, Voice to Queen Annalise, once one was properly introduced to the man — was a bit of a prat.

There was simply no better way to put it.

Alexis tried — she really did — but the man's particular blend of supercilious unctuousness really didn't lend itself to any other description.

He was, of course, eminently polite, accepting Alexis' apology with a tilt of his head and muttered "of course," but it came with sort of superior twist to his lips Alexis had come to associate with ennobled midshipmen and younger lieutenants who thought themselves above the others by virtue of their titles and not any particular skill they held themselves.

"I truly am sorry, Herald," Alexis offered again.

Braithwaite nodded. "Of course. It was, I'm certain, an honest mistake." He frowned. "And it is, now I've delivered the Queen's words, properly Lord Braithwaite — or my lord, if you prefer."

"Told you," Denholm murmured to her, then "Oomph!" as Julia elbowed him in the ribs.

"Will you stay for dinner, Lord Braithwaite? And you, as well, Captain Kayser?" Julia asked. "It would be our honor."

"Of course," Braithwaite said, "but, sadly, no."

It took Alexis a moment to parse that answer, after which she felt a pang of regret she hadn't dragged the man to the pig wallow when she'd thought he was simply a prize court agent.

If one must apologize, it's likely best to make the most of the opportunity leading up to it...

"No," Braithwaite went on, "we've a long journey back to New London — and a great deal of work to do along the way."

"Work?" Alexis asked.

Braithwaite nodded. "Of course, lieutenant — you've much to learn before your first appearance on New London, not to mention the investiture ceremony itself." He looked her over as though apprising a cow for sale in the market. "There's your manner of dress, of course, and make-up — something will have to be done with your hair. Comportment is a must, as well as learning to recognize those you might meet." His lips curved. "Wouldn't wish you to mistake the Queen for some sort of prize agent, after all."

Alexis stared at him as he continued on.

"Do you suppose the pigs are hungry at all, Grandfather?" she whispered.

Denholm cleared his throat and turned away, jaw clenched and shoulders shaking.

Braithwaite went on, "Proper etiquette at dinner, of course." He glanced around. "Given the conditions of your upbringing."

Julia sniffed.

"As well, your initial duties and responsibilities within the Order of the Founding; though after they'll assign you a squire to assist and see to your clothing properly and such."

Isom sniffed.

Someone cleared his throat, but between all the sniffing and her grandfather's muffled laughter, Alexis couldn't make out who. She glanced at Delaine, but he merely lounged to one side of the room, taking it all in with Gallic amusement.

Another cleared throat and Alexis looked beyond Julia to the kitchen doorway where Captain Kayser stood.

"It sounds a grand plan, mister, my lord, herald, and all," Kayser said, "only seeing as there was two named by the lady in her invitation, and seeing as you've given your own answer thrice or more over, might the other party give a single one, by your gracious leave?" He bowed slightly to Julia. "Heartily grateful to you for the offer, ma'am, and delighted to accept. Weeks aboard ship gives a man yearnings, don't you know, and the smells from your kitchen here have all but driven me to distraction from our fair herald's words already — so the full effect of a fine meal would be doubly appreciated, me having had the dearth of the former and a sufficiency of the latter aboard my own ship these many weeks."

Braithwaite's mouth pursed. "Captain Kayser, I'm afraid I must insist — time really is of the essence, and I must return to New London with Lieutenant Carew forthwith."

Kayser frowned, then nodded and shrugged. "As you will, but I don't see what that's got to do with me and dinner."

"Forthwith, Captain," Braithwaite said. "I expect we shall need to return to your ship and sail immediately — after the lieutenant's packed, of course, but I'm certain that won't take long."

Kayser scratched at his face and frowned. "My ship? You got more of them proclamations to deliver?"

"No, my duties are now to return Lieutenant Carew to New London."

Kayser nodded. "Well, then, see, *Carpathia* is a Royal Mail ship. Mails, sir, not some cruise nor passenger lorry — and with your message delivered, well, you ain't properly the mails no more, sir herald, and neither is the lieutenant here. Besides, *Carpathia* has a route and we're heading more away from New London than toward it for the nonce."

Braithwaite frowned. "You're not returning to Zariah?"

Kayser shook his head. "Not for twelve weeks or more, winds depending."

"Then how am I to return to New London with my charge?"

"Wouldn't know, sir, my lord, herald, but it won't be aboard *Carpathia*, that's for certain." Kayser shrugged and turned to Julia, offering his arm. "Now, ma'am, it's said I'm a fair hand with a knife and stir a pot with the best — would your dinnering endeavors be in need of a helpmeet, at all? One who'll sneak only the tiniest tastes of such fine fare as he's been so sorely deprived of in his journeys, and that's a promise, it is?"

Alexis braced herself, for Julia wasn't known for helpers in her kitchen — especially men, as she claimed her grandfather could dirty every pot on the farmstead in the boiling of water, leaving them all to her for the cleaning.

Julia narrowed her eyes but took Kayser's arm.

"Why, yes, Captain Kayser, I do believe I've a chore or two could be done for me by a man with some skills."

Denholm sniffed.

"Have you been with the mails long, Captain Kayser?" Julia asked, taking her place at the table.

The cream and purple varrenwood table glistened where it wasn't covered with plates and serving dishes, and Alexis noted Lord Braithwaite eyeing it appraisingly. That much of the rare wood itself would fetch a pretty penny from a merchant ship here on Dalthus and she wondered what it would sell for so far away as New London itself, especially as her grandfather'd made the table from a single huge piece.

"Oh, many a year, ma'am," Kayser said. "Went into the mails when I was but a boy and worked my way aboard the ships — so mails through and through, might say."

Perhaps we should look into selling closer to the Core, Alexis thought, still watching Lord Braithwaite. *Fewer middlemen to take their bits.*

She was trying to follow all of the conversations around the table, but with so many about it was difficult.

Julia and Captain Kayser at the far end, nearest the kitchen door — so that Julia could quickly return there if needed — and across from each other, leaving the very end unoccupied. Her grandfather sat at the table's head, as always, Braithwaite to his right and Alexis to his left. Thankfully Delaine was to her own left, where she could easily touch his foot with hers below the table for comfort.

Villars sat beside Braithwaite, looking decidedly uncomfortable at the proximity — he came up from his rooms in the village to join them most dinners, but seemed still stunned by the events he'd been hurriedly caught up on when he and Marie returned from their walk. Marie herself looked uncomfortable as well, but that seemed more from the stress of keeping her boy, Ferrau, from clutching at every bit of the good china Julia'd seen fit to put out.

It seemed everyone had changed for dinner, as well, all save Alexis and her grandfather. Villars wore his midshipman's uniform, though he was without an appointment at the moment, and Marie wore what Alexis thought must be the girl's finest dress. Captain Kayser had taken time from the kitchen to return to his boat and change into a dress uniform, while Julia'd found time from cooking to put on a dress Alexis had never seen her wear before. Lord Braithwaite wore some sort of New London finery which looked quite out of place, and even Delaine had changed into his uniform — looking quite dashing, Alexis had to admit. Perhaps she should ask him to wear it a bit more often, despite the fact that his navy no longer, strictly speaking, existed.

As for Alexis herself, while she'd found time to bathe and change from the clothes she'd worn back from her camping and then rolled about in the haybarn in, her own denim trousers and linen shirt were not so very different than her grandfather's. Damned if she'd put her uniform back on before she had to just to please Braithwaite — especially as he had no ship for her. Now, if the man had come with a commission instead of a knighthood, she'd have donned her jacket and beret happily.

But mightn't there be one in the works? she asked herself. *Surely a knighthood will strike Admiralty the right way — I'll be on New London itself, after all, and could visit their offices. I've heard the best commissions come to those who present themselves in person...*

They all took up their napkins to begin eating and Alexis saw it wasn't the common, Dalthus-made dishes they usually ate from, but the fine set her grandfather'd ordered up for Alexis' parents when they married — Alexis didn't think they'd ever been used, at least not in her memory.

Isom, her clerk and steward when aboard ship, poured the last glass at the table full, Julia's, and stepped back to the sideboard in what little room was left with the table so full — nothing in the farmhouse was quite large enough for how the number of occupants had grown, much less their guests. Isom usually sat with them at meals, but he'd given Alexis' look a quick head shake, and she assumed he'd reverted to his role aboard ship due to Braithwaite's presence, not wanting his charge to be looked down on by the visiting peer.

Julia might have done the same, bustling back to her kitchen to be free of such august company, but she seemed quite caught up in conversation with Captain Kayser, who'd shown no desire at all to make his way farther up the table.

"No ceremony here, Lord Braithwaite," Denholm said, taking a platter of roast chicken from the table's center and offering it to the man. "We're family and'll stay such no matter the visitors." He nodded at Isom, who was at the sideboard. "Even him, though he's got a stick-in. Sit down and eat, lad, if there's one thing I know a peer can do for himself, it's pour his own drink, isn't that right, my lord?"

Braithwaite pursed his lips. "Of course. As herald, I often have to live quite roughly."

"See, lad? Now sit."

"I —"

"It's all right, Isom," Alexis said, twisting to see. "If we're leaving tomorrow, on whatever ship, then this is our last dinner together for some time — and you are family."

"Aye, sir," Isom said, seeming to say that if it was an order, then he'd do it.

He sat next to Delaine and the table was soon filled with the clink of silver against plate and dish, as they all took up and passed whatever was nearest them.

"Is this a Macdonald set, sir?" Braithwaite asked, examining his butter knife.

Denholm nodded. "One of the few luxuries Lynelle and I allowed ourselves in the packing when we came." He shrugged. "It was a fair bit of our mass allotment, but the silver'd have had use in the printers, if things got dire."

Braithwaite's face went white. "You'd have melted down Macdonald?"

"I'd have eaten the Macdonald himself, carved with his own bloody silver, that first two years, if it'd given any break from the bloody yams," Denholm said. "There's little room for sentiment on a new world, sir, and less for fancies brought from the Core."

And that set the dinner on its way, with mostly common conversation, largely between Braithwaite and her grandfather, with Julia and Captain Kayser holding up their end of the table — all of which was fine with Alexis, as it gave her time to simply eat and ponder. Though her pondering was mostly a blank mind, wondering at how she'd got to the bit where she was sailing to New London with a peer of the Realm to be knighted. It did seem a bit unreal to her.

"You are feeling better, *mon cœur*?" Delaine whispered to her.

Alexis nodded, torn from her reverie. "I'm over the first bit of shock, at least."

She paused, then quietly, "Thank you — for not rushing after me."

Delaine smiled. "In some things we all need *le père*."

Alexis nodded, relieved. She'd have had some comfort if Delaine had followed her to the barn, but she was just as glad he'd left it to her grandfather. She'd been more ... vulnerable in that moment than she liked.

"Now you've had your proper dinner, Captain Kayser," Braithwaite called down the table as his conversation with her grandfather turned toward their coming journey, "are you certain that you might not carry us back with you aboard *Carpathia*?"

Kayser paused in his eating, which seemed to be his third plate, under Julia's approving gaze, and narrowed his eyes. "Not unless your desire is a dozen or more stops between here and any Core world."

"As herald, Captain, I do have —" Braithwaite cleared his throat. "— a certain stipend available, for travel and incidentals. I could make it worth your while, I think."

"The Crown cares for my whiles quite nicely as it is, Mister Lord Herald — quite nicely indeed — so never you mind your thoughts about my whiles, now. My whiles are full and satisfied — most of them," Kayser added with what Alexis thought looked suspiciously like a wink to Julia. "And for those left, I've no desire for you to be the one involved in their satisfaction."

"Of course," Braithwaite said with a frown.

Denholm cleared his throat and tapped his knife against a glass, drawing everyone's attention — including a grinning Kayser and an oddly flushing Julia.

"Well, I suppose a toast's in order before we end things," Denholm said, taking up his glass. "To the family's new knight?"

"Really, Grandfather?" Alexis asked, flushing herself.

Alexis saw it was already too late, as the others had taken up their glasses and were all staring at her with the most ridiculously pleased expressions on their faces. She felt her face grow hot. Even Isom had a glass in hand, and she wondered if he was the one to put the idea in her grandfather's head.

"Were you aboard ship and this news came, *mon cœur*," Delaine murmured, "you know there would be cheers from the crew. May your family do less?"

"Now, I'd thought to get away from all that folderol of titles when Lynelle and I settled on Dalthus," Denholm said, "but if one's to receive the first such title brought back here, I can't say there's a more deserving, nor one who'd make me prouder, than my granddaughter. It seems these last few years have been me reading the Naval Gazette with my knees knocking in terror and my heart swelling with pride at the stories — then her coming home and me realizing I should have felt both those twice as much or more from the truth in her eyes."

Alexis cleared her throat and swallowed hard, keeping her eyes down on her plate.

"Aboard ship, your *bloodies* would send you off with cheers and huzzahs, *ma lionne*," Delaine murmured in her ear. "It is nothing but your due."

Denholm raised his glass. "Alexis Arleen Carew, soon to be knight, and no better deserved."

"Here, here!" Villars cried, while the others echoed him in their own way.

Then — to Alexis' utter mortification and in proof that her lads had brought with them to the farmstead a ship's ability for news to run seemingly through the bloody aether — came her coxswain's, Nabb's, call from outside the dining room windows.

"*Hip! Hip!*"

"*Hooray!*" came a chorus of voices.

"*Hip! Hip!*"

Alexis shot Isom a dark look as the second call came from Nabb, as she was certain her clerk must have snuck away at some time to inform her coxswain of the event in time for him to gather what sounded like the farm's full complement.

"*Hooray!*"

Nabb's third call rang out just as the loud bang of an opening door came from the kitchen and a boy of no more than twelve rushed into the dining room, out of breath, chest heaving, and eyes wide.

"*Hip! Hip!*"

"Miss Alexis! Mister Denholm, sir! You're needed in the village! The man's gone crazed and they're like to murder him!"

"*Hooray!*"

Chapter Nine

Alexis and her grandfather were on their feet as the others simply stared at the boy in astonishment.

"Who's gone crazed, lad?" Denholm asked.

The boy heaved a deep breath, winded by his run from the village. "That Isliki boy, Mister Denholm!" Even with his gasping he managed to express his excitement. "He's gone after the whole bloody pub, he has, and they're spoiling for a fight!"

Alexis winced. It wasn't the first trouble they'd had with the family she'd promised sanctuary here from Erzerum. The farmer wasn't a bad sort, despite his having owned several New London spacers as slaves — he and the other natives of the planet had rather been forced into it by the pirates who'd taken over the system — but he and his family did have difficulties adjusting to New London's ways.

"I'm sorry, Grandfather," Alexis said, setting her napkin down as he did the same.

"Not your fault," Denholm said as he passed the boy on their way to the kitchen door.

"Mister Villars!" Alexis called back. "I'd be admiring it, did you follow along with the lads, we may have need of them."

"Aye, sir!"

"Brandon!" her grandfather called, as they left the kitchen for the farmyard filled with hands, both from the farm and Alexis' idle spacers, all of whom seemed confused by the bustle it appeared their cheering had brought on. "Bring a truck around and gather up a dozen steady hands — we've trouble in the village."

"Trucks're all at the fields, sir," the farm's foreman answered, then nodded toward an outbuilding spilling light through its open doors. "Save the one we brought in for maintenance and it's in pieces."

"Saddle horses, then, and follow on quick as you can."

"Nabb!" Alexis yelled just after. "Assemble my boat crew — Mister Villars will be along presently to take charge."

"Right away!"

"Aye, sir!"

Alexis strode toward the stables, just a bit behind her grandfather — though her stride, she had to admit, was more of a skip in order to keep up with his longer legs — he might be getting on in years, but that hadn't changed the steely determination he showed toward his lands and people.

Brandon, the holding's foreman, had sent two men dashing off ahead to saddle horses, and they had a pair out of the stalls already. One of them, she was happy to see, was a filly she'd come to know well in the time she'd been home — not the steady, sturdy trail horse she'd taken for her outing with Delaine.

Now Alexis dashed ahead, sacrificing a bit of dignity for more speed.

"Never mind the saddle, Tom, just a hand if you please?" she called.

By the time she arrived, the groom had repositioned himself and cupped his hands, which Alexis got a boot in easily and vaulted onto the horse's back. She grasped the horse's mane, clamped her legs tightly, and leaned forward.

"A bit of a run, Fancy?" she whispered.

The filly nickered back, tossing her head — perhaps confused that it was night, when a proper horse should be safe and sleeping in a warm stall, but still game because the person on her back was well-known to carry the sort of tasty bits one didn't often get in a stall.

"Alexis, a bridle, at least —"

Her grandfather's words were cut off as she gave a little kick and Fancy was off.

Alexis would normally not risk such a ride — bareback, in darkness, and with neither bit nor bridle to exercise better control — but she knew tensions between the Isliki family and the villagers had been escalating and the boy's words had spoken to a certain urgency.

Even with that, she found the ride exhilarating, and couldn't help but grin as Fancy's hooves pounded against the packed earth of the road from farmstead to village. The wind in her face, surroundings narrowed by darkness and intent to only the path before her in the dim light of Dalthus' moons, and the powerful horse responding to her commands, all combined into a neck-or-nothing dash she'd not felt the like of since Erzurum.

Is there something odd about me, that I only feel this alive when I've wound up in utterly foolish danger? she wondered.

That thought, as it often was, was pushed aside, this time by the need to watch their path for obstacles — though the village road was well-maintained, there was always a chance. An unseen rut or hole, a fallen tree, even one of the ubiquitous, bloody rabbits dashing across and spooking Fancy in the darkness.

She slowed as they entered the outskirts of the village proper, where the packed dirt and gravel of the road turned to pavement, then more as she neared the older part of the village where the oldest streets were still cobbled with river- and travel-smoothed stone.

Their way was lit here by dim streetlights and more light pouring from the windows and opening doors of houses and cottages as the residents responded to the unexpected clatter of Fancy's hooves. Men and women spilled out to watch her pass and then follow along, for a fast rider this late must be an event of interest, and not a one wished to be left out.

The village center was better lit, and there she could see the crowd ahead, gathered in the street near the largest pub.

A few heads turned as she neared, and they moved aside, but the bulk of those blocking the street were intent on what was occurring in the crowd's center.

"*Make a lane!*" Alexis yelled as she walked Fancy up to the crowd's back.

Either her words or Fancy's broad shoulders and sweaty, heaving flanks had the desired effect, causing the crowd, only about five-deep, to part and allow her through.

Path clear, Alexis turned her own attention to what had attracted the crowd and the source of the trouble.

"*Şeytanlar*!" Olcay Isliki yelled, holding some antique, paper book above his head. The family's younger son stood at the center of the crowd, facing off with several of the village men — Alexis couldn't tell how many exactly, because the crowd merged with the men's backs, both supporting them and egging them on.

"Speak the Queen's bloody English, boy! Or I'll whip you until you do!" one of the men yelled back moving forward with a riding whip in hand.

"*Belay that!*" Alexis added her own voice to the shouts and rode forward into the clear space. "*Enough!*"

She turned Fancy in place, staring at the crowd until they settled and quieted a bit, then eased the horse and slid off her back. Fancy's bulk and height might give her a more commanding presence, but the cobbles were slick and the crowd unruly. She might have the weight of her grandfather's authority here, along with her own to the villagers, but neither would do her any help if a drunken lout sent her for a fall, all saddleless as she was. Better to face them with firmer footing.

"You!" Alexis pointed at a face in the crowd she knew to be a steady man. "James Clark, come here and hold my horse, will you?" She saw him ease out of the crowd and start forward, so held Fancy's mane while she turned to the man with the whip.

"Put up that whip, Andrew Wood, or I'll take it from you and turn your backside bloody, you see if I don't!"

A few of those behind Wood stepped back, but enough stayed to embolden the man. He was clearly drunk, as were those closest to him — not an uncommon condition after a hard day's labor and, if Alexis hadn't lost too much sense of the calendar in her trip to the wilds with Delaine, tomorrow would be a rest day for most, giving the opportunity for more than the usual amount of drink.

"We're free men!" Wood yelled, looking around at the crowd. "Not your navy dogs to whip!" He glanced at those nearest him again. "Nor indentures! Mine's done and I'm bloody free and you've not a bit of power to whip me or any free man here!"

"My grandfather's never had an indenture beaten, Wood, and you well know it," Alexis said, knowing that, while it was true for her grandfather's lands, the same couldn't be said for other landowners on Dalthus. "And it's being a fool I'd whip you for, not an indenture."

The indenture system let each landowner set up their contract as they wished, including what punishments might be meted out for transgressions and crimes on the holding — if the man who signed it later came to regret his choice, well, decisions had consequences. Which was fine and good until some landowner took his liberties — which had happened with Wood and no few of those backing him up, she knew.

Her grandfather's lands had become a haven for more than the strays Alexis sent him — men and women who'd worked off the indentures they'd come to regret with others often made their way there once their contracts were done.

"But you have had men beaten, haven't you, girl?" Wood yelled. "Your navy ways, laying a man's back bare, and now you'd bring those ways here, wouldn't you?"

Alexis' face heated. She'd ordered floggings aboard ship, there was no secret to that, and, though she found it unpleasant, it was, indeed, the navy way. With so many men, packed so closely, for so very long a time, there were bound to be transgressions, and far from home or any planet, there was little other recourse for the truly grave of those — and, come to that, it was a system most spacers paid no mind to. "Over, done, and now forgotten," was the creed for both the crime and the punishment, once done, and most shrugged it off as such.

Still, a free village was no Queen's ship, and her grandfather's lands were not the lands of the more vicious holders.

"It's neither Admiralty nor my grandfather threatening to whip you, Wood, it's me," Alexis said. "You're the one with whip in hand and facing a boy but half your size. You want a brawl in the square, that's what I'll give you. So end your rabble leveler talk and let's settle this ruckus down." She looked back at Olcay. The Isliki's younger son was, indeed, holding a paper book in one hand and was scowling at her with every bit the anger Wood was.

Well, at least I've distracted them from each other, whatever the matter was.

"He's but a boy with a book," Alexis said, "what could he have done to so upset you?"

Wood glanced from her to Olcay, then back again. He grinned slowly.

"Oh, it's you who'll whip me, is it?" he said, stepping away from his supporters. "Man to ... man, in a fair fight?"

One of the men beside Wood grasped his arm. "You're drunk, Andrew. Be careful, man — you know who she is?"

Wood shrugged it off and stepped forward, planting his feet wide.

"Do I care for her grandfather? Know who she is? Know who I am — a free man!" He stomped his feet again. "On free land! Not like those slaves up on the farm!"

Alexis' face stilled and she felt a warm rush of anger and anticipation flow through her. There was going to be a fight, no matter what other words were said now.

"Listen to your friend, Wood," she said softly, knowing, almost hoping, that it would do no good. The man had transferred his anger, whatever its cause, from Olcay to her, and likely couldn't be turned from his rage. "I've seen slavery, Wood, and it's in no way practiced here."

"*Liar!*"

Wood dropped the whip, raised a fist, and ran toward her. One of the men with him, perhaps the one who warned him, tried to grab his arm again, but missed.

In future, Alexis would look back on it as one of the more disappointing fights of her life. It had been some time for her, and she quite anticipated a bit of a dustup, but, in the end, it was simply a forearm to redirect Wood's blow to pass over her head and twist his path, a sidestep to avoid his rush, and a tap of her foot to the back of his knee to bring him down.

Wood spun in the air as he fell, then lay still as the back of his head hit the cobbles with an echoing *thonk*.

Alexis watched him warily for a moment, but he made no move to rise and attack her again.

Two of his fellows came forward, slowly, giving Alexis a wide berth and respectful nod, to stare down at him.

"Weren't the grandfather I were warning you of, Andrew," one said to the still form.

Alexis ran her eyes over the watching crowd, but saw their initial anger seemed to have turned to chagrin. Few met her eyes, and those who did were grinning as though it had all been great sport, no matter the turnout.

She turned her attention to the original target of Wood's wrath, hoping to find out what the matter had been about to begin with.

Olcay still stood where he had when she arrived — alone, no backers from the crowd for him, and with his book only half raised now. He still wore clothes in the Erzurum style, layers for warmth and to keep the constant drizzle at bay, though they must be stifling here in Dalthus' warming spring.

He was Altu Isliki's youngest son, though three of the daughters were younger. Alexis hadn't learned his exact age, though she thought of him as a boy — he had a bare face, still, despite having broad shoulders and nearly a third of a meter more height than Alexis.

Olcay scowled at her as she approached, but she couldn't tell why. Perhaps he thought he'd be in more trouble for Wood being injured. There'd been more than one incident in the village so far, most involving Olcay, and she knew his father had promised to keep him more in line.

Poor luck with that, it seems.

Still, Alexis couldn't fathom what the boy might have done to illicit such an angry crowd.

She walked closer to him and spoke softly, hoping to show she wasn't angry with him, and slowly, as she knew he seemed to have had more trouble than the rest of his family in learning English on their trip to Dalthus. "Will you tell me what's the matter here, Olcay? And I've not my tablet with me to translate, so you'll have to speak English, I'm afraid."

Olcay's face twisted, turned red, and he lashed out, slapping Alexis' face with his left hand. It was a hard enough blow, and came so unexpectedly, that she didn't react to block it. Her head rocked and her face stung from the impact.

"*Bitch!*" Olcay shouted, adding a gobbet of spit to the sting on her cheek.

Alexis stared at him for a moment in shock, then nodded.

"Right, then," she said, driving her knee up into the boy's fork.

Chapter Ten

The village pub — the Jolly Weasel, a name she'd always thought was an homage to shite-weasel, what her grandfather had wished to name the planet's largest predator, instead of "bearcat" — was larger than Alexis remembered it from the few times she'd entered.

At first, she thought it was only her younger self's memory — she'd only visited with her grandfather, after all, when he had some business there. Most of her personal pub-visiting, at least on Dalthus, had been in Port Arthur, the planet's main spaceport. There was more tolerance there for the sort of drinking spacers got up to — and, when it came to that sport, at least, Alexis knew she was a spacer through-and-through.

The row of brick-clad columns running down much of the space spoke to the pub's having expanded into the building next door at some point — the space was far too large to be explained only by the pub's signage and windows, and the next store front appeared blacked over and empty from the street.

What had that been, then? Alexis wondered. There were so many changes to the village as the Dalthus population expanded, especially after the *gallenium* mines opened, that each return home seemed to be to a new place. *Wasn't it the —*

Yes, it had been a dress shop — the finest dress shop in the village, in fact — and one where her grandfather had once ordered her a truly atrocious concoction of pink frills and lace.

Alexis found herself unable to muster much sympathy for the dress shop's demise and found its having been turned into the darker half of the Jolly Weasel a just fate.

I'm certain their wares drove more than one poor soul to drink.

"Yer keepin' me custom out, Denholm," the pub keeper called.

Alexis' grandfather, who'd arrived shortly after she'd sent Olcay to his knees with an aching fork, motioned for Wood to be set on a nearby table. Alexis made the same motion to a different table, so that Nabb and a couple others could set Olcay there. The boy grunted as the men hefted him to a thoroughly unnecessary height to clear the chair backs around the table, then set him down with the gentleness of a rugby tackle.

"Nabb," Alexis warned quietly.

Her coxswain frowned. "I said handsomely, lads," he admonished the others, then grinned and glanced at Alexis. "Would you like us to try again, sir?"

"No," Alexis said with, she hoped, enough firmness to keep the lads from trying on their own, then turned her attention back to her grandfather and the pub keeper.

"Your custom's out brawling in the street, Nicholson," Denholm said.

Nicholson took up a glass to polish with a rag. "Not so much now, as your lads have sent them all scurrying."

"Back soon enough, I'm sure," Denholm said. He nodded to the two bodies taking up Nicholson's tables — Wood still unconscious and Olcay still moaning. "Can you say what these two were about?"

"Wood, there, was drinking with his mates," Nicholson said, "no rowdier than they ought to be, given the day's work they put in, when yonder —" He nodded at Olcay. "— come through the door, muttering his gibberish, showing his book like some bloody Papist casting out and such." Nicholson shrugged. "Thought he was just on about the drink as he's wont to be, but he walks right up to Wood and his gibberish goes ... more specific, if you take my point?"

"Specific?" Denholm asked.

"There's words said to a man what he don't understand — then there's words he might not ken the meaning of, but he bloody well knows what the other bloke's saying, aye?"

Denholm pursed his lips. "Aye." He turned to Alexis. "Did you get any idea what this was all about before you..." He scratched at his beard. "... put an end to it?"

"No, Grandfather" Alexis said. "I did gather that this one —" She pointed to Wood. "— has no affection for slavers, and sets those who hold indentures to be of the same cloth; and this one ... Nabb," she added warningly as she turned her attention back to Olcay and found her coxswain holding the boy's shoulders while two of her boat crew held his legs straight.

"Curling up'll just make his eggs ache all the longer, sir," Nabb said. He patted Olcay on the chest with enough force to belie the innocent expression. "Lad could do with walking it off, come to that." He nodded to the pub's rear door and the alley beyond. "If you like, me'n the —"

"No," Alexis said. "Let him be — and there'll be no 'helping him walk' in an alley. Tonight or any other, do you understand?"

"Aye, sir," Nabb muttered. "Only trying to help the lad, you understand. A man's going to go around sayin' an' doin' a thing as gets him a certain result, he ought to know how to ease his eggs after." He patted Olcay's chest again, drawing a cry. "Me an' the lads'd be happy to help him ... practice."

Alexis shook her head. Nabb and her boat crew, along with her grandfather's farmhands, had arrived just after she'd sent Olcay to the cobbles. They seemed to have got the whole story in the time it took them to pile off the farm's hastily reassembled truck and make their way through the crowd, and were none too pleased with the boy.

"That one," she told her grandfather, "has learned at least a bit of English since his family arrived."

"I see," Denholm said, then sighed. "Lexi-girl, this isn't the first time that boy's caused —"

Alexis' grandfather broke off as the pub's door opened. They all turned to see and Alexis nearly groaned, for it was Zehra, the Isliki's middle daughter and Olcay's sister. The rest of the Isliki clan wouldn't be far behind, she was certain, for they'd never let their daughter be out without escort.

That was a thing which kept the family more isolated than they ought to be, for the village women frowned on the practice — that and the head coverings the Isliki women wore.

The Dalthus colony held no particular religious beliefs — or, better to say, it held dozens. Unlike the nearby faith-based colonies like Man's Fall or Al Jadiq, the Dalthus founders, including her grandfather, hadn't written anything into the colony's founding contract that could be read as more than: *Best to keep it to yourself — but if you must talk about it, get off a man's bloody porch when he says to.*

The girl glanced once at her brother, who raised a hand and called to her, then scowled and rushed to Wood's side where she took the unconscious man's hand and gently stroked his brow.

"Oh," Alexis said, glancing from Wood and Zehra to Olcay, whose grimaces of pain had changed to scowls of anger.

"Ah," Denholm said.

"I'm sorry for the trouble, Grandfather," Alexis said.

They were riding back to the farm, side by side and walking the horses. The truck with Alexis' lads and the farmhands far ahead.

"Wood's isn't the first head to be cracked on a rest-day eve,"

Denholm said. "Nor Olcay the first brother to think he's defending a sister's honor or some such."

"No, but if I'd not brought them here —"

Alexis broke off.

Shortly after Zehra'd arrived, the elder Isliki, his wife, and all the rest of their children had rushed into the pub. There'd been quite a bit of yelling all around, most of which Alexis couldn't understand, but the upshot had been the Islikis helping their son back home while screaming over their shoulders at the daughter who refused to leave Wood's side even while bursting into tears in the midst of her own yelling back at them.

The village doctor'd taken charge of Wood, who'd regained consciousness — if not, Alexis suspected, with any greater wits than he'd had in the first place — and spoken with surprising tenderness to Zehra.

The pubtender's wife had then taken charge of the girl as the doctor took possession of Wood and, with a bit of emphasis toward the injured man, assured everyone that she'd have a safe place at the inn for the night.

"If you'd not brought them here, you'd never have repaid the debt you felt you owe them," Denholm said. "Nor felt ought but guilt over leaving them to their lives on ... what was it?"

"Erzerum," Alexis said, nodding as she had to admit the truth of her grandfather's words. "Perhaps I should encourage them to move on to Al Jadiq — I've enough funds to send them on without them being indentured for it."

Or, I suppose I have, provided the Zariahn Prize Court doesn't take it all.

Her grandfather shook his head.

"If I understand such things, they're the wrong sort for Al Jadiq," he said. "Something about which brother they bow to or some such." He waved a hand. "No, I'll send to Port Arthur — there's a man at their sort of church there who might come and speak to the Isliki's. Help them to understand how to live and let live with those different than themselves and such. He's done as much for some who've come back up the colonies from Al Jadiq after not finding it to their liking. Poor sots, them, with a double indenture."

"Thank you."

They walked in silence for a time, with only the soft thuds of the horse's hooves on the road along with the occasional *clack* of horseshoe against stone, then Alexis caught her lower lip between her teeth and worried at it before speaking.

"Grandfather, you've not said yet whether you'll come to New London for the ceremony — I know there's the northern harvest coming soon, and the southern fields should be prepared for winter there, but..."

Denholm sighed.

"I'd dearly love to," he started, and Alexis' heart fell at his tone, for whatever the next words might be, she knew what that start foretold. "Dearly, but there's the family to consider. Lynelle and I didn't leave home on the best of terms."

"It's been so long, and you've accomplished so much here, what grudge could our family still hold?"

"Not the Carews," Denholm said. "It's Lynelle's family. Her brother Angus, to be clear. He's written to me often over the years."

Alexis frowned. "But if he's written to you —"

"Blame and bile's what he's written," Denholm said, "and paid the post to put it before me every year since..." He took a deep breath and let it out slowly. "Since Lynelle passed."

Alexis' grandmother had died giving birth to her father and Alexis marveled at the pain in her grandfather's manner even after so long a time.

He loved her so much, she thought.

"He blames me, you see," Denholm said, "for bringing her here. Likely the whole family still does, and I'll not fault them for their feelings, but Angus ... well, he started with a surfeit of hate for me and he's gone to overflowing with it. I'd fear he'd make good on this vow to challenge me, did I set foot on New London."

"A duel? At your age?"

Denholm turned his head to stare at her.

"I mean ... um, you've sense enough, with maturity, that is, to see the foolishness of such things ... surely Angus must..."

"Hmph." Denholm turned his eyes back to the road ahead. "There are two times in a man's life when he might fight a duel without much sense — when he's young enough his brain's not yet baked through and when he's old enough his brain's gone wormy. There's some question whether Angus had much of a middle between the two."

"I see."

"There'd be no good outcome to such a thing, Lexi-girl. I'm sorry."

"No, I understand," Alexis agreed, trying to hide her disappointment.

Chapter Eleven

Port Arthur's landing field was filled to overflowing — not with ship's boats, but with tents and stalls and the numerous workers set about assembling them.

She'd said her goodbyes to all those not travelling with her — which was all except Isom and Delaine. Neither Alexis nor Denholm felt the need to drag things out, and Port Arthur was as good as being aboard ship, when all was said and done. It'd been a chore to keep Isom from packing The Creature for travel with them, but she'd managed to put her foot down and convince Isom that this long a journey, with her not an officer aboard ship, might present some sort of danger to the annoying mongoose she'd been gifted with. Julia had almost as unnatural an attraction to the thing as Isom, so it would be well cared for, much as Alexis might wish otherwise.

It almost occurred to her to reverse her decision and bring the bloody thing with, if there were truly that much danger — she'd then be rid of the thing after all.

Captain Kayser's boat had to set down at the field's far end, and they were all faced with a walk through the growing sea of canvas to the town.

"Thank you for the carriage, Captain Kayser," Alexis said. "It was far more comfortable than a local hauler would have been."

Kayser nodded. "Thanks're well and good, miss lieutenant —" He leaned close and spoke lower. "— but the promise of a word of praise to your sweet, the fine cook, Miss Julia, would settle well with me as well. *Carpathia* will be back this way, I'm sure, and a good opinion on her part would please me no end."

"I shall include a certain praise of you in my very next letter to her, Captain Kayser, but you should —" Alexis broke off. She'd been about to speak of a certain — unspoken so far as she could tell, but somehow sensed — bit of something between Julia and her grandfather. Julia herself had not seemed averse to Captain Kayser's attentions, though Denholm had been seen to frown a great deal.

Is it my place to warn of a thing that might not be? The Dark knows Julia's been alone all the time I've known her — yet so has Grandfather.

Alexis sighed. If the pair of them hadn't the sense to speak to each other about their feelings, being forever in the same bloody house, how was it on her to interfere?

People can be so very tiresome at times.

"I shall write to her before we leave Port Arthur, Captain Kayser," she said finally.

Kayser nodded while Braithwaite sighed heavily and looked about. "You shall have plenty of time for it, it appears. Not a single other ship in the system, you say?"

He strode halfway up his boat's ramp. "Good day to you, Mister M'lord Braithwaite, Lieutenant Miss Carew, good journeys!"

With that, he was back in his boat and the ramp already rising.

His boat crew had already unloaded their luggage from the rear ramp and, once all ramps were up, the boat lifted.

Isom nodded to her. "I'll stay with the luggage, sir. To the hotel?"

"Thank you, Isom, yes — until a ship with passenger space calls."

"There are hotels, at least, then?" Braithwaite asked. "You can speak to the finest, I assume?"

Alexis raised an eyebrow and Delaine chuckled. "I can speak to the hotel, my lord, there's but the one, after all."

Braithwaite closed his eyes and took a deep breath. "One ship in-system, one hotel — does this world have more than one of anything?"

"Dalthus has quite a lot of things we've need of, Lord Braithwaite." Alexis was beginning to anticipate weeks in close, shipboard quarters with the man. "But we're a young colony yet. The belt mining's had us grow faster than we ought, and rougher."

They started walking toward the town, taking a mostly open aisle of space between rows of tents and roped-off spaces.

"Surely these miners need accommodations," Braithwaite said, "yet only the one hotel?"

"There are other lodgings, *monsieur*," Delaine said, "if perhaps they are to your liking."

"Delaine —"

"What other lodgings?" Braithwaite asked.

Alexis elbowed Delaine in the side. "Pubs, gambling dens, and houses of a certain repute, m'lord," Alexis said. "Miners being as they are." She shrugged. "In all, I recommend the hotel, sir."

"I see."

They walked on for a time, dodging men with poles and coils of rope, while others were set about moving crates of supplies and equipment for the vendors and food stalls.

"Lieutenant Carew," Braithwaite asked, "is this some sort of festival time for your people?"

My people, Alexis noted, *as though we're some distant, just-discovered tribe.*

"In some way, m'lord," Alexis said, "An indenture fleet's in-system, as Captain Kayser said. Holders will be in town to sign contracts and there'll be some merchants and food vendors after their custom."

"A fleet? Soon, do you think?"

"An indenture fleet's made up of ships, m'lord, but not those set up for passenger travel — not as you'd expect. You'll find when you visit the chandlery later that there *are* ships in system, I'm certain, but they're ore carriers taking on *gallenium* at the lunar station — not the sort for passengers, either, my lord."

"Well, certainly not an ore carrier, but these indentures must have cabins, mustn't they? These ships are built for carrying people, after all. Perhaps as some will be hired on here, they'll have spare accommodations for us."

"You may ask after it, Lord Braithwaite," Alexis said, "I'm certain you'll let us know if you find their offer satisfactory."

Braithwaite, in his eagerness to find them transport, went straight to the chandlery once he'd seen the hotel's location, and Alexis wasn't certain who — Braithwaite or Doakes the chandler — she wished would have the best of the encounter.

She and Delaine continued to the hotel — a new structure built a few streets back from the landing field. It was now the highest building in Port Arthur at six storeys.

"We're nearly full up, Miss Carew," the clerk at the desk said, "but we put down reservations for all the First Holders when the indenture fleet announced, in case there'd be need. Is Holder Carew coming, do you know?"

"He's not," Alexis said, "I've sent him enough strays the last few years that we've no need of more workers right now."

"Right, then," the clerk said, tapping at his terminal between glances at her and Delaine, "two rooms is it?"

"One," Alexis said, "for the both of us. There'll be a Lord Braithwaite along from the chandlery soon for another."

The clerk looked up, glancing from Delaine to Alexis. "One? A lord?"

He seemed torn between the thought of her and Delaine sharing a room and the oncoming finery of a title.

"A lord," Alexis confirmed. "From New London and a Queen's

Herald, no less. If you've no other rooms left, you'll not want us taking up two of them when he arrives."

"What? No, of course not." He fumbled with his tablet. "It's only —" He glanced from Alexis to Delaine and back again, then leaned forward and whispered. "Would your grandfather approve, miss?"

"I'm twenty-one years old, man, and a naval lieutenant — a spacer, not some holder's daughter off on her first fling."

The clerk reddened and cleared his throat. "No, no, there you are."

Alexis' tablet pinged with receipt of the room's code. "Thank you."

She and Delaine started for the lift.

"Miss Carew," the clerk called.

"Yes?"

"I meant no offense, miss, it's only there was an incident — and complaints, you see."

Chapter Twelve

The indenture fair was to last five days and both the landing field and Port Arthur filled overnight, with the indenture ships' boats bringing down load after load of bodies for the tents. The colony's antigrav haulers worked through the night as well, and the city's population swelled.

Alexis and Delaine left their room early, only to find the hotel's dining area filled and with a long queue. The lobby bustled with late arrivals, some with reservations and those foolish enough not to have made one turned away to seek a room from the more enterprising residents of Port Arthur who'd let out a room, a couch, or even a cushioned bit of floor.

"I'm sorry, Miss Carew," the harried maître d' said as they peeked into the dining room. "The wait's an hour's time already and only to get worse, I fear. There's —"

An even more harried server rushed by the podium, whispering, "A cook's burned three trays of bacon and chef's like to kill him, sir."

"Miss Carew, I'm sorry, but I must —"

"Go, Charles," Alexis said. "We'll make do."

Alexis and Delaine made their way out onto the streets of a city transformed.

Despite the early hour, the street was as full as the hotel's lobby.

Pedestrians, horses, carts, and the occasional electric buggy vied for space in the street — space lessened by so many pedestrians forced into the streets by the sheer number of tables set out in front of nearly every building. Tea and coffee here, fresh baked goods there, and scattered about there were sizzling grills and venting steam tables of those who'd set up in front of their homes to sell any manner of thing the newcomers might wish to start their day.

Delaine stopped walking and stared at the scene. "*Mon Dieu.*"

"Did you not have indenture fairs in the Berry March?" Alexis asked.

"*Non.*" Delaine shook his head. "If the leaders of Hanover wish you to go to another world, you go. Do they wish you to stay, you stay. There is little to decide."

Alexis looked about. "It *is* more crowded than I remember them being."

They started on again, weaving through the moving crowds until they reached the landing field, which was just as abuzz with activity as the town streets, though with other customers.

The vendor stalls were all open and lines already forming as boats from the indenture ships disgorged their cargoes. Men, women, and whole families streamed off the boats from the indenture ships — more than Alexis would have thought a captain should allow packed aboard.

Spacers from those ships were at the boats' cargo hatches before the first indenture hit the ramp, tossing bags and crates to the grassy field.

The indentures rushed to find their baggage — some with only a canvas bag to sling over their shoulders. Others begging carts or assistance from the spacers — and paying dearly for it — to transport more bags and crates than they could carry.

Possessions sorted out, they crammed the wide aisles between roped off squares, searching for their assigned spots.

"Q194," a man dragging a heavy bag muttered, wide-eyed, as he passed Alexis and Delaine. "Q194 ... excuse me, sir, am I close to Q194?"

Delaine looked to Alexis.

"The rows up from the town there are the letters, crossed by numbers," Alexis said. She glanced at the nearest intersection. "That's L52, just there." She pointed. "So you've to go away from the town — that way — to your number, then to left a bit for Q."

"Thank you!" The man took a few steps, then turned. "Are you, by any chance, in need of an accountant? I have references here —" He fumbled for his tablet.

Alexis shook her head. "No, sir, I'm sorry — but there are a number of firms and families who will be. Dalthus is growing and prospering, I assure you."

The man smiled at that. "Is it? Thank you!" He turned again, then back, frowning. "Any, ah, recommendations?" he asked. "For good or ill?"

Alexis frowned. She didn't know much about the accounting firms, having Isom for her own numbers and being away so much of the time that she wasn't certain who her grandfather used for his holdings.

Still —

She stepped closer to the man so that she could speak quietly. "Goodwill, Warriner, Hollingworth, and ... Coalson," she said quietly, naming those families she knew to be harsh and unfair with their indentures. "Those are families to avoid, if you can."

The man nodded. "Goodwill, Warriner, Hollingworth, and Coalson," he repeated. "Thank you again!"

He rushed off.

Alexis and Delaine resumed their walk.

"Do you wish breakfast?" Delaine asked, nodding toward a stall.

"Perhaps coffee," Alexis said, "but nothing more at those prices.

A six pence for a butty? I think not. Their prices will drop in an hour or so when those off the ships are settled and the fair officially opens."

"But will there not be more customers then?"

Alexis nodded. "There will, but local folk who know what a thing should cost here. For now, they're counting on the spacers and indentures being too impatient to wait after weeks on ship's rations."

Indeed, there were lines at most of the stalls and Alexis shook her head at those paying a day's wage or more for a sandwich and a bit of juice. She glanced at the signs for several nearby stalls and shrugged. "There'll be no coffee for us at these prices, either. We should have got what we wanted back in the town."

Delaine chuckled and got in the nearest line. "I think my purse will extend to coffee, no matter the cost. I have my stipend from *La République* while they determine the fate of *La Marche des Baies* fleet, as well as pay from my time as captive."

They drank their coffee walking and, as Alexis predicted, the prices on the signs began dropping as the crowd changed, with the indentures finding their own stalls, the spacers moving off to the town and their own particular entertainments, and more of those native to Dalthus entering the fair.

Alexis led their walk back to an aisle with a particular concentration of stalls she'd noted.

"There, you see?" she asked. "The prices are a third or less what they were before — and since your purse is flush with coin you may begin making up for all the treats you didn't have the opportunity to give me these last years."

Delaine raised an eyebrow. "*Poupounette*, I *was* a captive of pirates much of that time."

"Which is why I shall forgive you and allow you to make up for your laxity."

She looked around at the tents and stalls.

"This one," she said, grasping Delaine's hand and leading him to a stall selling candied nuts. "And then an ice cream and one of those filled crepes."

Delaine laughed. "All at once?"

Alexis tugged at his arm to hurry him up. "It's been years since I attended a fair of any kind myself and I'm headed off-planet again — I'll make the most of this one, if you please. And, no, not all at once. The nuts will keep until we're past the food, the ice cream and crepe will have to be eaten now, of course, and we'll get a bit of floss later, but the toffee apples are always best to get early before they've sat too long."

"Ah, you have a plan."

"This is not my first fair, I assure you. The optimization of sweets is a thing I'm long familiar ... oh, dear, they have yellowman. I'll save that for later, but we can get it now."

Delaine laughed and Alexis tugged him along to their next destination, popping a few of the candied nuts into her mouth before tucking the warm paper package into her pocket.

"Is that all?" Delaine asked.

Alexis snorted. "Not nearly. We've not even got to the fried things, yet."

The flavors, once ice cream and crepe were firmly ensconced in her hands, served to more fully bring back her memories of fairs past — perhaps the tents were a bit dingier with age, the bunting a bit faded, and the smell of overused grease just a bit stronger than she remembered, but time would tell, wouldn't it?

The fair's rides, off along the field's edge, were certainly not so exciting looking as she remembered them, but even a brief glimpse of those bloody, spinning cups was every bit as sick-making as she remembered. No need for those — she'd ridden the masthead in a *darkspace* gale often enough to sate anyone's appetite for such jerking about.

Past the food were the merchants and craftsmen, where she hoped to pick up a gift or two for her folk before leaving for New London — she'd be gone yet another Christmas for this trip, so best to leave something behind.

"Alexis? Alexis, over here!"

The call drew Alexis' attention from a bit of leatherwork she was admiring — might be something fancy for her coxswain, Nabb, to add to his station-going rig. She looked up and smiled to find her cousin, Lauryn, waving — then narrowed her eyes to see who was with her.

"Coalson again," she whispered.

"They do seem much about each other," Delaine murmured back.

"Yes, I can't fault him, he's been nothing but proper, it's only —"

Alexis broke off as the pair approached, widening her smile in genuine delight as she hugged her cousin, then managing to keep it in place as she greeted the man with her.

"Lauryn — Mister Coalson."

"Miss Carew," Edmon Coalson said with a nod, then frowned. "Or is it still lieutenant? I can never keep straight which is appropriate when you're not in uniform."

"Alexis is fine, I'm sure, and Edmon," Lauryn said. "The two of you waste such time with this little formal dance every time we meet. Can it not be Alexis and Edmon and leave it at that?"

Coalson shrugged. "I assure you I have no objection, if you do not."

Alexis paused. She'd no love for the Coalsons, surely, but the son was not the father, after all — nor the grandfather, both of whom had done ill to her family. And Edmon Coalson did seem to have forgiven her — or at least forgotten — that she'd thrust his father out of an airlock.

Perhaps it is well past time to put the past behind us. And Lauryn wishes it so much.

"Of course ... Edmon," she said.

The man did support the change in law which will allow me to inherit our lands, she thought.

"Are you looking for workers for your grandfather, Alexis?" Lauryn asked.

Alexis shook her head. "Merely enjoying the fair."

"Well, then you'll walk with us, surely?" Lauryn asked. "Edmon and I are merely taking in the sights, though he does have some hiring to do later."

"Ah, yes, surely," Alexis answered with a glance to Delaine.

"Wonderful!" Lauryn said, then her cousin took Edmon Coalson's arm and started off.

"They seem to have become close," Delaine whispered.

Alexis took his arm and nodded. "They did ... and I can't help but feel that's a bit wrong."

Chapter Thirteen

"Must we, dear?" Lauryn asked as they reached the limits of the town's merchant stalls and arrived at the area set aside for the indentures from the ships. "They're still setting up, after all."

"I did say I must take a quick walk through to see what's available," Coalson answered.

"Oh, very well," Lauryn said, then almost hopefully, "Do you mind, Alexis?"

Alexis and Delaine exchanged a quick glance.

"Not at all," Alexis said.

The two couples continued on past the merchant stalls into the indenture area proper and the very tone of the fair seemed to change to Alexis' senses.

Where Dalthus' merchants and vendors had bright and gaily painted stalls and carts, the indentures had no such frivolity.

Some, mostly those who had some marketable skills much in demand on colony worlds, had tents covering their space, but most had nothing but their roped off square of land, unprotected from Dalthus' sun.

"It's all so gloomy," Lauryn whispered to Alexis. She'd dropped back from Coalson's side to walk with Alexis and Delaine, as Coalson himself concentrated on scanning the signs.

Each space had a sign listing the people available — sometimes just one, though in the case of families it might list everyone who was willing to work. A husband, wife, and even the older children if they were of an age where work was appropriate. After that came a list of skills and work they were willing to contract to perform, as well as the total of their indenture — the cost of their transport and board during their time aboard the ships, any debts or fines the indenture ship had paid for them to leave their last world, perhaps a bit the folk had added on themselves, to ensure it was saved and available to them when their indenture was done.

As a child, walking here with her grandfather, Alexis had always wondered why they might do that — then Denholm had pointed out the folk on their own lands who couldn't seem to hold onto a pence of their pay past the next leisure day.

A man of that sort, with the proper skills, might prefer to have a sum upfront, safe from his habits in a trust earning some few percents while he worked out his term, then receive enough for him to immediately set up his own shop at the end, while knowing he was free to spend the rest of his pay as he might without needing the discipline to save any of it himself. She'd noted that most of that sort had families and suspected it was the profligate man's wife who'd come up with the plan.

Those were what she'd thought of as the happy signs, though. The folk who'd left their home worlds hoping for a better life among the colonies of the Fringe.

They'd always looked so hopeful to Alexis, eyes bright — often with children playing and rushing about, happy to be off the close confines of the ships and with space to run and play their games.

Even as she thought that, she spied one such group rushing about in a chaotic muddle behind their parents' space. They'd pushed their parents and their parents' gear to the very front of their space and setup their own small football pitch, using bits of the rope partitioning their parents' space to form open nets at either end, and piles of luggage behind each to backstop their game.

That was poor defense against the enthusiasm of the players, though, as Alexis watched an errant kick launch the children's ball over their parents' heads to cross the walkway and smack firmly into Edmon Coalson's back as he read the signs opposite the game.

"*Bugger, what?*" Coalson exclaimed, turning, but not before Alexis saw the dusty imprint the ball had left on his jacket.

Coalson glared about then his eyes narrowed as he caught sight of the group of children, all hung heads and wide eyes now.

"Bloody hooligans," Coalson muttered, stalking toward the group.

"Sorry, sir, so sorry," one of the parents said as Coalson approached. "Children stuck aboard ship for so long, you see? Nowhere for them to run up there, you know?"

"I'll —"

"Edmon," Lauryn said, laying a hand on his arm. "They're only playing. Surely it was an accident."

Coalson drew back his foot to kick the ball, with such an expression on his face Alexis knew it would send the ball far away from the children, but as his foot started forward, Delaine's own darted out.

Delaine tapped the top of the ball with his toe, drawing it toward him just as Coalson's foot swept through the now empty space.

"*Allez!*" Delaine yelled, lofting the ball a few feet in the air with one foot, then hopping to kick it with the other.

The ball sailed over the parents' heads back to the children, landing neatly in the middle of the group, who then resumed their game as though nothing had happened.

Coalson glared at Delaine for a moment, before his face calmed. Delaine simply smiled and shrugged.

"Must we continue to the rest?" Lauryn asked as they arrived at the next row. "It becomes so dreary."

"It should be dreary, dear," Coalson said, "and it's among the transported that the best bargains are often found."

Lauryn looked around as they continued and Alexis had to agree that these ... well, there weren't proper stalls or even tents here. The roped off squares were smaller, which was likely because those here had less in the way of both luggage and family.

Most of the indentures here were single men and women with no more than a single duffel to hold their belongings.

The signs here also changed to now list the crime, or crimes, each had been convicted of on their home world ... or last world, as some had been transported more than once, with that history laid out before their little plot of the field for all to see.

Those would likely never be picked and would live out their lives aboard the ships, for they'd almost certainly offend again. What landowner would wish to see the bond he'd paid for disappear into worthlessness when the fellow next committed a crime and was transported yet again?

It showed in the transportee's attitude, as well, for many lounged about, ignoring the Dalthus holders who walked along the rows looking for the few who might be prepared to make something of a second chance.

"The indenture system is so abhorrent," Lauryn said. "We should do away with it entirely."

"Then how will the colonies get more workers, dear?" Coalson asked.

"From those who buy their passage," Lauryn answered. "I don't see why these folk can't be made happy on their home worlds instead of forcing them into such debt seeking another."

"We'd only see the wealthy land here that way, cousin," Alexis said, not happy that she and Coalson appeared to be on the same side of this. "Those willing to work the fields and mines for a time in order to build their future lives haven't the means to buy passage — the travel is quite expensive."

"Why don't they simply get a loan?" Lauryn asked. "There's more than one bank, even here on Dalthus."

"With communications taking so long between systems?" Alexis asked. "What banker would make a loan when they have no idea what system the borrower might alight in? Or even if the system would let them collect? Al Jadiq calls it usury and negates all out-of-system debts with interest attached."

Alexis' cousin frowned.

"And the indenture amount *is* a loan, when you get right down to it," Alexis went on. "The shipowner loans out what's needed to clear the previous system and the cost of transport, then it's paid back by whoever purchases the indenture."

"Perhaps," Lauryn allowed, "but it seems so ... so wrong to speak of it in terms of a man's life."

Delaine cleared his throat. "I do not know your ways well yet," he said, "but what more does one have to trade with than years and minutes? You may call them pounds and pence, or credits and tenths, but we all trade what time we have for the means, I think."

Coalson laughed. "No doubt! Some of us have minutes worth more than others, though, don't we?" He eyed a nearby indenture's sign. "Take this fellow here — transported for theft and not a skill listed beyond the strength of his back ... with his spindly-self just there to put the lie to that value."

He shook his head.

"No, likely spend his years in the ships with that cost — not enough years left to make up a single pound." He looked around. "Very well, I think there'll be no bargains to be found here. Shall we return to town and luncheon, my dear?"

Coalson took Lauryn's arm and steered her back toward the edge of the field and the town before she had a chance to answer, but she turned back to Alexis and smiled.

"Will you join us?" she asked. "I'll speak no more of politics, I promise."

Alexis jerked her attention away from the indenture Coalson had singled out. The man was hunched over as he sat on his half-filled duffel and his shoulders shook.

"Ah, I'm afraid no," she said. "Delaine and I still wish to explore the rest of the fair."

Lauryn laughed. "You were always one to prefer the stalls to a proper meal. Very well, we'll see you again before the fair ends, I hope?"

"Perhaps," Alexis said, though if Braithwaite found them a ship they might be gone before that time.

"Your *cousine* has opinions," Delaine said once the other pair was well away.

"She does," Alexis said. "I think she may be searching for her next crusade after our inheritance laws were changed a few years ago." She frowned. "I suppose she could do worse than to set herself against the indenture system — I don't see it going away, but there are abuses, I'm sure."

"Abuses she walks away with now, *oui*? You told the man — *le comptable* — to avoid this Coalson?"

Alexis shrugged. "There are ... anecdotes. And rumors. Nothing to bring to the Conclave, so far as I know. The Coalsons are known for squeezing every bit of value from a contract, but there's never proof they've broken the terms."

Delaine offered her his arm to continue their walk.

"A man may have two loves," he said, "but if those loves are money and a woman, he will soon lose one to the other."

"A moment," Alexis said as they started to walk away.

She turned back and studied the sign Coalson had mocked, then the man — his head still bowed and shoulders shaking.

A quick calculation told her the man's indenture would be eight years at the lowest tier. With no particular skills listed, he'd be put to the mines or fields, or some other work that required little wit, but some brawn — which the man clearly lacked.

"Give me your purse," Alexis said, reaching for her own.

"Purse?" Delaine asked.

"Wallet, *portefeuille*, whatever you call it. Give me whatever coin you have."

Without a word, Delaine reached for his pockets.

Alexis took a handful of coins from Delaine and added them to her own.

"Twenty-four shillings between us," she muttered. "The stalls will be less expensive the farther out."

"Are you hungry again so soon?" Delaine asked. "And your shillings and pence — why not the credit?"

"The Founders were touched," Alexis said, lip caught between her teeth and brow furrowed. "With genius or madness, depending on who you ask, but touched." She closed her hand over the coins, hiding them. "I'll be but a moment, please stay here."

Alexis went and knelt next to the crying indenture.

"Come t'mock me more as your friend did?" the man muttered.

"No friend of mine," Alexis said. "He's right, though, that you'll not get off the ships as you are."

"Think I don't know?"

Alexis slid her hand behind the man's heel where no one could see and set the coins on the ground.

"There's twenty-four shillings there."

"Wha—"

"Don't say a word and hide them well. Don't let others see or you'll be robbed, right?"

"I — yes, before I'd drawn another breath," the man agreed.

"Take one out, only one, on each world you visit," Alexis told him. "Use it to buy better food than ship's fare and stuff yourself full.

Start eating more aboard ship, as well, no matter how bad it is. Then exercise."

The man shook his head.

"No room on the ships for —"

"If you've room to sit or lie down, you've room for some," Alexis told him. "Walk the corridors, squat and lift your own body, then add your duffel for more weight. By the time those coins are done, you'll be fit enough for some work on these worlds."

She stood before the man could protest again. He'd take the chance to improve his lot or not — if he spent the coin on drink instead ... well, she couldn't force him to do what was smart.

She hurried back to Delaine.

Chapter Fourteen

The hotel had a private dining room, as they were used to accommodating visiting holders who wished not to mingle with other visitors or have their discussions overheard, and they were quite pleased to be able to accommodate Lord Braithwaite.

Alexis and Delaine wore their respective uniforms, the captains of the indenture ships wore theirs, and Braithwaite wore dinner dress, making him the plainest at the table by far, for both the navy represented and the merchant lines had far more in the way of ornaments than plain dinner dress.

There were four indenture ships and one naval escort in the mix.

The gold band around Captain Jordan's, the young naval captain's, beret gleamed to indicate his command, which Alexis had to admit she envied, no longer having one of her own — if there were a navy ship in their sector, even a tiny pinnace, then Admiralty could have called on her to command it if they liked. That they hadn't must surely be a sign of their displeasure, despite the Queen's summons.

Two of the indenture ships were owned by the Marchant line and their captains — the younger being the other's nephew, so they said — came resplendent in the line's uniform, complete with their own gold braids and hashes for rank and time in service to the Company.

Another captain, from a smaller line, was decked out in grey with bits of red that almost, though not quite, matched Delaine's uniform — the heavily modified garb, which had started as Hanoverese then been adapted by those of the rebelling Berry March Fleet he'd come with to New London.

The last of the indenture captains, though still more colorful than Braithwaite, could not be said to match his finery. He wore a cast-off naval jacket, faded, save where gilt had been removed — too shabby and worn to make a place in even the poorest midshipman's chest — and came to dinner only partially shaven.

He was ignored by the others of the indenture fleet through most of the dinner and seemed to prefer it that way, making only perfunctory answers to Alexis' attempts at conversation.

As for Alexis herself, she found the Marchant captains' disdain for the tattered captain also applied to herself, where they were short and dismissive, with a sense of underlying hostility, when forced by the conversation's flow to address her — something she found not unwelcome, for she'd always found Marchant Company officers to be the sort of haughty, disdainful fellows she'd not converse with by choice in any case, even when she hadn't known what she now did about the company.

These two might not be aware of the Company's involvement in the Barbary slave and piracy trades — it wasn't general knowledge among the line's captains, she suspected — but the Company almost certainly promoted only those they were confident would keep such a secret if found out.

And those they're mistaken about will find themselves at the receiving end of a bomb or some such — as Captain Skanes of the Hind had back on Penduli Station in the attack which had left Alexis injured as well.

Alexis had no proof now, and her knowledge was nothing to

confront two captains far from the Barbary with, but she was just as glad to have limited conversation with the men.

What conversation there was centered around Lord Braithwaite and remained the casual sort of idle news, gossip he brought from New London (him not appearing at all interested in any gossip the captains brought from their travels along the Fringe), and what each of the tellers thought to be amusing anecdotes.

As the last of the dishes were cleared, bowls of nuts set down, and glasses reset with the first of the post-dinner ports, Alexis glanced at the young naval captain, who raised an eyebrow back.

He was almost certainly a lieutenant underneath the courtesy rank of his command, and younger than Alexis, but he was active and in command, and the time in-service tabs on his shoulder were...

Bloody hell, I'm junior here ... Alexis thought.

She grinned acknowledgment, nodded to him, then, not being aboard ship where she might remain seated, rose, taking up her glass.

"Gentlemen," she said, "the Queen!"

"The Queen!" they all answered, taking up their own glasses. Except Delaine who answered with, "*La Reine!*" Drawing a glance or two from the others.

Braithwaite seemed a bit surprised — no doubt because it was a naval custom and the other captains were close enough to the Dark to have encountered it before — but took the opportunity to stand after Alexis sat and draw the captains' attention to himself.

"Indeed, Lieutenant Carew, and thank you, for such a toast does bring us to the purpose of this dinner — more than courtesy to you fine captains and your ships, I'm afraid.

"I am, as I've said, here on Dalthus as envoy and herald for Her Majesty. My task, delivering to Lieutenant Carew here Her Majesty's regards and to request and require that the lieutenant return to New London for investiture in the Order of the Founding."

That brought on a set of cheers from the other captains, along with another toast, though the two Marchant captains were noticeably silent and only touched their glasses to their lips without the hearty drinking of the others.

Alexis flushed and nodded thanks, though she suspected the enthusiasm had more to do with draining a glass of fine port and having it refilled out of Lord Braithwaite's purse than in thinking her honor so deserved.

"Of course, of course," Braithwaite said. "That said, I must say that I find myself in a most embarrassing position for the completion of my appointed task ... in want of transport, you see." He cleared his throat. "Which is where I hope you gentlemen will come in — for surely, with so many folk transported as indentures aboard your ships, there must be something in the way of accommodations available. It's but five of us in need of passage, and I've means of compensation. At least as far as Zariah, where there's enough passenger traffic to see us the rest of the way."

"Ah, Lord Braithwaite," Captain Jordan said. "It's not for lack of desire to accommodate your return, I assure you, but *Swallow* is no passenger vessel. She's but a pinnace, much as I love her." He glanced at Alexis for support. "Even at just the five of you, it'd be a crowd — and we've no cabins aboard, only a bit of thermoplastic panel between my cot and the quarterdeck."

Alexis nodded. "It's true, m'lord — *Swallow* would not be at all suitable for passengers. You've a crew of, what, eight, Captain Jordan?"

Jordan nodded. "And overcrowded at that. As well, we're contracted to the Marchant Company for this convoy —" He nodded toward those two captains. "— and bound by Admiralty orders to sail where they will."

"I see," Braithwaite said. He turned to the two Marchant Company captains. "But what of your ships, sirs? Surely the Company could accommodate us and take a bit of a detour?"

The two captains glanced at each other and the older Captain Hodgman scratched at his beard before speaking.

"We will surely accommodate you, m'lord — Queen's Herald and all. Even to one of us leaving off our route and sailing direct for New London — I've no doubt our superiors would support that. Crown business, and all —"

"Excellent," Braithwaite said, beginning to smile.

"*You*, m'lord, if I might stress that." Hodgman cleared his own throat and started to speak, then paused before going on. "It's awkward, m'lord, to say aloud, Company business and all, but we've instructions with regard to, ah, your guest."

"My guest?" Braithwaite said. "Do you mean Lieutenant Carew?"

Hodgman glanced at her, then away. He nodded. "Carews in general, but her in specific, m'lord, yes."

Alexis narrowed her eyes as she stared at the two Marchant captains. She supposed that it should be expected — she'd been with Captain Skanes at the end on Penduli, the both of them on their way to the Board of Inquiry to lay out what they knew of the Marchants' involvement in the Barbary space piracy and slave trade.

That had ended with a bomb — or not ended entirely it seemed.

Braithwaite blinked rapidly. "What possible instructions could you have?"

"With respect, m'lord, that's Company business — save to say we'd provide no carriage, sir, to the lieutenant or her entourage."

"With respect to the Company," Alexis asked, "would the nature of my denial be any of *my* business?"

She suspected, of course, that it was to do with her certain knowledge of the Marchants' involvement in slavery and piracy, but wanted to force the two captains to say as much as they would.

Hodgman shrugged. "You would likely know better than us, lieutenant — we only know there's a directive we're to refuse carriage to the Carew family on Dalthus in all respects." He glanced at Lord Braithwaite. "Orders, m'lord."

"I see," Braithwaite said, while Alexis pondered the Marchant captain's words.

The Carew family, he'd said — which would include her grandfather and carriage of goods for the homestead. While the family had little business with the Marchants in the past, it had grown recently with the colony's expansion.

Alexis sighed. She'd have to tell her grandfather she'd brought yet more difficulties to their table. Still, she ground her teeth at the slight, wondering what the line's "directive" would say if a Marchant ship were under attack, and she was in command of a nearby naval vessel.

"Tell me, Captain Hodgman," Alexis said, "does this directive extend to refusal of Royal Navy assistance, should a Carew be in command of the vessel so rendering?"

"I believe I've said what I must," Hodgman said with a shrug. "I've no knowledge of what passed between you and the line to cause this, and no desire to learn." He turned to Braithwaite. "So you see, m'lord, I'm limited in what passage I might offer you."

"Of course." Braithwaite frowned. "Of course." He looked down the table to the remaining captains.

The better dressed of the two non-Marchant captains raised a hand to forestall him. "I'm contracted to Al Jadiq," he said, "and only traveling in convoy for the protection." He shrugged. "Much as I'd like your coin, m'lord, if the convoy turns back here, even for a time, I'm afraid I must continue on."

"I see," Braithwaite said, frowning. "Captain Meiggs? What of your ship, might you have room for a few passengers?"

Meiggs cleared his throat and straightened his shoulders. "M'lord, I'm always set to serve the Queen, no doubt, but ... well, *Star of Tauric's* an older ship, and she's not set for passengers."

Braithwaite frowned. "Yet you carry these indentures, sir, do you not?"

Meiggs scrunched up his mouth. "Indentures aren't, strictly speaking, passengers, m'lord — not in the manifest regulations, do y'see?"

Braithwaite's frown deepened. "If not passengers, then what are they listed as?"

"Well, cargo, of course, m'lord."

"Of course."

"Still," Meiggs said, "there may be a way we can help each other in this."

"Indeed?"

"Well, m'lord, as the Marchant fellows here would offer you fine accommodations, I'm sure, but won't carry Lieutenant Carew, and as I've no room at all for passengers..." Meiggs glanced at Alexis and trailed off.

"Yes, Captain?" Alexis asked.

"It's only if you were willing," Meiggs said, "and not thinking it's beneath you, having your naval rank and all, but I note you're between commissions and ... well, I do find myself down a first mate. And my second not being of particularly fine material, come to that, and Dalthus isn't, no offense, known for its spacers here at the port." He shrugged. "I've one cabin I need to fill rather than let for coin, if you understand."

"You wish the lieutenant, on her way to be knighted by the Queen herself, to *work* for her passage?" Braithwaite asked.

"That sounds quite satisfactory, Captain Meiggs," Alexis said. She'd have done it in any case, but the near outrage in the herald's tone set her on edge and made her decision quite easy. "You've need of a mate and I've need of passage. A fair bargain."

She held out her hand and Meiggs took it gingerly with an eye toward Braithwaite.

"A bargain, aye," Meiggs said.

"There it is, then," Alexis said. "Lord Braithwaite and his valet will travel aboard the Marchant Company ship, and I will graciously accept Captain Meiggs' offer of employment aboard the *Star of Tauric*. It will be good to have some work to do on the passage and not remain idle."

She nearly heaved a sigh of relief at not having to be a passenger with Braithwaite for the entire journey.

"This is most irregular," Braithwaite said. "I am charged to deliver Lieutenant Carew to the Court — how am I to do that with her aboard a different ship?"

"It's only the first bit of our transit, my lord," Alexis said.

"That simply won't do. There's a certain propriety involved in this, as well as the time, you see, as I'm also charged with preparing you for your appearance at Court."

"We won't be riding the indenture ships straight in to New London, Lord Braithwaite — once at Zariah we'll be able to transit to a proper passenger vessel and it's nearly three months to New London from there." Alexis shrugged. "I'm certain that's enough time for me to learn not to embarrass myself —"

In truth, Alexis was a bit put out at Braithwaite's suggestion — she *had* been to a proper court, after all, in *Noveau Paris*. True, she'd wound up in a bit of a tiff with a French nobleman, but that had managed to bring the French into the war with Hanover, which was her purpose, after all, so in the end she'd handled it quite well, she thought.

"— don't you think?" she finished weakly.

"No, no," Braithwaite said. "If you are to be aboard this *Star of Tauric*, then I shall make my passage there as well."

Meiggs cleared his throat. "With respect, sir —"

The elder Marchant captain also spoke. "My nephew's *Almorah* is a fine ship, Lord Braithwaite, and more suitable than —"

"I've made my decision," Braithwaite insisted. "Please make accommodation for me and my valet aboard *Star of Tauric*."

Chapter Fifteen

"I'm sure you'll have a fine passage aboard *Almorah*, Lord Braithwaite," Alexis said. "The Marchants are well known for their hospitality."

"Yes, of course, yes," Braithwaite said, backing into *Star of Tauric's* airlock toward the boat sent from *Almorah*, eyes wide.

"We'll have our time together from Zariah on, once we can find a proper passenger ship," Alexis continued.

Braithwaite nodded, raising one hand to his mouth, and continuing to back away, as though watching to be sure nothing from *Star of Tauric* might follow him into the other ship's boat.

"It's only a small bit of the passage, after all."

"Of course, of course."

Behind Alexis, Isom muttered, "Mightn't we go with him?"

"They will not take her," Delaine reminded him.

There was a pause, during which Braithwaite nearly stumbled making the transition from the ship's artificial gravity to the boat's, only being saved by his valet's quick actions.

A moment later the far hatch closed behind him and Alexis

closed *Star's* hatch as well, allowing the airlock to cycle with no little groaning and hissing from the mechanisms.

Alexis looked around at what had sent the Queen's Herald running.

The *Star of Tauric* was not a well-kept ship.

If the state of the ship's boat and its lingering odors on the way up from Dalthus hadn't been enough to tell Alexis that, the cacophony and stink which greeted her as the airlock opened would have, and Lord Braithwaite had not wasted time in mentioning it.

Neither had Delaine, who grunted as though he'd walked into something solid, nor Isom, who muttered under what breath he was able to take.

Alexis turned from the airlock to face the chaos which had finally sent Lord Braithwaite packing to the, she assumed, relative peace of one of the Marchant ships.

The meter-wide companionway that ran *Star's* length here was cut effectively in half by the press of bodies and possessions. People sprawled against the bulkhead, feet and legs laying in the somewhat empty space she assumed was meant for those traversing the companionway, only pulling them back at the last moment as someone passed — and that only in the event they were awake.

The inner bulkhead was lined with folding bunks three high — much like the gundeck of a warship, only on *Star* it was nearly the whole of the ship's bulkheads, with a cot seemingly mounted on every vertical surface that would hold one.

Where there weren't bodies, there were bags — the heavy, durable canvas bags in which the indentures held their day-to-day possessions. Those things which couldn't be crated and settled into the ship's hold.

"Captain Meiggs will likely be on the quarterdeck," she said to Delaine, "we should see him before visiting the wardroom ourselves."

"I'll see to the stowing of your gear, sir," Isom said. "Should the wardroom not be taken up with ... passengers."

The ladder and companionway leading to the quarterdeck was, at least, uncrowded with the press of humanity found elsewhere on the ship.

There was no marine at guard next to the quarterdeck hatch as there would be on a navy ship, only a much-used and seldom-cleaned panel. Alexis reached to press the call button to request admittance, but the hatch slid open at their approach. Meiggs' voice echoed out into the companionway.

"You're owed what you're owed and transport to where you were hired on, no more," Meiggs was saying.

From the hatchway, Alexis could see him at the signals console, back to her and one hand to his ear as he spoke.

"Not a bit of it, lad," Meiggs went on, "I'm sorry and all, for your troubles, but it's none of the ship's concern now —" He paused. "Well and you should take that up with the driver of the bloody lorry, shouldn't you? Lad, but it weren't aboard *Star* and it weren't on ship's duties, so it's on your own head."

"Captain Meiggs?" Alexis called, wanting to alert him that they were present.

Meiggs held up a finger, not turning.

"No, lad," he said. "I'm sorry for you, sure, but I've done what I must. Speak to the Spacers' League if you wish more — they've funds for that, if I recall."

He pulled the earpiece from his head and set it on the signals console, then turned to the hatch. His face brightened in a smile as he saw who it was.

"And I'm glad to see you lot, sure," Meiggs said. He gestured to the signals console. "*Star'd* not be sailing, else."

"What's happened, Captain Meiggs?" Alexis asked.

She couldn't quite dare to ponder what else might have gone wrong aboard this ship — crowded and dirty as it was. She'd not seen a quarterdeck so ill-maintained since she'd stepped aboard that rogue

Dansby's smuggling vessel — and that had been a carefully applied veneer to throw off the revenue men. She rather suspected *Star* came by her condition honestly.

"I'm down another bloody mate," Meiggs said, scowling and waving a hand at the signals console. "That was him, there. Fool stepped in front of a bloody lorry — both legs broke and in hospital. Says he was pushed, but drunk's more like it."

"That's awful," Alexis said. "Will he be all right?"

"Aye, I feel for the lad, but he's expecting more than he's owed. He's got his pay and a voucher on *Star's* accounts back to his home system — most captains'll take that — but the lad wants coin in hand for his transport." Meiggs sighed. "Like as not the lad wants to find a berth after he heals — no interest in heading home — so'll pocket the fare." He shrugged. "Some captain'll buy the voucher, though at a discount. In any case, *Star's* met her obligations to him."

He glanced from Alexis to Delaine.

"So, then, lad, would you be up for working your passage and not lazing about?" Meiggs asked.

"*Mais oui*," Delaine said.

"May you what?" Meiggs asked. "Two of you want to talk it over? That's fine, and I've no care which of you is first or second, so long as you can both stand a watch."

Alexis and Delaine shared a look.

"Ah, no, *Capitai* —" Delaine cleared his throat. "Captain. It was only French for yes."

Meiggs frowned. "Less of that, then. It confuses folk."

Chapter Sixteen

Star's wardroom was at least neater and cleaner than the rest of the ship, if not what Alexis might reasonably describe as neat or clean without the recent comparison.

It consisted of four cabins of roughly equal size around a central space just large enough for a round table, four chairs, and a hatch to the steward's pantry aft.

As Alexis and Delaine entered, the reason for the space's relative tidiness became apparent as Isom exited one of the cabins with an armful of bedding, hair in disarray and a smudge of grime across his brow.

"Tidying as best I can, sir," Isom said, panting as he crossed to the pantry. "Fresh bedding's on your bunk and there's fellows coming to clear out the second mate's bits an get those down to him." He shook his head and entered the pantry. "Poor man."

Again, Alexis marveled at a ship's ability to transmit gossip to the crew at near light speed. They'd only just heard of the mate's mishap themselves and no one else had been near the quarterdeck to hear Meiggs take the call, yet word had already come this far.

"Poor man, indeed," a voice behind them said.

They turned to see a stout man with profound, greying sideburns, then moved out of the way for the man to enter.

"Norberto Slott," he said, holding out his hand for each of them. "Sailing master aboard this cursed ship."

"Alexis Carew," Alexis introduced herself. "To be first mate, I'm told."

"Delaine Theibaud," Delaine said. "Second mate, now, as well."

Slott nodded and made his way to the table where he poured a mug of wine from the bottles there.

"And may you have better of the positions than your predecessors," he said, drinking.

Alexis frowned. "Why do you say cursed, Mister Slott?"

"What else?" Slott asked. "Six men meet misadventure on one voyage, in barely three months now? What else to call it?"

A new voice answered him. "Best the crew not hear you at that."

"At the truth of it?" Slott asked. "Do you think they're not saying the same?"

The new man entered, stouter even than Slott, but without the facial hair to fully round out his features. He sat and pulled the bottle from in front of Slott to pour a glass for himself.

"Gilbertson, bosun," he said, glancing at Delaine and then Alexis.

"Alexis Ca —" Alexis began, but Gilbertson waved his hand.

"Carew and Theibaud," he said. "It's all over the ship already that we've replacements for Evens and Hughley." He drank. "Pay no attention to Slott's ravings and for the sweet Dark's sake don't repeat any of it in front of the crew."

"I'm aware of how a crew reacts to thoughts their ship is unlucky, Mister Gilbertson, and would never add to their tales ... but I *would* like to know the facts for myself. You say six men, Mister Slott, but we were only told of the first mate, who's said to have run, and the second who was struck by a lorry — hardly the stuff of dire tales."

"Evens never ran," Slott said. "This ain't the navy, he wasn't pressed. The man's first mate on a slack ship with easy runs, and married to the captain's niece! Set to inherit it all when Meiggs retires, so why run from that?"

"Clear enough if you'd met the captain's niece," Gilbertson muttered.

"Codswallop," Slott said. "Best thing for a man with such a wife is to have his own ship and return home only often enough to show he's not yet dead."

"And the others?" Alexis interrupted. She could see the sense of either argument. True, it might make little sense to run from a berth where one was set to inherit a ship, even one as Dark-beaten as *Star of Tauric*, but she'd also seen marriages where one might simply wish to be gone from the business all entire.

Slott poured himself a full glass and sat back in his chair, smiling. "Ah, well, there's tales enough of woe aboard this ship to fill an evening."

Gilbertson sighed.

Isom took the opportunity of a lull in the conversation to stick his head through the pantry door.

"I'll have supper prepared in twenty minutes time, sir," Isom said.

"Heard you had a man with you," Gilbertson said, sniffing at the aromas coming from the food. "Smells as though he knows his way about the pantry."

"He's a fine cook," Alexis assured them.

Slott nodded. "That's a relief. We had one of the indentures cooking for us, but she sold her indenture here on Dalthus and won't be returning — fine woman, good cook." He shrugged. "Once you got past the poisoning bit."

"Poisoning?" Delaine asked.

Gilbertson nodded. "Her husband. Hear he deserved it, though."

Alexis and Delaine shared a glance.

"She killed him?" Alexis asked.

Slott nodded, then frowned.

"Didn't Meiggs tell you?" he asked. "*Star's* a transport ship."

Gilbertson jerked his head toward the hatch to the rest of the ship.

"Murderers and thieves, the lot of them."

There was a shattering crash from the pantry, then Isom's voice.

"Be a bit longer on the dinner, sir!"

"The first was some fellow we'd just taken aboard," Slott said, tucking into the plate Isom set before him. "Investment scheme, was it, Gilbertson?"

Gilbertson shrugged and nodded to Isom as his own plate was set down. "I pay little heed to the reasons."

Slott shrugged. "Transported with six years on top of his fees, so some coin needed repaying." He shoveled in a mouthful of food, worked his jaw twice, then swallowed. "Headfirst down a companionway ladder and all in a heap at the bottom, that one."

"Indentures are injured every voyage," Gilbertson said. "We crowd them aboard and they've never seen a ship before — don't know the dangers."

"Never seen one manage to go out the airlock like that second fellow," Slott said. "Takes a bit of doing, that."

"The inner sensors had frayed," Gilbertson said. "We've maintenance issues aplenty aboard this ship — no need to blame any else."

Alexis nearly forgot her own supper, looking from one to the other as the sailing master and bosun first told and then excused the deaths aboard *Star of Tauric* since she'd last picked up indentures on Norington.

"Then was Edwards," Slott said, "landsman — crushed in the hold along with an indenture woman."

"Loads shift," Gilbertson said. "Especially if there's..." He glanced at Alexis then cleared his throat. "Activities, we'll say, of a certain energetic nature, near. The sort where folk don't heed what they're knocking about in their tos and fros, it is to say."

Alexis wasn't surprised at what Gilbertson was implying the pair were about. She'd wondered much the same when she came aboard and saw the number of women amongst *Star's* indentures. Throw the spacers with even a bit of coin amongst so many with so little for even a bit of time and transactions of a certain nature would certainly occur.

"Were none of these ... incidents captured in the log?" she asked, frowning, for four deaths aboard ship in such a short time was certainly unusual.

Slott looked to the wardroom's corner where the ship's log camera was mounted to the ceiling and shrugged.

"Log cameras are out in most of the ship. No sense replacing them when the indentures'll just knock them down again. They have their own dealings amongst themselves, the like of which they'd prefer no one have a record of, if you take my meaning."

Gilbertson nodded. "There's two worlds aboard an indenture ship, Miss Carew. The crew's and the cargo's — best they meet only as necessary."

Chapter Seventeen

Slott and Gilbertson left the wardroom soon after eating. The one to see to the stowing of stores and the reloading of baggage from those indentures who'd found no place on Dalthus and the other, he said, to review the charts of the system in preparation for their departure on the morrow.

Alexis pushed her half-eaten meal aside and saw, as Isom whisked the plates away, that Delaine had not eaten much more of his own.

"What do you make of our bosun and sailing master?" she asked.

"The *maître*, he likes to tell a tale, *assurément*."

"If he's to be believed..." Alexis shook her head. "It's not necessary a ship be unlucky, only that the crew believe it so for the unlucky things to happen. And with so small a crew, only two dozen plus the engineers, we could ill-afford more incidents than *Star* has already seen."

Isom filled their glasses, set the rest of the bottle between them, and retired to his pantry.

Alexis drained hers and stood.

"Come," she said, "let us take the measure of our new ship."

Star was, after their dinner, filled with more chaos than before, if Alexis was any judge.

First, she and Delaine made their way forward from the wardroom to the ship's sail locker, where Alexis made what examinations she could of the lock's controls and sensors.

"It's dirty, but appears in order," she muttered.

"You are thinking of the man, his name I forget," Delaine said.

Alexis nodded. "Yes, the one Slott said went out a lock. Gilbertson said the sensors were frayed, but if there's any maintenance I can't fathom a crew slacking on, it's the things that keep our air on the inside of the bloody ship." She looked around. "But I suppose anything is possible with the ship in such a state."

They made their way down the nearest ladder to the next deck.

"They are steep," Delaine said. "A man might well trip."

"Indeed," Alexis muttered, keeping her voice low to not be overheard by either the indentures who crowded the lower passageway or the occasional crewman rushing about. "That's not unheard of, even for experienced crew."

Aft again showed more of the same and they descended to the hold level and the purser's stores.

The man himself, when Alexis spotted him, was so unlike what she expected that she at first took him for some other member of the crew. Only the deference the working crew gave to his orders marked him as the one in charge.

Where naval pursers were, invariably in Alexis' experience, the sort of slick, sharp, quick-looking fellows one typically associated with a cup of dice, eagerness to learn a "new" card game, or the offering of investment opportunities in which the last fellow surely doubled his coin in only a few months' time — *Star's* purser was a rotund, friendly, almost jovial fellow, who sent his crew scurrying about with laughing good humor rather than pointed words and sharp orders.

"Aft with that lot, Armstrong!" he called out as Alexis reached the bottom step of the ladder. "It'll settle easier there and offset what we just stored forward." He laughed. "Balance, me lad, balance. Helps the ship sail true — much like me gut and buttocks, you know!"

Alexis waited for a time when the man's attention wasn't needed elsewhere, then spoke, "Mister Sams, if you have a moment?"

Sams turned and squinted. "What? Aye? Who're you, then?"

"Carew," Alexis said, "just hired on as first mate and this is —"

"Yer a girl."

Oh, sweet Dark, is it this again?

Alexis looked down at herself. "Am I?" She turned to Delaine. "Tell me it isn't so, Delaine. Am I a girl?"

"Sadly, I must say it is so," Delaine said, then whispered. "*Délicieusement.*"

Alexis flushed, hoping Sams hadn't heard or understood that bit. She'd have to speak to Delaine about propriety aboard ship once she had a moment.

And he'll have to put his list of French pet names away for the duration ... which is a shame, and'll likely tie the poor dear's tongue in knots for want of using them.

"It does appear you are correct, Mister Sams, through my own observation and independent confirmation, I find I am, as you say, a girl." Alexis sighed. "Yet, also, strangely, *Star of Tauric's* first mate. And since it is from the latter role I'm addressing you, may we forgo further comment on the former, distressing as it may be to yourself?"

Sams frowned. "Was just observing — no need to go on about it so."

"If that's the case, then I apologize, Mister Sams. There've been more than enough times others have gone on about it, you see?"

"No doubt," Sams said. "I've no doubt indeed." He nodded. "Is there aught I can help you with, Miss Carew?"

"Only learning our way about the ship, Mister Sams," Alexis said. "Seeing how she might sail, as I'm to have the watch as we leave tomorrow."

Sams glanced around the hold. "Oh, she'll sail like a spacer on his last night of leave, but it'll be no fault of my stowage, Miss Carew."

Alexis also glanced around and she could find no fault with how the stores were loaded in the hold. Things were, indeed, balanced as Sams had earlier admonished his crew, even if it might mean more work in their stowage and retrieval.

"Indeed, Mister Sams, it appears all is in order."

"I should hope so."

"So if not for your stowage," Alexis asked, "why do you say *Star* will ... what was it? 'Sail like a spacer on his last night', yes?"

"Sails worn thin, Miss Carew," Sams said. "A keel worn thin as parchment in places. Short-crewed and overloaded. You're like to have a lively morning if it's you taking us out."

"I see." Alexis frowned. "Well, I'll let you be on with your work, Mister Sams."

Alexis left Sams to his stowing and wandered down the central aisle of the hold, glancing between crates and vats to get the lay of things. She stepped a few paces away to where a stack of crates formed a head-high wall with only a narrow space between it and the next. She felt the straps which held each crate to its neighbor's and the stack to the deck. She crouched and peered into the narrow space between the stacks.

Crew often used such spaces in the hold for their own purposes. To hide a bit of gambling, drinking, or, in the case of *Star*, it seemed, for more private activities with the indentures.

Still, she could find nothing amiss with the work of Sams and his men — all was stowed well and the straps tight — even in a hard storm she didn't think the loads would shift much.

True, all that might have been done after the spacer and indenture were crushed in the hold — a pair of deaths would certainly make one work the harder and take better care.

"I see nothing amiss," Alexis said.

"Nor I," Delaine agreed.

They passed a pair of vats holding stores of beer. They were a bit oversized for *Star's* hold, reaching almost to the deck above. One of them had a maintenance tag hanging from its control panel.

"Down for service, much like the whole ship should be, I think," Alexis said.

Even that wasn't cause for concern, with such a small crew the other visible vats would easily keep the crew in beer, wine, and spirits between such close ports as the indenture fleet traveled through. Alexis wondered if the indentures were given any rations of alcohol or if they made due with water — and if there were any thriving trade between crew and passengers to make up for that.

If there were, it wasn't a concern of hers — *Star* had sailed many years without her and would sail many more after she left the ship at Zariah.

"This one may be soon as well," Delaine said, tapping at the other vat's panel.

Alexis walked over and checked, seeing that the other vat had added nitrogen twice in the last week, despite no beer being pulled from it.

"I'll mention it to the purser," Alexis said.

Nitrogen was added to the vats to replace the air at the top, keeping the contents from oxidizing or spoiling as quickly as they might and to keep up the pressure on the beer. If some was leaking, it was automatically added by the vat itself, but too great a leak would allow the contents to spoil or go flat, as well as adding extra nitrogen to the ship's atmosphere.

Alexis shrugged.

"I doubt it's the worst maintenance issue we might find aboard."

Chapter Eighteen

"Signal from *Swallow* — *Convoy, break orbit, form line, shape course for L5.*"

Alexis nodded, looked to Captain Meiggs who also nodded, and took a deep breath. She felt quite out of place — on a quarterdeck but out of uniform. Meiggs had his, but it was more of an odd assortment of castoffs than any proper uniform, and she simply wore her ship's jumpsuit as the rest of the spacers did — with only her rank tabs at the collar to identify her as first mate.

"Take us out, Miss Carew," Meiggs said.

Alexis took a deep breath.

She'd taken the quarterdeck of multiple ships, but never with a crew she knew so little of. After only a day aboard *Star*, she was uncertain of their quality and had time for little but an exchange of names even with the quarterdeck crew, who'd been busy until the last moment with stowing the indentures and their baggage before being called to their posts.

"Aye, sir. Signal to *Swallow*, Mister Joyce — *Affirmative*," she said.

Joyce glanced at her oddly and Alexis realized her mistake. On a naval ship of this size, the signals would be handled by a midshipman due the honorific. Joyce was simply an able spacer.

"Our typical place in line, sir?" Alexis asked Meiggs. "As *Swallow's* not indicated it."

Meiggs grinned. "Dead last, of course, Miss Carew. It's the bloody Marchants who run the show — *Star's* just a tagalong."

"Aye, sir," Alexis said, setting her face so as not to wince. Odd how she'd become so used to the Fringe Navy's choice that all officers be called "sir" and "mister" that she found it off-putting to be called "miss" aboard ship.

She watched the plot as first *Swallow*, then the two Marchant ships, left their orbits. The other indenture ship was leaving the convoy, as they were contracted to sail on to Al Jadiq and could ill-afford the detour back to Zariah.

She turned to the helm where Slott, the sailing master, stood beside the helmsman, his eyes on her.

I suppose I can't blame them — I am the newly here and they've no way of being certain I know my way about a ship.

"Ahead one quarter, Reynolds," she said to the helmsman, glancing at the speed of the other ships on the plot. "Roll thirty to port, come starboard to plus thirty on the ecliptic and down ten."

"Ahead one quarter, roll thirty degrees to port, starboard thirty and down ten on the ecliptic, aye," Reynolds said.

Alexis laid her fingertips on the edge of the plot, watching *Star's* plot against the others. She'd deliberately given the helmsman the target she wished to follow and not the helm inputs so that she could gauge how he chose to get the ship on course.

Too shallow and they'd fall behind the other ships before coming in line, but too steep and they'd likely overshoot their course, requiring a correction and leaving them bobbing about behind the others.

But Reynolds appeared to have a smooth hand, easing the ship into line with the others with no more gap between *Star* and the last Marchant vessel than the rest of the convoy.

"Handsomely done, Reynolds," Alexis said.

She turned and caught Slott's eye, giving the man a nod to say he wasn't the only one judging things here and that she'd found his helmsman's skills satisfactory.

Slott nodded back, then his face broke in a grin.

"I'll be in my cabin if I'm needed, Miss Carew," he said, leaving the bridge.

Captain Meiggs chuckled. "If you've satisfied that old fellow then I'm not needed either." He walked to the door to his cabin. "Call me for transition, Miss Carew, you have the quarterdeck."

Swallow, at least, held a steady pace, allowing Alexis, *Star*, and the other ships an easy time of it in following her. They made for the planetary L5 point, trailing the planet in its orbit, so using the orbit's change to bring the point closer to them even as they accelerated toward it.

Had Alexis been in command of a naval ship, she might have used one of the lunar points, which would be closer, but merchants preferred the larger planetary points which provided less chance of a nearby transition from another ship. Even the convention of entering a system at L4 and leaving at L5 didn't eliminate the possibility of an incoming ship confusing one for the other and transitioning atop one's ship. It was a small risk, but one best avoided.

"Signal from *Swallow*," Joyce announced. "*Transition in one hour.*"

"Thank you, Joyce," Alexis said. "Inform the captain, if you please?"

"Aye, ma'am."

A moment later, Meiggs appeared on the quarterdeck, glanced about to take in the state of things, then nodded to Alexis and left again.

I guess that means he's happy with the state of things.

"Very well," Alexis said. "Reynolds, bring us about. Joyce, signal the sail locker and inform Mister Theibaud he may commence stepping the masts momentarily."

"Aye, ma'am," they both responded.

Alexis' view of the stars outside the ship spun on the monitors as Reynolds brought the ship about, swapping ends so that their engines pointed in the direction of travel in preparation for slowing during the second half of the journey to the transition point at L5. There'd be a time where the engines were idle and they simply coasted through space within the Lagrange point, and that was when Delaine and the rest of the crew would have an opportunity to step the masts and ready the sails.

Another difference from a naval ship, as there she'd have had the masts stepped and the sails set during their deceleration.

The view on the monitors settled as Reynolds stopped their spin and Alexis nodded to herself as their course updated on the plot. They were within a single degree of *Swallow's* course — well within any reasonable expectations.

"Nicely done, Reynolds," Alexis said.

"Thank you, ma'am."

"Signal from *Swallow*, ma'am," Joyce said. "*Step masts.*"

"Acknowledge them, if you please, Joyce — and send the lads out."

"Aye, ma'am."

The forward cameras, images brought inside the hull by long runs of fiber so that no electronics would be exposed to the radiations of *darkspace* once they transitioned, showed her the bow sail locker open and vacsuited figures emerge.

Alexis picked Delaine out immediately as his suit was the newest of the lot, having been purchased after his rescue from Erzerum where the pirates had taken all of the captured spacers' belongings. In a moment, he had the men about their tasks.

First raising the lower sections of the masts, then the lower rigging which would hold them in place.

The masts rose from their storage positions against the hull, hinged at their base, before locking upright.

Star was a hermaphrodite sloop, with square-rigged fore- and mizzen-masts at the bow and stern, and a fore-and-aft rigged main-mast midway down her spine.

Alexis felt a tingle of excitement as the masts were locked in place. She'd never had the opportunity to command such a ship. She'd heard they were touchy in storms or high winds, but the square-rigged sails would allow her to run well before the wind, while the fore-and-aft rig would let her come up closer to the wind than a fully square-rigged vessel.

She was eager to put *Star* through her paces and learn how well she performed — the purser's criticism of the ship's sailing character notwithstanding.

Once the masts were locked in place, the suited figures on the hull extended the next sections — telescoping out of the main. Then the next and the next, all with the seeming kilometers of rigging necessary to support them.

Alexis reached out and rested her fingertips against the plot table.

All ships had a different feel. The thrum of the fusion plant, the vibrations of the crew — and in *Star's* case, the indentures — moving about, a bit of a rattle when a course was changed as loose fittings and bits adjusted, and, most of all, the vibrations of the masts and rigging working with and against the ship's momentum.

It was only slightly noticeable on *Star* now, being in normal space without the *darkspace* winds and with the engines off, but Alexis felt she caught the hint of it.

Joyce interrupted her reverie.

"Signal from *Swallow*, ma'am — *decelerate one-eighth, relative to L5*."

"Acknowledge, Joyce, and inform Mister Theibaud."

"Aye."

"One-eighth on the engines, Reynolds," Alexis ordered.

"Aye, ma'am."

Outside the hull the work paused for a moment as men grasped a nearby stay or handhold, ensuring they were set for the change. They resumed in a moment, though, adjusting to the resumed thrust.

The spars went up, and the mainmast's long boom, then the sails, though those would remain furled until after *Star's* transition to *darkspace*.

Alexis watched Delaine take a turn about the hull, checking each bit and issuing an order to tighten this or loosen that.

A spike of longing shot through her.

There was something to be said for the hot, heavy work outside the hull, with little except the rasp of your own breath and the crackle of the radio — and not even that once the ship was properly underway in *darkspace*. Perhaps she'd arrange for Delaine to have the quarterdeck for their next evolution, and she'd go out on the hull herself.

It would give her an opportunity to get to know the men at their work, after all, and she was first mate on this trip, not the captain who had other duties to attend to.

"Mister Theibaud reports the ship is fully rigged and ready for transition, ma'am," Joyce said.

Alexis glanced at the monitors. She'd been lost in longing to be out on the hull and missed the crew reentering the sail locker.

Far too long since I was aboard ship, she thought. *I've missed this so.*

She smiled at the images of the masts and furled sails, ready to be dropped and catch the winds. *Star* looked like a proper ship now, not just some characterless tube tumbling through vacuum. She only lacked the coming transition to *darkspace* to be fully in her element.

"Signal to *Swallow*, Joyce — *ready in all respects*."

"Aye, ma'am," Joyce said, then a bare moment later, "Acknowledged and *cut all thrust*."

Alexis glanced at the images of the other ships in the convoy, all of whom had their own masts and sails rigged and in place. *Star* must have been the last to complete the evolution, which was disappointing, but she'd not fault the crew for that.

Star had fewer men than the other ships for her size and they'd done a competent job of it.

"Cut the engines, Reynolds," Alexis ordered. "Let us get back to where we belong."

Chapter Nineteen

Dishes clattered and clinked through Captain Meiggs' small cabin as Isom served them.

"Your man's a fine cook, Alexis," Meiggs said as he took a second bite.

"He is, Captain Meiggs," Alexis answered. Despite the assurances of Meiggs and the others — Sams, the purser, Gilbertson, the bosun, and Slott, the sailing master — Alexis couldn't bring herself to address a captain by his given name. "He's a fine hand at many things and I've been lucky to have him by my side."

"Well, this is a far cry from our normal fare, I'll tell you," Meiggs said around another mouthful.

"I hope there'll be no ill-feelings from your normal man," Alexis said. "What with Isom taking over this meal."

Meiggs had asked them all to dinner and for Isom's services if Alexis didn't mind — she suspected after hearing from Slott and Gilbertson that the food in the wardroom had improved with Isom's arrival.

"Oh, I take on someone from the load of indentures for that work," Meiggs said. "There's always someone willing to do a bit of cooking and cleaning for access to my pantry and the cot there. He'll likely find a place in-atmosphere in a stop or two, so no cause for jealousies there — and my man, Powell, doesn't cook."

"I see," Alexis said.

Meiggs swallowed. "So what do you think of my *Star*? Saw you clambering about the hull on your off-watch — all ship-shape?"

Alexis hurried her fork to mouth while Meiggs was speaking so that she'd have the excuse of chewing to form her answer.

She had, indeed, been clambering about the hull on her off-watch and she, along with Delaine, had compiled a list of things she'd dearly like to address. The question was, would Meiggs respond well to what he might take as criticisms of "his *Star*" and her current state.

"She's a fine ship, sir," Alexis said, "and her rig is quite interesting. I've never sailed a hermaphrodite before and I can see some advantages — we'd be all out of the system ourselves by now with the fore-and-aft rig."

The convoy was two days out from Dalthus — past the worst of the shoals, but still within the system's influence and the *darkspace* winds were expending all their energy toward the system's center, forcing the two Marchant ships to take a long, spiraling course, as they couldn't sail as close to the wind as *Star* and the pinnace *Swallow*.

"Indeed we would," Meiggs said, "but that'll be made up for when we're running with the winds — can't keep up with the sail area on those ship-rigs there. Lucky we've got *Swallow* in the same fix, otherwise the Marchants would leave us well behind."

Alexis nodded.

"What will you change?" Meiggs asked.

"Pardon, sir?" Alexis asked. It was Meiggs' ship, after all, so why was he asking her that. In fact, other than a bit of maintenance, she hadn't planned to issue any changes to the way *Star's* crew was used to operating — only being aboard for a short time, she saw little reason to break them from their routine.

"You're first mate, charged with running the ship," Meiggs said. "I expect you'll want a bit more spit and polish than my lads are used to. All the better, that." He grinned. "It'll do them some good to feel a stricter hand and they'll love me all the more once you're gone, then."

Alexis allowed herself to join in the general laughter that greeted Meiggs' statement.

"Well, sir, since you ask," Alexis said, "I was thinking of exercising the guns."

"Did that a fortnight ago," Meiggs said, eyes on his plate.

"I did see that in the log, sir," Alexis said, "then, out on the hull, I wondered at it." She paused, thinking of how to phrase it. "The gunports seem to ... well, have not been opened in some time."

Meiggs swallowed and grinned. "Regulations say we must practice running the guns in and out and simulate firing, Alexis. Don't say we must open the ports."

Alexis blinked. That was, she supposed, the merchantry's license regulation — she'd had Isom look it up — but it certainly didn't satisfy the spirit.

"I see," Alexis said. "Perhaps, even so, we might —"

"Have you *seen* our decks, Carew?" Gilbertson asked.

"I ... have," Alexis admitted, and she took the bosun's meaning.

Star's maindeck, where the guns were located, all four of them, was the same mass of too much humanity crammed into too little space that the rest of the ship was. Only a small section aft wasn't perpetually crowded with indentures and their baggage, and that only because it was partitioned off for the crew's bunks.

"Have to herd all those indentures down into the hold," Meiggs said, nodding. "Cheek and jowl down there and they'd not like it a bit." He switched to shaking his head. "No, I'm afraid there'll be no running the guns out the ports — hard enough keeping the indentures in line as it is."

"I see," Alexis said. "Perhaps, then, we might simply trim the hull around the ports? That would help our preparedness quite a bit."

Out on the hull she'd had trouble even finding the gunports, so scoured was *Star's* hull. The ship's passage and the dark energy winds had driven the fine bits of dark matter permeating *darkspace* along the ship's hull for so long that they'd smoothed over and nearly sealed the seams around each port.

"'Preparedness,'" Meiggs said with a laugh. "That's your navy showing, Alexis. I'd sell the guns off if the regulations didn't require ships in the Fringe to go armed. Naught we need preparing for, I think."

"We have had piracy here, sir," Alexis said, "even near Dalthus, and *Swallow's* a fine ship but she's only a pinnace."

"Oh, of course," Meiggs said, "but the Marchants didn't hire *Swallow* to convoy with them for pirates. Pirates aren't interested in indenture ships, as a general rule, after all. Not a lot of value in our cargoes."

Alexis frowned. "There are slavers out there."

"Oh, aye," Meiggs allowed, "but we're not in your Barbary here." He shook his head. "No, pirates here want something they can sell quickly and quietly, not a shipload of mouths to feed and complain."

Alexis had to allow Meiggs was correct in that, at least. While there were worlds who'd look the other way to a load of workers arriving at some reduced cost, they weren't many in number.

It'd been some time since she'd worked the guns, even in training, and she'd been quite looking forward to it.

"I see," Alexis said, trying to keep the disappointment out of her voice.

"Perhaps the rigging, then," she said after a moment. "I did note some lines are frayed and stretched."

In fact, she was worried some lines might not take the strain if they encountered any real weather and she'd noted the rigging was so stretched that the masts were swaying a great amount — so great she wondered at how the topmen could keep their breakfast on the inside.

"Hmmm," Meiggs murmured, brow furrowed. "Have to be when we're not at any great speed — perhaps once we're in orbit again."

"We're barely able to keep up with the others as it is, save against the wind," Slott added. "Fall behind and the others'll leave us."

Alexis frowned. "*Swallow* would do that?"

"It's the Marchants' convoy," Slott explained.

"Aye," Meiggs agreed. "The Marchants set the destination and pace, as they're the ones hired *Swallow* for the escort. Any and all might tag along with an escorted convoy, such is the law, but it's tagging along we are. Neither slowing nor deviating from the course is to be allowed."

"I see," Alexis said. She pondered the last item on her list and nearly sighed, knowing what the answer would be. "I did note the keel could do with reinforcing, perhaps we could work at that?"

In fact, she'd noted the keel was very nearly worn through in places — the constant scraping of invisible bits of dark matter had gnawed away at it until she could see the massive plate of thermoplastic flex and twist as the ship sailed.

"Really? How so?" Meiggs asked.

"It..." Alexis thought of how best to describe the wear she'd seen, though she was at a loss to understand how Meiggs didn't know. It was the man's own ship, after all. "Wobbles," she finished finally.

"Wobbles?" Meiggs asked.

Alexis flushed. There was simply no proper naval term for what *Star's* keel was currently doing.

"In fairness, Buckley," Slott said to the captain, "the ship's keel *has* taken to waving about a bit. Plays all hells with the helm."

"Hmm," Meiggs said. "Well, if you say so, Norberto." He turned to Alexis. "Only what may be done without affecting our speed or course, mind you."

"And don't schedule so much maintenance as it interferes with the men's time ashore," Gilbertson advised. "Hard enough to crew an indenture ship as it is."

Alexis took a deep breath and let it out slowly.

"We're not the navy, Alexis," Meiggs said with a knowing smile. "No need to fill every moment of the day with toil."

Chapter Twenty

Eidera's landing field was much as Alexis remembered it from her time aboard her first ship, *Merlin*.

The town was a bit larger, she thought, though not so much larger as Port Arthur back home had grown. Eidera didn't have the influx of gallenium miners and the need for businesses to support them as Dalthus had now.

"That's the lot, Alexis," Gilbertson, the bosun, told her as the last of the canvas totes and bags were unloaded from *Star's* boat.

"Thank you, Mist — ah, Gilbertson," she said, finding herself still unused to *Star's* laxer form of address amongst the ship's officers. She sighed. "You may release the men to their leave now."

"Aye, they're waiting for that," Gilbertson said.

Alexis watched as he made his way to the boat's crew, who were gathering about the rear ramp in anticipation.

Very nearly all of *Star's* crew were present, with only four, including Delaine as watch-stander, still aboard the ship. All the rest had made their way down with the boat's last load of indentures and their baggage.

The words releasing them were hardly out of Gilbertson's mouth before the group scattered into the rows of tents and stalls making up Eidera's indenture fair on their way to whatever recreations they had foremost in mind — Alexis' wish for additional maintenance aboard *Star* evaporating with them.

It was all well and good to tell her to rerig the ship and reform the keel while the ship was idle in orbit — until she'd reviewed the norms of watch-standing aboard *Star* and discovered so much of the crew was typically on leave.

Cancel that and the crew would think her a Tartar and take to rolling shot canisters down the companionway nearest the wardroom.

Alexis sighed.

She'd at least managed to have the worst of the rigging marked as the masts were unstepped and folded during *Star's* approach to orbit. There were fresh lines made for most of those runs and laid out to be replaced as the masts were stepped once more — though she'd then found *Star* was low in some stores, especially for the ship's printers, and nearly half the lines needing replacement would have to wait until the first batch of old, frayed lines could be brought down for recycling.

The argument between Moore, the ship's carpenter, and the purser, Sams, over where the fault lay had been entertaining, but not so much so as to offset her displeasure over the lack of stores.

At least she'd convinced Captain Meiggs to authorize refilling the ship's stores a bit more than usual here on Eidera.

Which, speaking of Meiggs, it was time for her to make her report that all indentures were unloaded and the bulk of the crew released to their own devices.

Alexis made her way around the boats from the other ships to where the new indentures, those leaving Eidera, either by choice or not, were forming up in lines to hear the ships' offers.

Meiggs was there, along with representatives from the Marchant ships, *Belvedere* and *Almorah*, though not their captains, as well as Lieutenant Jordan from *Swallow*.

There were a dozen voluntary indentures and about half that of involuntary, those who the system had deemed unrepentant and, due to debt or crime, undesirable.

Meiggs noticed her approach and nodded to her.

"All squared away, Alexis?"

"Aye, sir," Alexis said, unable to bring herself to more casualness with the ship's very captain, no matter the norms aboard. "The indentures are all off to their spaces and the crew's released for forty-eight hours."

Meiggs nodded. "Very good. You may take your own leave as well then."

"Thank you, sir."

"Though I'm sure you'd prefer it if your young man was in-atmosphere to enjoy it with you," Meiggs said with a grin.

Alexis flushed. "Someone does have to watch the ship, sir," Alexis said.

"Well, you'll have two days with him once Norberto goes up for his watch."

"Indeed, sir."

"Ah, the auction's starting," Meiggs said as his tablet pinged and all attention turned to the indentures and the Eirdiran representative who'd just arrived at the head of the line.

"Gather closer, all of you," the new man said, standing near the indentures and beckoning the ships representatives closer. "I am Scrupulous Jones and I'll be handling the auction for you today. Who might you all be?"

"Albi Lloyd for the *Almorah*, sir," one of the others said.

"Zakaria Scott for the *Belvedere*."

Meiggs stepped closer and Alexis followed. She'd never seen this aspect of a fair and found herself curious.

"Meiggs, captain of *Star of Tauric*," he said.

"Thank you, gentlemen," Jones said. "You're all old hands at this, I take it, so no explanations necessary for you, I'm sure. Are all your contracts standard? No added clauses or changes?"

"Standard," Lloyd said immediately.

"Standard as well," Scott answered.

"We've struck clause seven," Meiggs said.

"Indeed," Jones said, then turned to the waiting indentures. "Very well, you've heard it — the ships *Belvedere* and *Almorah* offer the standard contracts you've reviewed, while *Star of Tauric* has struck clause seven, minimum berthing space." He tapped at his tablet for a moment. "Please acknowledge your awareness of the terms."

Jones waited a moment while those in line tapped at their own tablets and finally nodded.

"And *Star*, of course, carries mostly involuntaries," Meiggs added. "So there's that."

"Very well. All disclosed as is proper," Jones said. "Lieutenant?"

Jordan stepped forward and took a deep breath.

"In accordance with the Terms of Planetary Charter," Jordan bellowed, "as passed by Parliament, this world, Eirdira, may do as its rulers wish in all things, save these."

For a moment Alexis thought he might go on to read the entire Act, but then he went on, skipping to the bits about free travel and indenture.

"Term the fourth," Jordan yelled. "That whosoever shall wish to leave the world may be neither hindered nor harnessed in any way from this. That from time to time those wishing to leave the planet Eidera may gather at such time and place as the planet's rulers shall determine and may board any ship which agrees to carry them. Yet this time shall not be less than twice per planetary year and this place shall be made accessible to all.

"Term the fifth," Jordan went on. "At the time and place described above, the rulers of Eidera shall put forth those they wish to be taken from their world, and all ships engaged in traffic of the Fourth Term shall, without fail, agree to carry all that they are able."

Jordan stepped back and the auctioneer, Jones, stepped forward again.

"Lot One, then, we have a family of four. The man's a skilled weaver, but willing to take any work. His wife's a housekeeper and will be offering herself for work as well. Their baggage is eighty-seven kilos under the allotment. Questions?"

"Yes, a question," Lloyd from the *Almorah* asked. "Why do you wish to leave Eidera, sir?"

"That's in the packet sent to your tablet," Jones answered.

"It is," Lloyd said, "but I've a wish to hear from the man himself. How he presents himself will be a factor in how quickly he finds a place."

"Oh, very well," Jones said, then gestured to the man first in line. "Answer him, then."

The man nodded. "Yes, sir." He cleared his throat. "I'm a weaver by trade, as it says there, sir, but we got the patch-back some years ago and the flocks..." He shrugged. "Think there's two islands with flocks ain't got it now. Hard to weave when there's so little wool, you see?"

Lloyd nodded. "But you say you'll do other work – why not here?"

"I'd like to get farther out, you see?" the man said. "If I have to make such a change, well, why not someplace where a man can build more? Work off the indenture and then build something to pass on to my sons."

Lloyd nodded again.

"Other questions?" Jones asked.

"No," Scott, the other Marchant representative answered.

Meiggs shook his head.

"Very well," Jones said, "we'll start the bidding at twenty-five pounds per head for this family of four – do I hear twenty-five?"

"Twenty-five," Lloyd said.

Jones glanced at Scott, who shook his head, which made sense since they were both Marchant ships and it would be bad business to bid against each other.

"Twenty-four," Meiggs said, followed immediately by Lloyd's, "Twenty-three."

"Twenty-two," Meiggs said.

"Twenty-one," Lloyd said nodding.

"Twenty," Meiggs said, "and eighteen for the children."

"Nineteen pounds, ten shillings for the adults," Lloyd said, "seventeen for the children."

"Seventeen each for the lot," Meiggs said.

Lloyd opened his mouth, then pursed his lips and shook his head.

"Seventeen pounds," Jones said. "Going once? Twice?" Both Lloyd and Scott shook their heads. "Thrice and done."

Jones turned to the indentures. "Do you accept *Star of Tauric's* price of seventeen pounds each under standard contract less clause seven for carriage?"

The man, the indenture, who Alexis realized hadn't even been asked his name in all this, blinked.

"What's this clause seven bit, exactly?" he asked finally.

Jones sighed. "Read your contracts, please, everyone," he called out, then, "minimum space. *Star of Tauric* does not guarantee you a minimum amount of bunk space aboard ship during your journey."

"Oh," the man said, then huddled with his wife for a moment.

"Quickly, if you please," Jones said, "we've much to be about today."

"I'm worried about the space thing," the man said, "what with the children and all."

"Do you reject *Star of Tauric's* offer, then?" Jones asked.

The man swallowed, glanced at his wife, then nodded.

"Very well, the lowest remaining offer was nineteen pounds, ten shillings each for the two adults and seventeen pounds for each of the two children from the *Almorah* — do you accept that?"

The man glanced at his wife again, who gave him a short nod.

"Yes, yes, we'll take that offer."

"Very well, then," Lloyd said. "I've certified seventy-three pounds cost for your passage. Make your way to *Almorah's* boat there. Next up, Lot Two, a single man with no skills of note, though young and strong. Questions? No? Then we'll start the bidding at twenty pounds, shall we?"

Alexis watched as events played out much the same, with Meiggs eventually making the lowest offer, but the indentures refusing the offer and accepting one of the Marchants'.

"You're wondering why I bother," Meiggs whispered during a lull while another family gathered their baggage and made their way to a Marchant boat.

"I am," Alexis whispered back. "It seems a pointless exercise with everyone preferring the Marchants."

"Can't blame them. The lack of space over months and more aboard *Star*? Then there's the involuntaries to be surrounded with?" Meiggs shook his head. "No, I don't expect any of these to accept our offer." He leaned closer and spoke lower. "*But* I can bring the Marchants' offers down and save these folk a bit of coin, so there's that."

"I see," Alexis said.

Meiggs shrugged. "They allow ships like *Star* along on their convoys only because we'll carry the dregs they've no desire to. Still, I can cut into their profits a bit."

Indeed, Alexis watched Meiggs do exactly that for the rest of the auction, with Meiggs bidding down the offers of carriage and the indentures rejecting those offers to travel with the Marchants until all of the voluntary indentures had been settled.

"Will they do the same to you, now?" Alexis asked. "Bid down the involuntaries, there?"

Meiggs shook his head. "No, watch."

Alexis did, seeing the representatives for both Marchant ships walk away, waving to Jones as they did so.

Jones then approached Meiggs.

"We've six for you, Captain Meiggs," Jones said. "Five debts and an incorrigible drunkard — be careful, he either sings or fights when he's in the cups and I'm not certain which is the worst."

"What's the total of the debts?" Meiggs asked, then nodded when Jones told him. "I've enough in *Star's* accounts for that and will settle up with the other ships for their shares later."

Jones nodded and Alexis let her attention drift as the two began negotiations on what Eidera would pay to have *Star* carry away these folk the planet deemed undesirable. Perhaps they'd find a place on some other world, perhaps the experience of being uprooted from their homes and sent traveling to others on such a ship as *Star* would put a stop to whatever behavior had put them here.

Chapter Twenty-One

The walkways of Eidera's port town were bustling with activity and the pavement so crowded that Alexis and Braithwaite were forced to walk at its very edge, close to the equally crowded street.

Eidera was older and more populated than Dalthus, even with the latter's influx of miners, and there wasn't a single horse in sight. Instead of the comforting *clop-clop* of hooves on cobbles or concrete, there was the constant *whish* of tires and the whine of the passing vehicles' electric motors.

Alexis would have found it a pleasant walk, save for her current company.

"I'm told there is a fine restaurant in the hotel ahead," Lord Braithwaite said. "Hardly up to New London standards, I'm sure, but we may be able to begin some instruction there."

"Instruction?" Alexis asked, quite wishing it were Delaine walking at her side, rather than Braithwaite, but she couldn't very well tell the man she didn't have time for him or pretend she had anything other to do than have her first dinner in-vacuum for weeks.

Especially since Captain Meiggs had handed her over to the herald with an almost gleeful smirk and an offer to show them to the finest hotel in the port.

"Of course," Braithwaite said. "A formal Court session and dinner on New London has certain ... etiquettes best followed."

Why is it, Alexis asked herself, *that I'm so often assumed to embarrass myself at formal functions?*

First that Foreign Office fellow Eades on their way to *Noveau Paris* and now Braithwaite.

"I think I'll do fine. This is not my first visit to a Court, after all," Alexis said.

"No?"

"No — in my time on *HMS Shrewsbury* we visited *Noveau Paris* where I spent some time at their Court."

"Indeed?" Braithwaite asked. "And how did that go?"

Alexis opened her mouth, then paused, thinking of the rather inebriated and obnoxious French youth she'd almost come to blows, if not a duel, with.

"Tolerably well, I think," she said finally.

There were, after all, no deaths, and the French did enter the war with Hanover for the Berry March.

"Indeed?"

Alexis flushed. *Did Braithwaite have some report on her time there and know about the incident?*

"There were no incidents regarding which fork I used, at least," she said finally, "and I'm to be only one of hundreds receiving awards and honors. I very much doubt anyone will even look at me twice."

"Indeed?"

Alexis flushed further.

Damn the man, he's —

A sudden blow to her back drove her forward and she shuffled to regain her footing, but something caught at her legs, and she was falling.

The direction of the blow and her own twisting to recover sent her not to the pavement, but off the curb and into the street.

Tires squealed, her hands burned from catching herself, and her vision filled with the front of an oncoming lorry.

Chapter Twenty-Two

"Ouch."

"We must clean these before the bandage, *mon cœur*," Delaine said.

The storage compartment that doubled as *Star's* infirmary was tightly packed with Alexis, Delaine, and Isom, along with shelves of supplies and a medical table along its wall.

Alexis sat on the exam table in her underthings while Delaine dabbed and swiped at the scrapes covering her palms, elbows, and knees. To one side, Isom stood with her jumpsuit in hand, examining the rips at elbow and knee. She'd chosen to return to the ship and have her minor wounds treated there, rather than planetside. She'd let the task fall to Delaine, rather than call what passed for *Star's* surgeon up from Eidera.

"I know that," Alexis said, "but it still stings."

Delaine chuckled. "You did not complain this much even when blown up."

"I think that hurt less than whatever you're using."

"Some of these are deep. You must have fallen hard."

Alexis paused, thinking back.

"The blow was hard," she said, "and the trip unexpected. If I hadn't managed to twist and slap the concrete to absorb the impact, it would be my head you were swabbing."

Delaine sighed.

"You are certain it was a blow and no accident?"

Alexis nodded. "I know the difference — this was no accidental bump. And the trip ... well, it lifted my leg, not just something getting in the way."

"Not sure I can repair the holes, sir," Isom said. "I'll have to put a patch behind some."

"It's all right, Isom," Alexis said. "Do what you can, and I'll use it for the dirtier work that — *ouch!*"

"Nearly done," Delaine said, holding one of the deeper cuts open to squirt it with water.

"*Owie!*"

Delaine laughed, then sobered.

"Who would have done such a thing?"

Alexis shook her head. "I've no clue. If the lorry had been a meter closer when I fell, I doubt we'd be talking right now. I've no enemies I know of on Eidera and I hardly think it's the sort of place where such things are done at random."

"Probably those bloody Marchants," Isom muttered.

"I've no cause to think that," Alexis said. "No doubt the higher ups at the Marchant Company have no love for me. Those in the know about the Marchant involvement in piracy and the slave trade in the Barbary, but that must be a closely held secret. I can't imagine they've told all their captains to try murdering me for what I know or some such."

"You know no one on Eidera?" Delaine asked.

"No. I've only been here a few times, first on *Merlin* then on *Nightingale*, and there was never any ... well, on my first visit here with *Merlin* I suppose I did embarrass a foreman at the chandlery, but that was years ago."

She sighed as Delaine wrapped her hand with gauze.

"You saw no one?"

"No — by the time Lord Braithwaite helped me up, a crowd had formed. It was quite the ruckus, with the lorry nearly hitting me. I recognized no one in the crowd."

"No one from the ship?" Delaine asked.

"It does sound quite similar to what happened to the first mate back on Dalthus, doesn't it?" Alexis said. "But no. I saw no one from the ship before or after — only Lord Braithwaite and he saw nothing either."

Isom glanced up.

"No," Alexis said. "You may not like the man, but it certainly wasn't him who pushed me. He was a bit in front of me the whole time and we weren't looking at each other while we talked."

"Someone from the ship," Delaine said.

Alexis nodded. "I'd wager on it. For *Star of Tauric* to lose two mates within a few weeks' span might be coincidence, but three would be quite careless. The question is *who* and for what purpose? *Ow!*"

"We will be done soon, *minette*." Delaine glanced at the door, then said quietly, "*Monsieur* Gilbertson? Or *Monsieur* Slott? Either might be promoted to mate, *oui*? If an opening occurred? And a man making such an opening is known to happen from time to time."

"Neither seems discontent in their positions," Alexis said. "Nor would it explain the other deaths — the man who fell down the ladder and those crushed in the hold."

"You think they are part of this as well?"

"*Ouch!* Yes, I do, for while three losses might be careless, seven is sure to be deliberate, I think." She took a deep breath. "Evens, the first mate, disappeared without a trace; Hughley, second mate, pushed in front of a lorry; then myself the same. Edwards, the able spacer crushed in the hold along with an indenture ... we'll have to find out her name and more about her. One out the airlock and the indenture — we'll find his name as well — fallen, more likely pushed, down a ladder."

"Did Lord Braithwaite object to you returning to *Star*?" Delaine asked.

"A bit, but only because he wouldn't be able to quiz me on the difference between salad and pastry forks. He was in front of me, as I said — do you suspect him of hiring it done?" Alexis asked, only half teasing.

"A bit smaller than the dinner for salad, sir," Isom said, "and might have a thicker left tine for cutting the lettuce — but the pastry might as well, so it's a tricky one. Best look to where it's placed." He paused. "The salad might have a bit of a notch at the tip, for spearing and such."

"I'm aware, Isom, and I believe it was you who made me so. Frequently."

Delaine didn't answer for a moment. "I would not think it of *Le Héraut* — but these men, your Marchants, *les rapaces*, truly fear what you know and did not stop at killing others before, *non*? Might they trick you away from home?"

Alexis pondered that for a moment. How deep might some Marchant plot to get at her again go? Braithwaite had simply shown up and whisked her away. She had only the man's word he was a Queen's Herald, after all — if the Marchants were willing to bomb a station to silence Hinds, might they not...

No, that was too unkind a thought about the man, and likely only because he *was* so blasted full of himself. Only a true Queen's Herald could display that sort of blind arrogance.

"A man sent to kill me would be quite more likable, I think."

Isom snorted, making Alexis think about what she'd just said.

"Not quite what I meant, but not far off the truth, either. An assassin, at least, I could respond to in kind." She shook her head. "No, the other deaths aboard *Star* make that unlikely and there would be easier ways for the Marchants to kill me than a plot so convoluted as to include a false Queen's Herald. Much as I might wish, since it would mean there's no bloody knighthood and I could go home." Her brow creased. "No, this must be somehow related to the other deaths, but how? I've not been aboard *Star* long enough to make an enemy, even of a killer."

Alexis bit her lower lip, frowning.

"This does, though, make finding the truth of this killer all the more important — I fear with my surviving this attempt he may become all the more brazen, whatever his agenda may be."

Chapter Twenty-Three

For nearly a fortnight out of Eidera things were peaceful and routine aboard *Star of Tauric.*

The convoy bore away from the direct route to Zariah to pick up one more planetfall along their way. Much to Lord Braithwaite's irritation, Alexis was sure. It added nearly three weeks to their transit time, but the indenture convoy was still the quickest way to reach Zariah and the more regular passenger service available there.

Gilbertson and Slott had much to say about Alexis' incident on Eidera, but little of use.

To them, it was a topic of fantastical speculation, which typically degenerated into the simple belief that *Star* was becoming a bad luck ship — a belief that began to be echoed by others on the crew, despite Alexis' and Delaine's efforts to put a stop to it. Besides being first- and second-mates, they were newcome to the ship and known to be leaving it at Zariah — the crew would follow their orders, but not their lead.

While on watch, Alexis read and reread what little there was about the incidents in *Star's* logs.

Daniel Dixon - indenture - dead by misadventure (ladder).

William Sals – indenture – dead by misadventure (airlock).

Oscar Edwards - able spacer - discharged dead by misadventure (cargo shift).

Alathena Baxter - indenture - dead by misadventure (cargo shift).

Dunton Evens - first mate - run.

Ashley Hughley - second mate - injured on planet, discharged (planet Dalthus).

The full logs for the day of each incident, as full as they might be given *Star's* lack of maintenance to the log cameras, contained little more mention of the dead than this — each surrounded by the mundane, rote entries of a ship underway.

"Signal from *Swallow*, Miss Carew," Joyce called from the signals console, drawing Alexis' attention from the logs. "*Come ten degrees to starboard.*"

Alexis nodded to the helmsman. "See to it, Reynolds."

"Ten degrees to starboard, aye," Reynolds nodded.

The quarterdeck hatch slid open and Delaine entered, causing Alexis to check the time. The morning watch was nearly done, and she'd spent its entirety reading and rereading the ship's useless logs searching for some clue as to who could be responsible for the deaths aboard *Star* — and the why of it.

Delaine crossed to her at the navigation plot, and she longed to reach out to him, but settled for a small smile.

"Shall I relieve you, *mon ange*?" Delaine asked.

Alexis caught her lower lip between her teeth and shook her head, seeing the corners of Delaine's mouth quirk. The double *entendre* was clearly intentional.

"Sshh," she said glancing around. Such flirtations were inappropriate on the ship's quarterdeck.

Delaine shrugged, knowing full well what the Gallic shoulder movement did to her.

"*Ils n'ont pas de Français,*" he whispered.

"They may have no French," Alexis whispered back, "but they certainly know what a blush must mean, and I'll thank you to leave me some dignity ... much as I might like to lose a bit from time to time."

Delaine smiled and nodded his head toward the log displayed on the navigation plot.

"Have you found a new thing?"

"No." Alexis shook her head. "I think I'll take a look at the hold again, perhaps I'll ask Captain Meiggs to..."

She frowned. She hadn't seen Captain Meiggs during her watch and, though the captain wasn't one to haunt the quarterdeck when he wasn't needed, it was normal for him to check in.

"Joyce," she called, "call the captain's steward and ask if he's up and about yet, will you?"

"Aye, Miss Carew."

Delaine frowned. "Is there something —"

Alexis shook her head. "The barest start of a feeling — nothing to it, likely as not. It's only with so many other incidents aboard ship —"

"No answer from Powell, Miss Carew," Joyce said.

Alexis' frown deepened. "I don't know. I have a sudden feeling things have gone amiss," she whispered to Delaine, then to Joyce, "My compliments to Mister Gilbertson and might he join me at the captain's cabin with two men."

"Is something —"

"Handsomely, Joyce, and with no speculation, if you please."

"Aye, Miss Carew."

Alexis turned to Delaine. "You have the deck."

"*Oui.*"

Alexis left the quarterdeck, stomach churning. She might look the fool, when all was said and done, for waking a captain who'd simply decided to sleep in, but for neither Meiggs nor his steward to answer her call gave her a sick feeling.

Meiggs, lax as he might be, still wasn't the sort to ignore a call from the quarterdeck when such a call might mean trouble for his ship and livelihood. The man might not care for spit and polish, but he did love *Star* and cared for his crew.

She made her way to Meiggs' cabin and tapped the call button.

"Captain Meiggs? Captain Meiggs, it's Lieu ... ah, Carew – Alexis, I mean. Are you awake?"

Gilbertson arrived with two spacers and Alexis tapped the call button again.

"Captain Meiggs? Powell? Are either of you awake?"

"You asked for us, Alexis?" Gilbertson asked.

"A moment," Alexis said. Another tap at the call button also brought no response.

She took a deep breath, caught her lower lip between her teeth, and stepped back.

"Open it."

Gilbertson blinked. "Open ... it?"

"The hatch," Alexis said. "Open it."

"I ... ah, that's the captain's –"

"Indeed," Alexis said, becoming more certain something was seriously amiss. She turned to the two spacers. "Lads, this is likely the only time breaking into the captain's cabin won't get you hung, so have at it with a will."

Gilbertson nodded to the men, and they set about opening the hatch's control panel. In less than a minute, the hatch slid open.

Beyond the now open hatch, Meiggs' cabin was dark and silent.

Alexis took a deep breath and shivered. She felt a moment's dizziness, putting it down to the rising tensions as she saw the two spacers shake their own heads as they stepped back from the hatchway.

"Captain Meiggs?" she called again. "Powell?"

There was no answer and no sign of movement.

"Newman," Alexis said to one of the spacers, "run along and fetch Stewart, will you?"

"Aye, Miss Carew."

"You think that's necessary?" Gilbertson asked, voice almost a whisper.

Alexis nodded. Stewart acted as *Star's* surgeon, though also rated able spacer and was primarily responsible for those duties.

"Captain Meiggs, I'm coming through," Alexis called out, then squared her shoulders and crossed through the hatch.

Alexis took two steps into Captain Meiggs' cabin.

The cabin itself was representative of those on most ships — dining and office space at the fore, with a steward's pantry and quarters to one side, and sleeping quarters set off by a light partition at the rear.

The light from the companionway cast a bit of illumination as far as the captain's dining table, but no further.

"Captain Meiggs?" she called out.

She took a deep breath, wondering what she was most afraid of — the righteous wrath of a captain disturbed in his slumber or that her suspicions of something dire would be borne out.

"Compartment lights on," she said, finally.

The lights came on and Alexis saw the hatch to the steward's pantry was open and the space beyond empty. Powell's cot was folded down from the wall, blankets rumpled as though the man had just left his bed, but no sign of him at all.

Alexis crossed the dining space and peered around the partition to Captain Meiggs' sleeping quarters. She saw the still form in the captain's bed and her shoulders slumped — there was a difference in how one lay, between sleep and death, and she'd become all too familiar with the latter.

Gilbertson called from the hatchway, "What is it, Alexis?"

Alexis sighed and stepped back.

"Is it the captain?" Gilbertson asked.

"It is," Alexis said.

"Is he..."

"I fear so," Alexis said.

Alexis raised a hand to keep Gilbertson at the hatchway, though he'd shown no inclination to enter, and made her way to Meiggs' bedside to be certain. The captain's cheeks held an oddly bluish tint in the cabin lights.

A touch to the man's neck confirmed it, though, stone cold skin even before detecting no pulse.

"Mister Gilbertson," Alexis called, backing away and making her way to the hatch, "I'd admire it did you call for a man with recording equipment. I'll want images of everything in the room, close up and full spectrum, if you please."

"Images?"

"The captain is dead and Powell is missing, Mister Gilbertson," Alexis said. "Until Powell's found and the cause of the captain's death is determined, we must treat things as suspicious. I'm certain there will be an inquiry when we arrive at our next port ... especially given *Star's* other incidents."

"Aye, Alexi — aye, Captain."

Alexis sighed — yes, she supposed she was captain of *Star* now. Which she was certain she'd hear about from Delaine once the initial news of Captain Meiggs' death settled. He often teased her that she seemed unable to travel anywhere without, somehow, winding up in command of something.

"See to the images, will you, Mister Gilbertson?" Alexis said making her way back to the hatch. "And the search for Powell. I must signal *Swallow* and inform them of what's happened."

Chapter Twenty-Four

"And there has been no sign of this Powell?" the elder Captain Hodgman, of *Belvedere*, asked.

"Not from the initial search, no," Alexis answered. "Mister Gilbertson is conducting a more thorough search of the ship as we speak."

She glanced around *Belvedere's* captain's cabin, which was larger than *Star's*, though not by much. The Marchants, as well, it seemed, valued additional space for their indentured cargo over their captains' luxuries. Or perhaps that was a decision they left to their individual captains.

The space was now filled with the elder Captain Hodgman, his nephew — the Captain Hodgman of *Almorah* — Lieutenant Jordan from *Swallow*, Lord Braithwaite, and Alexis herself, as well as the elder Captain Hodgman's steward.

"And the cause of Captain Meiggs' death?" Hodgman asked.

Alexis glanced at Jordan. Properly, as the naval head of the convoy, it was his task to ask such questions, but he seemed perfectly content to leave the questioning to the Marchant captain, just as he'd offered no objection to their meeting aboard the Marchant ship — not that she could fault him for that, as the current company would double his little *Swallow's* inhabitants.

She'd returned to *Star's* quarterdeck from finding Meiggs and signaled *Swallow*, but had barely finished her request that Jordan come aboard when *Belevedere* had begun signaling herself.

Rather haughtily, Alexis thought, and ending with an imperious — and entirely inappropriate — *Captains To Repair On Board.*

She did understand that the Marchant ships were footing the bill for the convoy's naval escort, but that did not, she was sure, put the merchant captains in charge of the thing.

Swallow, however, had signaled Jordan's acquiescence and Alexis, lacking an active naval commission, didn't see how she could object.

The younger Hodgman from *Almorah* had joined them as well, along with Lord Braithwaite.

"Undetermined," Alexis said in answer to Hodgman's question. "*Star's* surgeon is examining the captain's body, but there were no visible injuries."

"Then why are we here?" the younger Hodgman asked. "Captain Meiggs was not, to look at him, any picture of health. Men do die."

"They do," Alexis allowed, thinking she'd seen far more of that sort of thing than Hodgman had, "however, given his steward's absence and the other events aboard *Star of Tauric*, I believe there's cause for suspicion — and concern."

"Hmph," Hodgman said. "A few deaths and injuries — no more than one should expect from such a ship."

"I've reviewed *Star's* logs, Captain Hodgman," Alexis said, "and until recently she's been a safe ship."

Lieutenant Jordan nodded. "The more reason to think there's something odd about these incidents."

Lord Braithwaite cleared his throat. "The more reason to have Lieutenant Carew moved aboard some other ship."

All eyes turned to Braithwaite.

"She *is* summoned by the Queen," Braithwaite said. "And if this theory is correct there's already been one attempt on her life." He squared his shoulders. "Captains Hodgman, I must insist that you grant Lieutenant Carew passage aboard one of your ships."

The elder Hodgman shrugged. "Insist you may, m'lord, but it changes nothing about our duty to the Company and our instructions."

"I'd not leave *Star*, in any case," Alexis said, causing all to look at her. "I accepted a contract with Captain Meiggs and I'm bound to see it through. In the event of his death or incapacitation, *Star of Tauric* is to be brought to a world capable of transferring the indentures to other ships and the ship itself to pass on to his heirs. Given the incidents aboard, a world with a proper magistrate would be desirable, as well."

"The nearest world of that sort would be Zariah," Jordan said.

Alexis nodded. "It would be best, I think, if we were to alter our plans and head directly there."

"Absurd!" the younger Hodgman said. "This convoy, and our ships, have already been hijacked to change our course once. Now you want us to skip the few, profitable worlds along this new route and bow to your whims!"

"We must put Captain Meiggs' death before a magistrate instanter," Alexis said. "And the further risk to his ship is too great to simply continue on as before." She turned to Jordan. "Lieutenant Jordan, you have a duty to keep this convoy, all of it, safe. In your mind, is *Star of Tauric* safe to continue on as though nothing has happened?"

"I —"

"Remember who pays the bills, lieutenant," Hodgman said.

Alexis took a deep breath. "Lieutenant Jordan, as master of *Star of Tauric*, I am informing you that my ship is in jeopardy —"

"You can't know that!" Hodgman shouted.

"In *dire* jeopardy," Alexis repeated, "and I will be sending you a formal note for *Swallow's* log to that effect."

Jordan swallowed, eyes wide.

Alexis hated to put him in this position. With such a note in

Swallow's log, any further incident aboard *Star* would reflect quite poorly on him in the eyes of Admiralty — yet refusing the Marchants' wishes would do so as well.

Braithwaite cleared his throat.

"I believe, Lieutenant Jordan," the Queen's Herald said, "that I will also be sending you a note for your log. As my charge is aboard *Star of Tauric*, then my charge is in jeopardy as well. This is now a matter which could well receive the attention of the Queen herself."

Jordan closed his eyes and sighed.

Alexis could see the weight of his decision drive his shoulders down and bow his head.

"Very well," he said finally. "We will sail for Zariah immediately."

"But —" Hodgman began.

Jordan held up a hand to stop him. "Immediately," he repeated. "Upon arrival, *Star of Tauric* will no longer be part of this convoy, and we will then sail on to wherever you like, Captain Hodgman."

Alexis sighed with relief.

Jordan frowned as though he faced another decision.

"I should tell you all, though," Jordan said finally. "I fear a storm is building in our new direction, so we may face some rough sailing."

"A storm?" the elder Hodgman asked. "All seems clear to me — I reviewed the images just this morning."

Jordan glanced away. "I ... sometimes have a sense about these things. Something about the way to starboard and ahead seems ... off to me."

"Ah, a sense, is it?" Hodgman chuckled. "Well as you get older, you'll have the sense to trust the images on your optics, and the ship's computer to analyze them, not such feelings."

Jordan flushed.

"I only wish us to be prepared," he said.

Chapter Twenty-Five

"Mister Slott, Mister Gilbertson," Alexis said. "Please have a seat."

Alexis was uncertain about moving into Meiggs' cabin, especially with no real knowledge of how he'd died – though she supposed if it was Powell who'd done the deed, she was safe enough behind a locked cabin door with the man missing elsewhere.

Still, it was important for the crew, small though it be, to know who was in charge aboard ship, and Isom, at least, seemed perfectly happy to move in.

Though he had disposed of all the food in Meiggs' pantry (for fear of poison), the bedding from Powell's bunk (for the man being somewhat unsanitary), the bedding from Meiggs' bunk (for there'd been a corpse in it, after all), and various objects from around the space (for reasons he refused articulate, but Alexis did observe him sprinkling salt in odd places and thought she might have to have a word with him about it when she had time).

Slott and Gilbertson seated themselves at the table where Alexis and Delaine had already taken places.

"Thank you, gentlemen," Alexis said. She waited for Isom to fill their glasses, then, "I do hope you don't find it unseemly of me to make use of Captain Meiggs' cabin, at least for our dinner. It does offer us more privacy than the wardroom."

Slott nodded. "Not unseemly, I think. Captain Meiggs was a decent man, but dead's dead, and the ship goes on."

Alexis looked to the bosun.

"The lads like to know who's in charge," Gilbertson said. "Important to them."

"Indeed," Alexis said. "And it will be only for a short time."

That raised their eyebrows.

"The decision, in consultation with Lieutenant Jordan and the two Captains Hodgman, is that the convoy shall sail directly for Zariah, there to carry out the instructions left by Captain Meiggs for this eventuality. The passengers will be offloaded, and *Star* will be left to the offices of Captain Meiggs' agent there — likely to be sold, as his heir was the missing Mister Evens."

"Shame, that," Slott said. "Evens would make a good captain."

"Perhaps the agent will leave some time for Evens to make himself known."

Gilbertson snorted. "I think we can say Mister Evens'll be late for that — and all else, given what's gone on aboard this ship."

"Perhaps," Alexis allowed. "The likelihood of some misadventure being behind his disappearance does seem rather strong."

Gilbertson snorted again.

"Any word on what done for him?" Slott asked. "The captain, I mean."

"*Non*," Delaine said. "The man, *le chirurgien*, says he lacks the equipment and skill to tell."

"Both *Belvedere* and *Almorah* offered to send their own surgeons aboard," Alexis added, "but I'm loath to trust the Marchants. I fear they'd label Captain Meiggs' death of natural causes and that might taint the magistrate's opinion once we arrive at Zariah. Better the cause be listed as unknown until then."

"A fair point," Slott said.

"Bugger every Marchant," Gilbertson said.

"I cannot disagree with the sentiment, Mister Gilbertson," Alexis said.

"What'll happen with the crew once we arrive at Zariah?" Slott asked. "If *Star's* to be turned over to the captain's agent?"

Alexis nodded. "I'm sure they're wondering. There are provisions in Captain Meiggs' instructions for his agent to pay off the crew — with a good bit of severance added on."

"They'll be happy to hear that," Slott said. "There's some wondering if they're working for no gain now."

"You may assure them they are not," Alexis said. "Which does bring us to an issue with crewing the ship ... if I am to take over the duties of captain, we're short a mate." Alexis paused. "Would either of you wish the position?"

Alexis glanced at Delaine. There was a bit of a test in the question — if the ship were to be sold, none of the crew, including the bosun and sailing master, were likely to be taken on by the new owners. A mate's rating, no matter how short the time, would allow one to apply for such a position on another ship. It was a step up for either Slott or Gilbertson — and she and Delaine still held some suspicions about the two men and their possible motives.

Gilbertson shook his head. "I work for a living," the bosun muttered. "No offense."

"None taken," Alexis assured him with a grin.

"No," Slott said. "Captain Meiggs asked me as well, but I'm content as master. I'm far more at home dealing with a ship than a crew."

Alexis didn't sigh with relief, but she felt it nonetheless.

If either man were the killer and their motive was promotion, they'd have taken the offer — and possibly be done with the matter. With both declining the opportunity, she felt she could trust them a bit more.

"Very well, gentlemen," Alexis said. "*Star* will sail a mate short for Zariah. It's not a long voyage, so should not be too much of a hardship. In the meantime, we must continue our search for Powell — perpetrator or victim, he must be found. And if victim, then we must be doubly on our guard, for the killer will know there's a magistrate awaiting him when we make port."

The others nodded, grim-faced at the reminder there was a killer aboard — still uncaught.

"Can't imagine where Powell is," Gilbertson said. "Searched the whole ship, questioned all the indentures, and no hint of the man."

"Can't trust the indentures to say," Slott warned. "They'd protect a killer just to spite us."

"I can't imagine they'd do that," Alexis said. "I've reviewed the records and most of the passengers were transported for minor crimes — debt, a bit of theft — not the sorts of things that lead to protecting a murderer."

"Oh, we've murderers aboard," Slott said.

Alexis nodded. "A fit of anger or a drunken brawl gone wrong are quite different than the sort of premeditation necessary for these acts. I would think even the most violent of men aboard, based on their records, would balk at a half-dozen cold-blooded murders."

Slott grunted but didn't argue the point further.

"We must find Powell," Alexis said, "to determine if he is the killer. Perhaps he harbored some grudge against the ship or Captain Meiggs; perhaps he is another victim of the real killer. Either way, we must determine the truth."

Chapter Twenty-Six

Alexis woke the next day and found herself, oddly, at loose ends.

As *Star's* captain, she no longer stood a scheduled watch as she was, for all practical purposes, available to the ship at every hour.

She wandered to the quarterdeck, but Slott had the watch and there was little for them to do as they were on a full-day's run toward Zariah, with no change of course planned until the morrow.

She spent some time in the wardroom, but it was empty save for the officers' new steward. Delaine was asleep in preparation for his own watch and the rest of the ship's complement were off supervising yet another search for Powell.

Isom voiced some suspicion that perhaps Captain Meiggs' cabin contained some secret compartment, and Powell was hiding there even now.

Alexis dismissed the idea where any of the crew might hear, but did spend a bit of time in the cabin tapping walls and pulling or twisting anything that might be pulled and twisted. Her time spent with the rogue and smuggler Avrel Dansby had given her some experience of such things and she couldn't entirely dismiss Isom's suspicion.

Still, she found nothing and left Meiggs' cabin to wander about the ship, sometimes watching the active search, sometimes moving on to areas the crew had already searched in the hopes she might sight something they'd missed.

Following along behind her were Isom and a spacer named Wells, whom Gilbertson had assigned to watch *Star's* new captain at all times for fear of another attempt on her life.

There was still no sign of Powell, but she did note unease amongst the crew and the sort of sideways glances that caused her some unease herself.

Alexis ordered Isom to box up Captain Meiggs' things so that she could fully move into the captain's cabin — perhaps that would give the crew some sense of stability and normalcy.

She retired to the quarterdeck then, for Isom wouldn't stop his following of her if she were anywhere else, and it was near the end of the first dog watch before he returned to the quarterdeck to inform her all was squared away.

Alexis said her good-days to the quarterdeck watch — much to their ill-concealed relief, for no one wished the ship's captain watching over their shoulder while they went about routine work — and made her way to what was now her cabin.

No sooner had she left the quarterdeck than Delaine appeared to pace her.

She glanced back at Isom and Wells, also following her.

"I've no need of my own convoy for the few steps from quarterdeck to cabin," she whispered.

"I only wish to see you safely there," Delaine whispered back.

"Well, here I am." She keyed the cabin hatch open and raised her eyebrows.

Delaine glanced inside and Alexis followed his gaze.

Isom had put the place to rights after the multiple searches had set things to disarray. Captain Meiggs' personal effects were gone now, boxed up in the hold, and the cabin appeared quite bare, for Alexis had not brought the personal effects she might have for a deployment.

"I should accompany you," Delaine said.

"We've had this discussion," Alexis said, "and my reasons stand."

"*Mon cœur*, you wound me," Delaine said. "I only mean I should wait within to keep you safe." He grinned. "To watch over your sleep, *oui?*"

Alexis sighed. She would, very much, like Delaine to watch over her sleep, even if there'd be little sleep involved if she let him in.

"Isom will be right there in the pantry," she said, "and Mister Gilbertson has assigned a guard to watch the hatch."

Delaine shrugged, which always had a peculiar effect on her insides. "Another set of eyes is always helpful."

"It's not your eyes I'm concerned about." She placed a hand on his chest. "We'll be at Zariah soon and be nothing but passengers after that. For now, I'll be safe enough with Isom inside and Wells at the hatch."

"As you wish, *ma belle*."

"None of this is as I wish," Alexis said. She gave his chest a little push. "Off with you now, you've watches to stand on the morrow."

Delaine grinned. "*Oui, mon capitaine!*"

Alexis watched him leave, then entered the cabin, followed by Isom.

"Might do you good, sir, to have a bit of —"

"Isom," Alexis warned.

"— extra guarding," Isom finished. "Things being as they are."

"I'm sure it will be fine, Isom," she said. "We've a guard on the hatch and Powell, if alive and our culprit, is certainly in hiding — the whole crew's looking for him and even the passengers have been shown his image. They may not be the sort to tell things to the authorities under normal circumstances, but they surely understand the danger these murders have put the ship in."

Chapter Twenty-Seven

Muffled, urgent voices pounded against Alexis' ears, demanding entry in much the same way the entire universe seemed to be demanding entry to her very skull – by pressing in from all sides until she felt her head must surely implode from the pressure.

"Go away," she tried to say, but couldn't seem to draw enough breath to do so.

Her lungs moved, but it was as though the air was so thin as to be nonexistent – yet she felt no real distress.

It was as though some even greater weight sat on her chest, pressing on her lungs until they'd emptied themselves and keeping her, no matter how urgently she worked her diaphragm, from drawing a bit of air into her lungs.

She opened her eyes, or tried to, the lids seemed weighted as well. When she finally did get them open, nothing was in focus, only so many blurs rushing about in front of her.

More voices – she could tell they were voices, at least, even if not what they said; then something covered her nose and mouth.

She raised an arm to bat it away, shocked at how weak her arm felt and how she couldn't seem to tell her hand to do more than flop about. Had her injury from the bombing on Penduli had some delayed effect?

Oddly, the thing covering her nose and mouth seemed to make her breathing easier, and she felt the weight lift from her chest. Her lungs expanded, then pushed the air back out forcefully, as though anxious to take the next, new breath.

The air flooding her nose and mouth was cool and she fancied it tasted sweet.

"— coming around —"

"— sir? Can you hear me —"

Coughing and then more coughing, some she knew was hers, but there was more, and deeper, than she could account for from just herself.

"— move her farther —"

"Turn on the bloody blowers, will you?"

"Aye!"

Alexis' eyes focused even as a roar of rushing air filled her ears.

She was outside Captain Meiggs', hers now, cabin, being dragged along the decking toward the ladder up to the quarterdeck. That last order — something about blowing, she thought — had been Wells.

No, the blowers — she recognized the sound from emergency drills. A compartment was being vented somewhere — great fans sucking out air and, if the ship's systems weren't up to cleaning it, venting the air out to the hull and *darkspace* beyond.

"Don't vent the whole ship," she mumbled, "there's no telling what the cartage fee on air will be next system. Mister Sams will be quite cross with you."

"Sir? Can you hear me?"

That was Isom, his face furrowed in worry and right in front of hers.

"I can, aye," Alexis said. She focused on her clerk's face and took another deep breath. "What's happened? Is the ship alright?"

"The ship is fine, *mon cœur*." Delaine, this time. He came into view above her, his angry face partially blocked by Isom's. "Can you stand, *Alexis*? I'd like to get you away from your cabin, if we may."

Alexis thought standing quite a grand idea, since lying about the deck in her underthings wasn't the most captainly image she could imagine. She saw there were several crewmen about, as well as some of the indentures behind them.

Whatever the excitement had been, it had certainly drawn a great deal of attention.

"Of course I can stand," she said, setting hands which still flopped a bit concernedly to the deck and pushing herself up.

Sitting felt better — in the way that one felt better when on a good drunk.

The watching faces detached from their bodies and spun about like planets orbiting a star — with the star being whatever point Alexis tried to focus on. Her stomach roiled.

"Oh, dear," Alexis managed, before her dinner made a second appearance.

"Take her to the quarterdeck!" Delaine ordered. "Isom, you stay with her and let no one near!"

Alexis closed her eyes to try and stop the spinning, wishing she could close her ears against the painful roar of the voices.

"And vent that cabin to bloody vacuum!" she heard Gilbertson yell.

The trip to the quarterdeck, carried by those she couldn't put a face to with her head spinning so, went quickly, and she felt oddly better as they left her cabin behind. She was even, once set down near the navigation plot, able to sit up and rest her back against the plot's pedestal without spewing again.

"Here, sir," Isom said, kneeling beside her. "You lot hold this."

Her clerk handed a blanket to two crewman — she suspected those who'd carried her, but still couldn't see properly.

They spread the blanket out to act as a screen and Isom tugged at her undershirt, rolling it from the bottom so as to cover as much of what she'd deposited as possible when he tugged it over her head.

"What a state," he muttered. "Just wrap this blanket about you, sir. There'll be clean clothes along in a moment, as soon as they've vented the cabin."

"What ... happened?" Alexis managed. It was still difficult to breathe — or, rather, difficult to use her breath for speaking, as her lungs seemed to want to retain every bit they possibly could.

"Some gas, sir," Isom said. "Went all woozy myself."

Alexis shook her head to clear it, regretted that, then took a deep breath. She held that, relishing lungs that felt full and satisfied, while Isom slipped a fresh shirt over her head.

"We must find ... the source," she said. They'd searched the cabin so thoroughly after Meiggs' death, then again before Alexis moved in — she didn't see how they'd missed some way of introducing a gas.

"Aye, sir," Isom agreed. "The compartment's sealed and re-airing now. Wells is stationed at the hatch, and we'll start a search soon."

"How —" She took another deep breath, feeling much better. "How was I found? Why weren't you affected."

"He was, *mon cœur*," Delaine said, kneeling beside her. "But he had a clever plan to alert us."

"What?"

"Deadman switch on my tablet, sir," Isom said. "Had a finger on it all night long — whatever gas it was, I couldn't think straight myself, and my finger slipped."

"That alert was sent to me," Delaine said, "and I had Wells open the hatch."

"I was on my feet," Isom went on, "couldn't think straight, but I could see. Knew all was wrong when the lights come on and you're not tossing as you do without Boots to calm you."

"The Creature does *not* calm me," Alexis protested.

Isom patted her shoulder. "There's your proof of some gas, sir, confusion and all, and here you are saying such a thing."

Chapter Twenty-Eight

Alexis had Gilbertson leave her cabin sealed until she felt well enough to walk, then pulled on a ship's jumpsuit borrowed from stores, as her own clothing was still in her cabin. The thing was far too big for her, and she felt as she had aboard her first ship, *Merlin*, when she'd not had time at first to have their smallest tailored to her size.

Hoping the sight of rolled up sleeves and legs wouldn't do too much damage to her authority with *Star's* crew, she made her way back to her cabin's hatch. The deck there had already been cleaned, thankfully.

She keyed the hatch warily, despite the knowledge that it had been vented to vacuum and then re-aired from the ship's stores.

Hatch open, she put off Isom's protest that she send someone else in first. Perhaps if the Creature were along, she might have tossed it in to try the air.

If the Creature were along, I'd likely be dead, as no doubt Isom would have saved the vile thing first and left me to my fate.

She turned on the lights, more than just the one Isom had used, and stepped through the hatch, sniffing as though she might smell something off. She saw Isom had his hand across the hatch coaming, as though to keep the thing from closing.

Will either of us see this compartment as anything but a deathtrap hereafter?

She sniffed again, feeling no ill effects.

"Mister Gilbertson, Isom, come have a look about. Wells, keep the hatch open, will you? I'm not ready to feel safe in here all shut up."

"Aye, sir."

Alexis went first to the air quality detector on the aft bulkhead. It had been printed in *Star's* carpentry shop and installed after Meiggs' death. It came loose from the bulkhead with a click of magnets releasing, and she pried the back off.

Inside, all appeared to be as it should. She looked closer.

No, there was a bit of something between the battery and its terminals, which would explain why it hadn't gone off.

Explain why it didn't go off, and make it clear these deaths are no accident — Slott said they'd tested the new detectors, and this would never pass in this state.

She set the detector on her dining table.

"Webb, do you have a bag of any sort?" Alexis asked, thinking there might be fingerprints or something of the sort to identify whoever'd sabotaged it.

I should have thought of that before touching it, I suppose.

Assuming *Star* had anything aboard to check for such things. Perhaps one of the other ships did — with such a large crew there were investigations necessary at times and the Marchants might have such kits. Though she thought *Swallow* was more like to rely on the ship's log and its record of what happened in every public space.

She looked around her cabin here on *Star*.

There was only a single camera for the log, and that trained on the small dining table off to one side. It wouldn't take in the sleeping area or the cabin's hatch.

"Is that companionway logged, Wells?" she asked.

"No, sir," Wells answered. "Not a thing."

Alexis took up her tablet from beside her cot. Isom and Wells were opening cabinets and examining bulkheads. She brought up *Star's* log to search it.

The table there, the quarterdeck, and the feeds from the hull, she mused, seeing what was recorded. *Some few cameras in the hold, to discourage pilfering, I'm sure, but most inactive as Slott said.*

Wells, searching the cabinets above her cot, coughed and gasped, turning away and quickly slamming a door.

"What is it?"

Wells exhaled, doubled over, then took a deep breath, shaking his head.

"Inhaled as I opened that cabinet, sir," he said, pointing, "and regretted it." He grasped his chest. "Felt like a normal breath, but then my head went all spiny as though I'd got no air at all."

Alexis approached her cot slowly and reached out to the cabinet. She stood as far back as she could and held her breath as she opened it.

Isom had used this cabinet, less accessible than most, for odds and ends, mostly clothing. An old uniform that might be useful in a pinch, but not so fine that folding for storage would do it harm, some food stores which hadn't fit in the pantry, and a bit of extra bedding for some reason.

There was nothing amiss, but the top of the cabinet wasn't solid — it was a mesh to save on mass — and above it was the cabin's main air vent.

"Get me something to stand on," Alexis said.

In a moment, Delaine and Isom had the dining table set next to her cot and a chair atop it, which Alexis used to clamber up to the top of the cabinet and peer into the air vent.

"Does anyone have a light?"

"Here," Wells said and passed up a small torch.

Alexis shined it into the air vent, but saw nothing except the bare walls of the conduit. She pulled at the vent cover and it came off easily enough with just a little resistance from the magnets that held it in place.

She was able to see farther in now and saw that there was a junction just a meter from the vent.

Placing both elbows inside the vent she was able to leverage herself in. The conduit itself was wide enough — she reckoned a full-grown man would have no trouble making his way here, provided he wasn't too large.

"Careful, sir," Isom called out.

"I'll not get stuck," Alexis said, "there's plenty of room. I just want to see what's around this corner."

She shuffled her way until she could get the light and her head past the junction to see down the other shaft and her breath caught.

"I'm coming out with something — will you lot give my feet a tug?"

"What is it, sir?"

Alexis felt hands on her ankles.

"It's a vacsuit air tank," she said, grasping it and maneuvering it around the corner as she was pulled backwards.

Once out of the vent, she handed the tank down to Wells and clambered down herself.

They gathered around the tank, which had an odd sort of nozzle and some sort of circuit attached to its valve.

Alexis reached out to grasp valve.

"Careful, sir," Isom said.

"It's not a viper, Isom," she said, twisting the valve and finding that it was partway open, but closed easily. Her hand brushed the cold surface of the tank and she shuddered.

There's a viper involved, though — a cold one, who'll poison to meet his goals.

She took up the cylinder and set it on her table beside the detector, only thinking then that she'd touched the valve the killer had and likely covered any sign he'd left behind.

It seems I'll never make a career as a policeman, she thought.

"Valve wasn't open much," she told the others. "Only part way."

Wells looked around. "Enough to fill the cabin slowly. More than once."

Alexis nodded. "A trap set to spring as I slept, once my compartment was sealed for the night. Once Captain Meiggs was settled in," she corrected herself, "and then left for me as well."

She looked around — swallowing to keep down bile, either from the lingering effects of the gas or how very close she'd come to never waking. "There'd be some airflow from the vents to the companionway, but not much. The gas would fill the cabinet first, then seep out over time."

Wells nodded. "Diabolical."

Alexis frowned. "It might seem so, but it's very inexact. Who's to say I wouldn't notice it before taking to bed?"

"And if you did, sir?" Isom said. "A headache and bad stomach? What would you do then?"

"There is that," Alexis allowed. "I'd have a drink to settle things and take to my bed, most like." She sighed. "A drink to settle things might not go amiss just now, come to that. Isom?"

"Wine, sir, and naught stronger."

There were times Alexis thought Isom took his duties as her clerk and steward too far — or, perhaps, added nursemaid to them — but, in this, she rather agreed with him. She still felt woozy from the gas and too strong a drink would strengthen, rather than settle, that.

"Very well. Wells? I think you can be allowed a draught yourself, if you wish."

"Thank you, Captain."

She and Wells seated themselves at her table to silently regard the malicious tank and detector while Isom brought wine.

"Sit, Isom, and ponder over a glass with us."

"Thank you, sir," Isom said, retrieving a glass he'd already poured for himself from the pantry.

"I'll want a list of everyone who's had access to these cabins during the day," Alexis said.

"Powell —" Isom started.

"Our villain may not be Powell," Alexis said. "There's every chance he may be dead as well as Captain Meiggs and his disappearance is merely intended to throw us off the track. I'll want a list of everyone who's accessed the cabins since our last port." She paused. "This tank could fill the cabin with gas nearly twice over and it's empty, so make that since the first death — if Captain Meiggs was a target all along, that's when the killer's plan may have started, waiting only for the right moment to set it in motion."

"That'll be ... a great many names," Wells said.

Alexis raised an eyebrow.

"Powell wasn't one to say no to a bit of help with his work," Wells explained. "Likely half the crew and a good number of indentures have been through here helping for a bit of comfort from the captain's stores."

Alexis sighed. "And no log of who or when, I presume?"

Wells looked uncomfortable, but didn't deny it.

Alexis turned her attention back to the tank she'd taken from the air vent. "What's this bit here on the nozzle," she asked. "I've not seen the like before."

Attached to the tank's valve was an automated nozzle, but with a bit of extra circuitry attached. It was clearly printed from the ship's printers, as *Star's* name and logo were printed on the green board.

Wells and Isom leaned closer to look.

"Something to control the flow from the nozzle, looks like," Wells said.

"In all likelihood," Alexis agreed. "But is it a timer of some sort or remotely activated?"

Wells shrugged.

There was a knock at the open hatch and Alexis glanced over to find Gilbertson there. The bosun's face was set and angry.

"Another search, Captain," he said, "stem to stern and no sign of that bastard Powell."

Alexis nodded. "I begin to doubt Powell's complicity in this matter — he didn't strike me as one who was adept at subterfuge."

Gilbertson nodded.

"Wells," Alexis said, "would you be so kind as to take this tank to Mister Sams and have him identify this odd circuit? If he's any records of who asked for it to be printed, I'd admire the information."

"Aye, Captain."

"Mister Gilbertson, I think we must search once more for Powell," Alexis said, "this time for where one might stash a body."

Chapter Twenty-Nine

Alexis signaled the latest events to *Swallow*, but there was no response other than the acknowledgment. She rather imagined Lieutenant Joyce had his hands full with charting the convoy's course, as his promised storm was showing signs of brewing across their path to Zariah – much, she hoped, to the Marchant captains' chagrin.

She wandered the ship again, observing the latest search, which was concentrating on places Powell might fit, rather than where a man might hide. As such, it was causing even more disruption to the indentures than the previous searches, as Gilbertson seemed intent on having the crew remove every possible panel that might cover such a space.

Alexis eventually found herself in the hold near the site of the second deaths – the crewman and indenture killed by shifting cargo.

She examined the crates and pallets stored about the hold, all of which, though stacked high, were strapped down quite securely. Even with a naval eye, she couldn't fault the purser's stowage, though she did wonder if the current state might not have been due to the two deaths.

A bit more care after such a tragedy wouldn't be unthinkable.

Just aft of the crates began the massive vats of the ship's beer stores. Narrower at the top and bottom, the side-by-side vats formed little tunnels and crawlspaces Alexis remembered fondly from her days as a midshipman.

There were long hours one could while away in those spaces, all the better to be out of sight, and mind, for those officers who might assign a task to idle hands.

Alexis glanced from the stacks of crates to the space between the vats.

There were other, darker, uses one could put such spaces to, and though the initial way between the vats might be tight, it opened up where their four curved bottoms met.

A closer look at the nearest vats made her pause. She'd noted the one being empty and the other with a maintenance tag at the time — one it still bore.

"Did you not have these filled back at Eidera, Sams?" she asked the purser who'd accompanied them into the hold, along with the bosun and several of his hand-picked men.

Sams shook his head. "The one's a bad pump — no way to fill until that's fixed and it's low on the maintenance list." He shot Gilbertson a look.

"Low, ma'am, because we've so many beer vats and rarely between systems so long as to use it all." The bosun shrugged. "More important tasks, you see?"

Alexis nodded, wondering what those more important tasks might be, since to her view there wasn't much in the way of maintenance being done aboard *Star* at all.

"And the other?" she asked, nodding to the one with a maintenance tag still hanging from it.

"Gas leak," Sams said. "Nitrogen's getting out somehow — nothing urgent."

"Gas?" Alexis frowned. She looked up at the tops of vats. "Mister Gilbertson, a ladder, if you please, and lively with it."

A ladder arrived and was hooked to the short rails atop the broken vat.

"Let me send a lad up," Gilbertson said, but Alexis shook her head.

"There's little room up there and I'm the smallest by far. No need for one of the lads to be uncomfortable when nothing may come of it."

She set a boot on the last rung and tested the ladder with her weight. It was flexible to drape over the curve of the vat and had to be raised with the help of poles to hook it at the top.

Even as her head rose above the vat's top she knew that something had, indeed, come of it. A thin, flexible tube ran from the closed maintenance hatch of the vat she was on and across to the hatch atop the empty vat next to it.

"Mister Gilbertson, send word to Mister Theibaud," she called down, "and I'd admire a full party of trusted spacers to us instanter."

"Have you found something?" Gilbertson asked as he nodded to one of his men and sent him off.

"Perhaps," Alexis said, looking closer at the tube.

She scrambled the rest of the way onto the top of the vat and examined it even closer. The hatch was sealed, but the tube caused that seal to be broken slightly. That would explain the nitrogen loss. Or would it?

"Mister Sams!" she called. "Is nitrogen denser than air or lighter?"

"Would I be knowing such a thing?" Sams asked.

Alexis grumbled. "You should know your vats, I should think — would a small gap in the seal —" She estimated the gap caused by the tubing, not the tubing itself. "— say, six millimeters, cause the nitrogen loss you've observed?"

"No," Sams said immediately. "It's not as though the thing's pressurized so much — we just replace the air with nitrogen to keep the oxygen out."

Alexis frowned. "Wouldn't the carbonation increase the pressure?"

She wished Isom was here instead of in her cabin, for she had no doubt her clerk would be able to tell her exactly what she wished to know — why her clerk would have a thorough understanding of beer storage, she'd never asked, but she was certain he would, as he seemed to know everything else.

"Not carbonated yet," Sams said.

"What? Do you mean all these vats are flat?"

"Aye, ma'am. Less space in storage that way and it's a use for all the carbon we scrub out of the air. It's carbonated when we draw it for use."

Alexis shook her head, not knowing much about beer, but certain that process couldn't be good for it — carbonated with what the crew exhaled? Certainly it was just carbon, no different than any other source, but still — they said the ship's recycled water was clean and pure, too, but a taste would put the lie to that, easy enough.

She'd thought the tube might just be some lads draining off a bit of an extra ration, but that didn't explain the lack of nitrogen — and even the most desperate spacer might think twice about such effort for a flat pint.

"Mister Gilbertson, another ladder, if you please?"

She started for the side of the vat to make her way back down and up the other, to see where the tube led, but then eyed the gap. It was nearly a meter between the tops, given the vats' curvature, much as it was at the bottom.

Alexis knew it was a pointless surrender to her own impatience, but she didn't want to clamber down and wait for another ladder, or have the one they had repositioned.

Instead, she crawled right to the edge.

Perhaps a meter? she thought. *A bit of a stretch, but certainly something I can accomplish.*

It wasn't something she could leap, the hold's overhead being just above her with no more room than to crawl on all fours.

Alexis put her knees just against the short, few centimeter, rail around the vat's top — more to hold the hooks of a ladder than anything else — and let herself fall forward, arms outstretched. She caught the other rail, knees atop the first vat's rail, then wondered what to do.

Bloody curiosity — cats and such — of course a meter's a fair distance when one has only half that again to spare.

"Ah, Captain?" Gilbertson called up.

"Yes, Mister Gilbertson? I'm a bit occupied at the moment."

"Just to let you know, we've that second ladder you asked for."

A moment later the hooks of a second ladder clattered onto the rail of the second vat — around the front, of course, not the side where Alexis was — and which was blocked by the curvature of the two vats meeting.

Self-restraint and patience — I really must do a bit of work on those.

Now she was stuck, though, with no way to push herself back to the first vat, so it was forward on.

Alexis walked her feet forward, bending at the waist, so that she was perched, hands and feet on either vat with her head down and backside touching the overhead.

Perhaps I should call Isom down and have him take an image? I could look at the bloody thing every time I don't want to wait a half minute.

She put her right hand on the vat's top, still clutching the short rail with her left, then twisted a bit and kicked off with her feet, so that her right leg caught the new vat's rail, and she could scramble the rest of the way atop it.

"No need for that, Mister Gilbertson, I have it quite in hand."

"Of course, Captain."

Alexis rolled onto her back, sighing, then got to all fours again and examined this vat's hatch. The tubing from the other went through this one's hatch as well. She grasped the handle, turned to release it, and peered inside.

"Has anyone a torch? I can't make out the bottom."

A moment later, a spacer appeared atop the ladder and passed her a torch.

"Thank you."

Alexis clicked it on and shone it on the tubing hanging down into the vat, following it to the bottom where it attached to one of the ship's portable compressors, normally used to fill the vacsuit tanks.

Well, that explains what was used to try and kill me — and likely did for Captain Meiggs.

Further movement of the light revealed a still, crumpled form at the vat's bottom.

"Mister Gilbertson — I believe we may call off the search for Powell."

Chapter Thirty

"Done in by his own gas?" Isom suggested.

Alexis shook her head.

Quite a crowd had gathered to watch Powell's body be removed from the vat and Alexis held back on her initial thought to have the bosun send the lot of them back to their work. She scanned the faces in the crowd, hoping for some look that might tell her who the culprit was, but saw nothing.

"No, the tubing was firmly attached to the pump, no leakage, and the air in the vat was fine. Powell had the same bit of blueness to him as Captain Meiggs, suggesting they'd both been murdered there, in this cabin, by the same gas."

"Then why move Powell? And how?"

"Likely to throw suspicion on the man — we did spend a great deal of effort looking for him, after all. As to the how —"

Alexis pondered that. How indeed? On a ship so crowded as *Star*, with indentures in every open space. She glanced down at the deck.

"Perhaps the crawl spaces?" she suggested.

There were tunnels, if one might call them that, holding the ship's wiring and piping, beneath the decks.

"From here to the hold?" Gilbertson looked down at the deck as well. "That might take determination."

Alexis nodded. The spaces were small, barely enough to hold a man without the addition of wiring and pipes — how would one even begin to drag a body the full length of the ship in such a space? Still, she couldn't imagine the indentures remaining silent about a spacer, or even one of their own, striding through the ship with a corpse slung over his back.

"Perhaps," she said. "Perhaps we'll never know the truth of it." She turned to the purser. "Mister Sams, I'd admire it if you were to dispose of the remaining beer in that vat."

"But what am I to do with it, Captain?" Sams asked.

The purser's face held a pitiful look as though he knew exactly what Alexis would suggest.

"Run a hose to the recyclers and draw it off into the tanks. We'll have plenty of water in a day, at least."

"Recyclers? But —"

The agony on Sams' face was nothing compared to the two spacers with him.

"We'd, ah —"

"Be happy to help, ma'am," the second finished for the first. These were merchant spacers and not tied to the naval convention of all officers being called the same, regardless of gender. "Not wishing there to be such waste and all."

Alexis shook her head.

"We've no way of telling what our culprit might have done to it. We'll not take the risk."

The spacer's shoulders straightened. "For the good of the ship, ma'am," he said. "There's risks and risks, aye?"

"I'm afraid not," Alexis said. "We've plenty of beer aboard without this one vat, and can refill at the next system easily enough, so no need to chance it."

All three men frowned, expressions turning to winces.

"If you insist," Sams said slowly.

"I'm afraid I do."

Sams nodded and gestured to the two spacers, who moved as slowly as they thought they could get away with, perhaps thinking with enough time Alexis might reconsider her heretical course.

You'd think I'd asked them each to cut off a foot and toss it in the beef vats for starter.

Hoses were brought out and laid from the half-filled vat of beer to the recyclers. The activity brought an audience of indentures from their nooks and crannies to observe the action, though, thankfully, the majority of the crew was still out on the hull making sail to avoid the oncoming storm.

Star's hull creaked, and Alexis adjusted her footing, as did the others.

Bugger your inertial compensators — she still moves.

The hoses were laid, the connections made, and Sams stepped to the half-filled vat of beer, hand to the lever which would send its contents gushing to the ship's recyclers, where they'd be separated into pure water — or what passed for that aboard ship — and a sort of organic-mineral sludge which would go to feed the beef vats and the purser's limited vegetable rows.

Sams strained at the vat's release lever and grunted. "I — can't —"

"Is it stuck?" Alexis asked. Yet one more problem to do deal with?

"No," Sams said, stepping back. "I can't make my arm do it..."

"Oh, for —" Alexis moved forward, grasped the lever, and *Star* gave a mighty lurch, nearly sending her to the deck if she hadn't been holding onto the lever.

Sams did stumble, saved only by crashing into the vat's side, while Slott fell to his hands and knees.

Sams yelped. "Shoals?" he asked, looking about the hold as though he expected to see a gash in *Star's* side, or some gaping hole exposed to the vacuum outside.

Alexis laid a hand on the vat's side, frowning and feeling for the ship's vibrations. Underneath the steady thrum she'd expect to be transferred from taught rigging and a well-regulated fusion plant came a sort of flutter.

"A torn sail?" she suggested, and could see the other spacers relax, though Sams didn't seem comforted. "They'll have it down and replaced in a moment."

A split sail happened, though it was rarer outside of an action when one might be pierced by enemy shot. Some defect in the fine, metal mesh might cause a link to part, and, once started, the force of the dark energy winds would make their way through, tearing at the links nearest until those too split and the sail fluttered to the ends of the rigging in tatters.

Delaine would have the matter in hand shortly, she was certain — in fact, the flutter had already stopped, indicating they'd cut the particle projector to that sail, leaving it uncharged and inert to the winds while they cut it loose and replaced it with new.

Alexis grasped the lever again. "No respite for the beer in that, lads, if that was what you were hoping for."

Star of Tauric jerked again, nearly throwing Alexis to the deck this time, and she shared a look with the bosun. That had been a bit more than a sail, and then the hold was plunged into darkness.

Chapter Thirty-One

The darkness lasted only a moment — though there was time for shouts of fear and dismay from those in the hold — before the hold's emergency lighting came on.

That they'd gone out at all, though, was cause for concern, for they shouldn't have, without something damaging the ship's lines.

The switch from that power to the ship's batteries left the lights as bright as any, but off-putting in some way Alexis couldn't describe. She could only say that from one moment to the next, her feeling of the *Star of Tauric* had gone from an able ship, well-in-hand, to one of distress, and she found herself dashing for the nearest ladder out of the hold.

"Mister Sams, to your station! Mister Slott, Mister Gilbertson, get the crew into suits, instanter, there's something amiss!" The nearest ladder to her position was behind a veritable wall of indentures, set to watch the fun of recycling a vat of beer, and now clutching at each other, eyes wide with the terror of something they didn't understand happening in an environment they knew nothing of.

Alexis' tablet pinged and she pulled it out to take a call from Joyce, working the signals console on the quarterdeck.

"From Mister Theibaud," Joyce said, "the winds have picked up and we've lost our port power and data lines forward of frame forty-seven."

Alexis nodded — *Star* had redundant wiring to carry power and data from bow to stern, run through conduits to either side of the ship. A problem with those power lines could explain the brief outage, though she'd have expected the ship's batteries to make up the lack before the other lines could take the load.

"Which power lines?" she asked — given the lack of maintenance aboard *Star*, it wasn't unexpected that some of the lines would fail and need patching or replacement. The ship's crew had been so lax for so long that they'd likely run the lines so that the normal working of the hull to and fro had caused them to fray. What Alexis needed to know was which systems, other than the hold lights, might be affected.

"All of them, Captain," Joyce said. "All starboard lines forward of frame forty-seven are gone. Data and power, both."

Alexis paused, taking that in.

"That's not maintenance," she muttered.

She pointed to the nearest two spacers.

"The two of you, with me — the rest of you into your suits and get outside to work the sails."

She turned to leave the hold for where the damage had occurred, but found herself facing a crowd of indentures, their curiosity about the emptying beer vat replaced with near panic at the power loss and sudden activity of the crew.

"Make a bloody lane!" Alexis shouted.

They might not understand the order, but those indentures between Alexis and the ladder were clear on her intent. They parted like rows of wheat before her rush, pressing each other against the sides of the narrow space between crates and vats of the ship's stores.

She made her way to the orlop deck and forward, mentally counting the slight ridges in the companionway's wall that indicated the ship's futtocks, or frames. There should be painted numbers, but

Star's were worn to indecipherable fragments where they weren't hidden by the crowded indentures lining the companionway.

"Clear a space here," Alexis ordered, arriving and motioning the indentures to move forward and aft of frame forty-seven.

One of the spacers with her pulled a panel from the overhead, exposing knots and tangles of wiring, as well as a wafting bit of acrid smoke.

"Boost me up, Garlan," Alexis said, motioning for one of the spacers to make a cradle of his hands.

They'd brought no ladder with them and Alexis wanted to see the damage for herself before continuing on to the quarterdeck.

She put her boot in the man's hands and he heaved, getting her up to where she could grasp the edge of the opened conduit and pull herself up to peer inside.

The conduits were supposed to be large enough for a full-grown spacer to crawl in and work, but it seemed like *Star's* crew might never have pulled out any of the old lines when replacing them, so there was much less space. Alexis noted fresh marks in the dust and grease coating the conduit's floor, then saw the damage — every line in the conduit was cut. Not frayed or worn, cut through cleanly and all nearly in the same place.

"Well, our villain assuredly wasn't Powell," Alexis muttered, edging out of the conduit and dropping back to the deck.

"Wait here for the carpenter," Alexis told the spacers with her. "I'll be on the quarterdeck."

The shuddering came again as Alexis neared the quarterdeck, this time greater, and though the indentures lining the companionway didn't seem to notice, Alexis certainly did.

She hurried through the quarterdeck hatch to find Delaine there on his watch.

"It is Jordan's promised storm, I fear, *capitaine*," Delaine said as she entered, no trace of teasing in his voice or manner, which told Alexis the situation must be more serious than a simple storm.

"This storm is stronger than we thought," Delaine added as she reached the navigation plot, where she was able to tell that was the case herself.

While the plot was still able to show the ships of the convoy, the images brought in from outside the hull by the ship's optics were blurry and nearly unreadable. *Swallow's* lights were barely visible in the haze of dark matter stirred up by the strong dark energy winds. *Belvedere*, being closer and larger, was more visible, but still indistinct.

"Where's *Almorah*?" Alexis asked.

"Here." Delaine tapped the plot.

"Why are they to windward?"

Delaine shrugged. "*Swallow* made us come to leeward, but *Almorah* was slow to respond and fell out of line — by the time she began her turn, she was more even with us, so came up into the winds. I think to come about and fall in line behind us, having lost the speed to resume her position, but then fell off again."

Alexis keyed up the plot history to see the maneuvers.

"She's square rigged and trying to come about — in these winds that will never happen. She'll be taken all aback."

Delaine nodded. "Such was my thought."

Alexis studied the plot and saw there would be no way for *Almorah* to resume her place in line, now that she'd fallen back more. Even without, the risk of a collision, especially in these winds, would be too great. Nor could she come about, for she hadn't the speed to make it through the eye of the winds by turning into them and coming full circle to fall in line behind.

She scanned the ship's status to see what changes Delaine had made while she was below.

"Projectors to ten percent," she ordered. "Signal to *Almorah*, *resume your place*."

By slowing *Star*, she could allow *Almorah* to come down off the wind without fear of collision, though it meant losing sight of *Swallow* and possibly *Belvedere.* She could only hope that with *Almorah* back in line, signals from *Swallow* would be relayed to her.

"*Almorah* is turning to starboard, ma'am," Joyce called out.

"Not starboard, port, you fool," Alexis ordered.

"He is trying, yet again," Delaine said.

As Alexis watched, *Almorah* now turned up into the winds, her turn slowing quickly once more as she faced them more and more.

"You Dark-cursed fool," she murmured, "you don't have enough way on you."

Still *Almorah* turned.

Alexis's eyes went to the navigation plot, measuring the strengths of the gusts they'd encountered so far. She thought of what she'd seen of *Almorah's* rigging, just a merchantman's and nothing like a naval ship — yet even with such rigging, she'd not wish to be taken aback by these winds. Not in a frigate, not in anything less than a liner, and, even then, not at all.

A single gust and...

"Douse the fore and main!" Alexis ordered. "Fifty percent on the mizzen! Hard to starboard — put us on the port tack! Signal to *Belvedere — Imperative.* Almorah *is dismasted,* Star of Tauric *to render assistance.*"

"But she's not —"

"Send the signal, Joyce!"

Even as she spoke it happened.

Almorah was taken all aback, the winds fell on her square-rigged sails, and without enough way to make it through her turn, those sails were pressed back into the masts and spars, gust after gust shoving the other ship fully backward against rigging meant to take such pressures from astern.

"Douse your sails, you thrice damned fool," Alexis whispered.

But it was too late.

Almorah's mainmast snapped, her yards swinging wildly with one side freed. That put more pressure on already stressed stays, which parted as well, sending the yard to swinging and striking the mizzen's stays. Those snapped at the impact — starting a cascade of failure that left *Almorah's* mainmast snapped at the lowest yard, her fore and mizzen cracked nearly at the hull, and all — rigging, sails, spars, and mast — collapsed back along her side as her sails finally went dark.

Alexis studied the image for a bare second, seeing how the wreckage lay.

"Signal to *Almorah* — *clear your starboard quarter, prepare to come alongside*."

"Aye, Captain."

"Alongside?" Slott asked. "In these winds?"

"If not, they are doomed," Alexis said, eyes never leaving the plot. "She's not a scrap of sail left — in these winds, she'll broach and roll, cracking her hull like an egg."

"And what of us?"

Alexis paused for a moment, assessing the state the other ship was in and the best way to bring *Star of Tauric* alongside to assist.

"Mister Theibaud, take a party to the hull to grapple *Almorah*. Mister Slott, we shall fall off the winds, come about, and let *Almorah* fall down to us."

"Grapple her?" Slott protested. "In these winds?"

Alexis shrugged. "What else? *Almorah* cannot maneuver as she is, she'll broach and crack at any moment. Are we to leave all aboard to that fate?"

Star edged to port, first a bit and then more, falling off the wind to eventually run before it, gaining distance from the stricken *Almorah* before continuing to come about onto the port tack and close once more. Alexis could see the vacsuited figures of *Almorah's* crew now out on the hull and hacking at the fallen spars and rigging that clattered against the other ship's hull.

"Hard a'port, Reynolds," Alexis ordered. "Put her on the starboard tack now, but only barely."

"Hard to port to the starboard tack, aye," Reynolds answered.

Star came up into the wind as *Almorah* had tried to, but with more way on her and without the handicap of the ship's-rig. Still, the ship slowed her turn, slower, until Alexis wondered if they, too, would be caught aback.

The advantage of *Star's* fore-and-aft rigged mizzen showed, though, and her bow eased past the winds, taking the next gust on her starboard bow. The mizzen's boom swung to port, the sail filling with the crack that shuddered through to the quarterdeck.

"Ten percent on the mizzen's projectors," Alexis ordered. "Full out on the keel — I want nothing more than to hold us here and let *Almorah* come to us as gentle as a young maid's first kiss, if you please."

Alexis could see *Almorah's* crew had much of the wreckage cut away to be carried off by the winds.

"Ten percent on the mizzen, drop the keel, aye," Reynolds said.

"She'll come to us," Slott muttered, but Alexis could tell he disapproved.

Star was making little headway, simply fighting the gusts as Alexis adjusted her heading and the strength of the sail's particle projectors to keep her almost in place and near enough to *Almorah's* course as could be — such as the other ship's wind-whimmed jerking about could be called a course. The gusts of dark energy winds were knocking the other ship about, sending her first one way, then another, with little in the way of consistency at all.

Delaine had only two men on the hull to attempt grappling *Almorah*, all that could be spared of *Star's* small crew, with others working the sails and trying to repair the damaged wiring below. Still, though, as *Almorah* drifted close enough, those two fired lines toward the other ship, just as *Almorah's* vacsuited spacers fired their own toward *Star*.

Few enough of those lines were able to make the journey and

reach the other ship, with most being blown far afield by a sudden gust of wind, but it was enough to connect the two ships and begin gingerly pulling them closer together, always allowing them to slacken as the spacers felt their ship move with a sudden gust that might snap the lines by throwing the two ships apart.

More lines followed, and, finally, there were enough lines connecting the two ships that one might expect them to survive the gusts as they were brought in, gradually drawing *Star* and *Almorah* together until their hulls touched.

A grinding, prolonged shudder ran through the ship as the two hulls scraped against each other, despite the fenders put in place, *Almorah* rolling as she had no sails to offset the force of the winds on her keel and hull.

Alexis could well imagine Mister Gilbertson, the bosun, looking up from his work to repair the damaged wiring and wonder what she'd just done to what he certainly considered his ship — at least the general condition of it. She knew, though, that the two crews would soon have additional lines running between the lower hulls and dampers in place to reduce the rolling. With *Star's* sail and *Almorah's* larger keel, the two ships would soon be able to act as one — even if one with a certain wallowing inability to do much else than, hopefully, ride out the storm.

"Signal from *Almorah*, ma'am," Joyce said.

Alexis looked up — the crews must have got some connections between the two ships, more than just the lines connected, for they were both too close and *Almorah's* masts and rigging too damaged for the usual reading of signal lights to be of much use.

"What is it?"

"Ah, so it's — *Captain to repair onboard*, ma'am."

Alexis could well understand Joyce's hesitation, for it was, possibly, the most absurd and ill-mannered signal *Almorah's* captain could make under such circumstances. Not only would it be dangerous for Alexis to leave the quarterdeck while the two ships were still being made fast to each other, but utterly foolish to try and cross from one to the other at this time.

Even leaving off entirely the fact that it's his *bloody ship which is disabled and in need of rescue*, she thought.

"Reply *Negative — Will not comply*, Joyce," she said after a moment's thought — Joyce would have to spell that last bit out rather than using the standard *Cannot comply* signal, but she dearly wished Captain Hodgman the Younger to understand she was refusing, not unable, to rush to his beck and call.

The nerve of the man.

"Aye, ma'am."

"Anything at all from *Belvedere*?" She knew Joyce would have told her had there been any reply, but felt compelled to ask.

"No, ma'am."

Alexis resisted the urge to tell him to inform her instanter should any signal from the other two ships of the convoy be seen — Joyce well knew the importance of not being left behind by the others.

Chapter Thirty-Two

"What is this nonsense of refusing to comply, Carew?" Captain Hodgman the Younger nearly yelled.

Their two ships had been made fast and umbilical connections made to allow for transferring data and video calls between the two. The connection was still jerky and filled with static due to the severity of the storm lashing at their hulls, and Alexis was glad she'd been able to allow her crew to leave the hull — *Star's* fore-and-aft rig on the mizzen was so much simpler than a ship-rig that it only required a few lines to work and those could be run into safer, enclosed spaces for the crew to work shielded from the worst effects of the storm.

"Captain Hodgman," Alexis said, "I will not leave my ship in these conditions. Certainly not for a specious, unnecessary meeting with you. The issue we now face is that your helm is not following my orders and is dragging us all off our line."

At first, Alexis had been confused at why every time she ordered a helm change to put the two ships before the wind, *Almorah's* helm had not complied — in some cases even working in direct opposition and dragging their course back to take the winds on their port beam. It had taken some time to realize *Almorah* was not merely ignoring her orders or that her helmsman was incompetent, but that he was *deliberately* countering those orders.

"*Your* line," Hodgman said, "and you'll bloody well leave your ship when I order you to!"

"I am *not* under your command, Captain Hodgman," Alexis said, gritting her teeth to keep from raising her own voice to match the volume of Hodgman's.

"I am *senior!*"

"*Star* is an independent ship, Captain Hodgman. Your seniority within the Marchant company is not impressed upon me — and I'll remind you, sir, your ship is dismasted and adrift while *Star* has way on her — you are derelict and you will take your orders from my helm, sir."

"Your orders take us off course! We must come to starboard so that we follow the line of *Belvedere* and *Swallow* and catch up!"

"We must come to *port*, sir, and run before the winds, else both our ships will be lost. *Star's* mizzen is not strong enough to hold the mass of both our ships in counter to their strength."

"Then raise sail on your fore- and mainmasts!"

"Not in these winds, sir."

Alexis was beginning to regret her decision not to board *Almorah* for an in-person meeting.

Never have I met a man in so dire need of a knee to his fork.

Instead, she carried on attempting to explain what should be self-evident to any spacer.

"We must run before the winds until this blows out — only then can we return to our course."

"That will put us days, perhaps weeks, away from the others! The cost is immeasurable."

And that was, of course, Captain Hodgman's first concern, for those days and weeks would further delay their arrival at Zariah, even further delaying the Marchants from moving on with their journey and profiting.

A shudder ran through the ship.

"Winds hard on the starboard beam," Slott whispered from the helm so he wouldn't be heard by the other captain.

"Hard a'port and keep her there," Alexis ordered. "Captain Hodgman, you will put *Almorah's* helm in harmony with *Star's* or I will cut your ship loose and leave you to your own devices."

Alexis wasn't certain she could carry through on her threat — doing so would certainly leave the other ship to be battered and broach. *Almorah's* passengers and crew should not be left to suffer that fate due to their captain's stubborn pride, yet *not* doing so would almost certainly doom *Star* as well.

Even through the static and jerky image, Alexis could see Hodgman scowl.

"You'd threaten us?"

"I will save my ship, Captain Hodgman, if you refuse to let me save yours, that is on your own head." She turned her head. "Signal to Mister Theibaud, if you will, Joyce — *a party to the hull and prepare to cut* Almorah *loose.*"

Alexis returned her gaze to the video pickup, as though to stare Hodgman in the eye. The other captain was silent, though his face spoke volumes.

"My uncle will hear of this, Carew, and Lieutenant Jordan as well. The Company will complain to Admiralty itself!"

"And you may thank me then for the opportunity to whinge about it," Alexis said. "Now, sir, will you bring *Almorah's* helm in harmony with *Star's*?"

Hodgman said nothing and silently broke off the call, but a moment later Joyce announced:

"*Almorah's* acknowledged your orders, Captain."

"Coming hard a'port, Captain," Reynolds added a moment later. "Coming to run before the wind."

Alexis nodded, silently thanking the Dark she'd not have to make the decision to cut *Almorah* loose in order to save her own ship.

"Five percent on the projector," she ordered, "and take another reef in."

The storm worsened and continued throughout the day, and Alexis stayed on the quarterdeck throughout. Though there was less work to be done on the sails, now that they'd reached a sort of balance with the winds and were simply running before them, there were still a myriad of lesser tasks to keep her and the crew busy — *Star's* already weak lines needing more urgent replacement under the current strain, monitoring and adjusting the lines and dampers between *Star* and *Almorah*, seeing to the needs and reassurance of those passengers being frightened and knocked about, the repair of *Star's* damaged power and data lines, which was proving difficult, for there was far more damage than Alexis had first thought, as well as the search for whoever might have sabotaged them.

In all, it drove both Alexis and the crew quite ragged and Delaine even more so.

The wearying day moved on to night, and finally at the start of middle watch, Delaine arrived on the quarterdeck with Isom.

"You must rest, *Capitaine*," he whispered to her. "The ship is stable and now we only wait."

Alexis nodded — she was quite tired. She'd already sent half the crew to their bunks at the start of the watch.

And knew she must get some rest herself, otherwise she'd be useless when something that did require her attention occurred.

"No need to glare at me so, Isom," she said. "I've no intention to argue."

"Hmph," Isom grunted, moving as though to herd her toward her cabin.

"Wake me if there's any change, Mister Theibaud."

"Of course, *Capitaine.*"

It was, perhaps, a measure of their situation that Delaine used no French endearment, though Alexis did admit that captain in his accent was not entirely lacking in effect.

"Cycle the men midway through the watch, as well, so we've fresh hands."

"*Oui, Capitaine.*"

Alexis woke with a start, something alerting her to a change, though she'd slept well despite the ship's constant shudders and jerking.

She swung her feet over the edge of her bed, even as a light went on in Isom's pantry quarters and he slid open that hatch. She blinked as her cabin lights came on and gradually brightened.

"Heard you moving, sir," Isom said. "Is aught amiss?"

Alexis had to grant that, as though her clerk and steward was as finely attuned to her movements as she was to her ship's, and wondered if he fancied himself her captain — before admitting that was almost a certainty.

"I don't know about amiss, but something is certainly different."

Alexis frowned as her tablet beeped along with the cabin's intercom, and a moment later, both declared, "Captain to the quarterdeck."

Alexis rushed through dressing, then hurried from her cabin to the quarterdeck, still fastening her jumpsuit.

"What is it?" she asked.

"*Monsieur* Slott has felt a thing," Delaine said.

"Wouldn't say it like that," Slott said.

"A bit of a shudder?" Alexis asked. "Different from the winds or a torn sail?"

Slott nodded. "That's it."

Alexis reached the plot and brought up both the images from outside the hull and their course. Neither was particularly useful — the views from outside the ship were hazy with the bits of dark matter kicked up by the winds and the plot of their course was, at best, only just as hazy a guess.

Between the winds, the former struggle against *Almorah's* helm, and their own maneuvering, both the computer's and her own dead reckoning of their position were suspect.

"Signal to *Almorah* — ask for their thoughts on our position."

It would likely only give Captain Hodgman an excuse to criticize her for getting them lost, even though his own calculations would be equally suspect, but there was a chance combining the estimates might bring the plots into some sort of consensus.

"Aye, sir."

Alexis froze, fingertips on the edge of the plot, straining to feel something that seemed there, but so faint she couldn't —

"There it is again," Slott said. "Do you feel it?"

Alexis nodded while Delaine shook his head.

"It's different than the winds," she said, "but so faint."

"Aye," Slott agreed. "From her bones, but so faint I can't tell what."

Alexis nodded agreement, studying the plot. For their calculated position — or the range of them — they were in as clearly open space as they could hope for. Yet what she'd felt, along with Slott's description, made her feel something.

"It was almost like a shoal," she said. "Yet ... threadier? Shorter and gentler?"

Slott nodded. "Aye, it has that feel to it, but a light shoal — more like passing through a belt's orbit than a planet."

The winds could make a ship shudder and shake when they struck, straining at the sails and that transmitted through spars, masts, and rigging to the hull. A shoal — that dark matter accumulating over normal-space masses — was more like a sudden, jarring shock as the accumulated dark matter jerked at the ship's keel and even hull, as though to stop her in place.

Yet shoals were only formed in *darkspace* over normal-space masses, so were limited to the space near systems where the planets, moons, and the star itself created heavy shoals and left lighter trails behind in their orbits.

The plot showed no systems nearby, yet there were some scattered around their path to either side.

"Response from *Almorah*," Joyce called out. "Sending it to the plot."

Even as he spoke, more lines appeared on the plot, laying out the estimates of *Almorah's* computer and officers. They were, near universally, to one side of *Star's* own dead reckoning.

Alexis frowned — with so much difference between the two, both the officers and computer on one of their ships had made a significant error.

Or both —

And it felt, to her, that both were, indeed, quite wrong. She'd had enough experience with her own navigation exercises to find a certain sense of when a plot was wrong just by looking at it.

What have we forgotten?

Alexis' eyes jumped past *Almorah's* plots to where they might be if both ships had underestimated the curve of their course and her blood chilled.

"Raise the keel! All of it!" she ordered. "Signal to *Almorah — Imperative. Raise your keel, instanter.*"

"What is it?" Slott asked.

"We're all wrong," Alexis muttered, fingers flying over the plot to recalculate their probable position. "Bloody hell, how does one tell this thing our keel's larger?"

"Our keel?" Delaine asked.

"Signal from *Almorah*," Joyce called out. "Captain Hodgman calling."

"And our mass!" Alexis yelled. "We must account for both ships, not only our own!"

Alexis spared a finger tap to accept the call, sliding Hodgman's image to the side so she might continue calculating what she was now certain was the error in their course.

Am I overreacting? she wondered. *If the winds were ... thus — and the two ships together, thus —*

"Carew!" Captain Hodgman fairly bellowed. "What are you on about now?"

"Is your keel raised, Captain Hodgman? If not, I require it, instanter."

"What is it?" Slott asked, coming to the plot from the helm. He looked questioningly at Delaine. "Do you see it?"

"Raising the keel will let the winds at us," Hodgman was saying. "We'll lose even *more* distance from our proper course!"

"We are in an Oort shoal, Captain Hodgman, and coming on the system itself. Raise your bloody keel!"

"What —"

"Gentlemen, our course is thus."

Alexis swept a finger along the plot, drawing a course well past *Almorah's* projections.

"Nonsense!" Hodgman objected as Alexis sent it to *Almorah's* plot as well.

"How?" Delaine asked.

"The keels and our mass, gentlemen — *bloody* computers. How does one change the ship's keel and mass in this mess?"

"You can't, but why would you want to? It's already got all of *Star's* data and — buggering Dark," the sailing master muttered.

"*Merde*," Delaine whispered.

"Bosun reports the keel's in twenty-percent," Joyce called out.

"Tell him, lively now," Alexis ordered, fearing it was already too late, especially with Captain Hodgman's resistance.

The ship's sailing profile went into the dead reckoning calculations, both from the ship's computers and her officers — every bit of it.

The mass of the ship, cargo and crew, the amount of sail, minute by minute, the charge on the projectors, the depth of the keel let out of the hull — all of it plus the strength of the winds, the resistance of the dark matter they sailed through, every change to the helm. All of it went into the calculations that told them where they might be in the vast expanse of the Dark.

For their ship.

Not for two bound together.

Another shudder, stronger than the last, rolled through the hull and this time Delaine nodded as well.

"What are you all babbling about?" Hodgman demanded.

"The calculations for our course require information about the ship, Captain Hodgman, which —"

"I bloody well know that, Carew!"

"For *our* ships, Captain Hodgman! Each of them on their own — that's why *Star's* and *Almorah's* projections are so different. *Almorah* has more mass and a larger keel, so your projection is offset to ours, but with the ships bound together —"

Hodgman's eyes went wide and he looked down at his own plot.

"*Raise the bloody keel!*" he ordered. "All of it!"

A moment later the heavy shudder and violent jerk that ran through both ships told of both their actions coming far too late.

They must have been past the Oort, into the system itself and at the orbit of some planet. Alexis could determine later if they'd simply crossed the line of dark matter left behind in the planet's orbit or had the bad luck to strike the shoal caused by the planet itself, but either was sufficient.

Both ships slowed abruptly, the added force on *Star's* sails snapping her sheet and letting the boom and sail swing forward freely. Had the line not parted, or had Alexis left any sail at all on the ship's fore- or mainmasts, *Star* might have been dismasted as *Almorah* had been earlier. As it was, her ship then faced far worse damage as *Star's* worn and weakened keel snapped at the impact.

Almorah's keel held, though she could be said to fare the worse for it. The heavy mass of thermoplastic ground through the line of dark matter, bringing both ships to such an abrupt halt that their inertial compensators let through so much force that Alexis and the others on the quarterdeck were knocked from their feet to sprawl on the deck.

Alexis knew it would be worse throughout both ships, with the passengers packed in so tightly and their baggage alongside them, there'd be injuries for certain.

Chapter Thirty-Three

"Mister Theibaud," Alexis ordered, "I'd admire it did you meet Mister Gilbertson at the keel and assess the damage, as well as a crew to the hull and get more lines between us and *Almorah*."

She could feel the further grinding of the hulls as the winds and shoals worked differently on the two ships, causing them to roll and grate against each other.

"We should cut her loose," Slott said quietly, almost whispering. "With her mass and her keel still out, she'll never work her way loose from this."

"We've only just struck and can't know that yet, Mister Slott," Alexis said as Delaine left to carry out her orders — though she suspected it was true. The force of the impact spoke to a large shoal, possibly even one carried by a planet itself and not just its orbital trail, and one there'd be no easy escape from for the larger ship. "And there are hundreds of people aboard her — I'll not just abandon them."

"*Almorah* has a larger crew," Slott said, "what can we even do to help them?"

"With no masts and no sails of her own," Alexis said, "she'll only run up against another shoal, should she make her way off this one without us."

"But —"

"Attend to *Star's* immediate needs, Mister Slott — I will attend to the futures of both ships."

"Aye, Captain," Slott muttered, returning to the helm, but Alexis could sense both the bitterness and fear in his manner.

She also feared he was correct. With *Almorah's* greater mass and her keel extended, her crew would likely not be able to free her from the shoals — yet with *Star's* own keel damaged, they, too, would be at the mercy of the winds and further shoals even should they work their way free from this one. *Star's* fore-and-aft rig offered some advantage there, as, even without her own keel, she might make some maneuvers, but not what was needed to escape whatever system they were in — the force to leeward would drive her on.

Without her keel to cut into the dark matter, *Star* would make more leeway than not, no matter what point of sail Alexis put her on.

A broad reach, perhaps, Alexis thought, *certainly no more than a beam.*

They could set out an anchor, she thought. If set into the shoal, it might hold even against these winds.

With the storm's winds now blowing directly toward the system's center, drawn there by the mass of whatever star laid there, running before the wind as *Star* must with her damage would only dash them up against the larger shoal amassed there. Without her keel, *Star* needed *Almorah* as much as the other ship needed *Star's* sails to have much chance of survival.

"Signal to *Almorah*, if you please, Joyce — *Interrogative. Your keel?*"

"Aye, Captain."

A moment later Captain Hodgman was again requesting a call and Alexis answered it, shocked at the change in the man's appearance after so little time since their last. His uniform jacket was askew, as though hastily donned or rebuttoned, and his hair was wet with sweat. As well, in the background she could see that he was not on *Almorah's* quarterdeck, but deep within his ship's hold where the machinery to raise and lower her keel was located. The look on his face was one of defeat and despair.

"Cut yourselves loose, Carew," he said flatly. "The motors burnt out a few minutes ago — we've tried to crank the bloody thing in by hand while those are being repaired, but to no avail. I've men on the hull to cut it loose as a last resort, but..." His shoulders slumped. "I fear —" He closed his eyes and took a deep breath. "We'll continue to try, of course, but I see no way we'll work our way off this."

"*Star's* own keel is lost, Captain Hodgman," Alexis responded. "We've less than ten-percent of it left to us."

Hodgman chuckled, clearly understanding the implications of that in these winds, already inside a system's shoal patterns.

"Aren't we a pair?" he said, then sighed. "You'll still have the better chance."

"Perhaps if you lighten *Almorah's* load?"

Hodgman shook his head. "Already started — I've half my crew toting bulkheads to the port airlocks and my pumps are spewing every bit of water, vatjuice, and beer we might spare out the side." He closed his eyes briefly. "It won't be enough — most of our portable mass is the indentures and their belongings. Which the latter I've already started out the side as well — nearly had a riot at that until I agreed to forgive their passage." He chuckled again. "Uncle Rawls'll not thank me for that ... should we ever meet again."

Alexis was silent for a moment, taking that in.

"We could cut our keel loose, I suppose," Hodgman went on, "but then we'd be in no better shape than you — worse, perhaps, as you've at least got that hideous mizzen of yours." Another chuckle gave the lie to his words. "No, even without the keel all entire, I fear we'd be mired here still. My bosun tells me we might need to lose another twenty or thirty tons of mass after all else is out the ports — and that's as well as cutting loose all the damaged spars and rigging, leaving us only a short foremast to step once loose."

Alexis frowned, trying to think of any way the other ship might make up so much mass — some way Captain Hodgman had not thought of and mentioned already.

"Have you considered the passengers, Captain Hodgman?" she asked, quickly doing some calculations — *Almorah* carried over three hundred indentures, at average weight they might make up some twenty tons or more.

Hodgman's face went cold. "You can't be suggesting —"

"No!" Alexis said quickly, shocked he'd even think she was. "Of course not. My thought was to transfer them to *Star* temporarily — then back once *Almorah* is off this shoal and the winds have died."

Star would certainly have to jettison some supplies as well, else the added mass would keep her stuck to the shoal as much as *Almorah* was, but sailing for Zariah immediately after the storm would take no more than a few weeks, so they could spare all but what was necessary for that journey. All — ship, crew, passengers, and what supplies were left — would be going separate ways at that point, so there was little need to think beyond that port.

"A moment," Captain Hodgman said, turning to the side and speaking quickly with someone outside the camera's range. He turned back a moment later, nodding. "It's possible that will be enough." He sighed. "If the worst comes, they'll be safe, at least."

It took some time to arrange the transfer of *Almorah's* passengers to *Star*.

First came the rigging of a docking tube from *Almorah's* port side to *Star's* starboard airlocks. They couldn't use the locks where the two ships met, as they were tightly bound together, hulls barely a few centimeters separating them with the fenders to reduce them rubbing and battering against each other.

They used a series of emergency docking tubes, strung together, to make the journey, and nearly all of both ship's crews that could be spared from the more vital work of keeping each ship intact spread out along the tube's length to pass passengers from hand to hand in the zero gravity.

Star's passengers were no more happy at the news their own belongings would be going out the locks than *Almorah's* were, but Alexis assured them, and placed it in *Star's* log as a binding contract, that their debts and cost of transport would be forgiven. They'd still be listed as transported, and likely have to take transport again to some other system as the Zariahn authorities were unlikely to want them there, but at least their new indentures would be only for the cost of transport and nothing else.

Captain Meiggs' heirs might also object, but Alexis assumed they could litigate the matter with the Marchants, as she'd logged the full reason for needing to free up mass on *Star*.

The transport of the passengers from *Almorah* to *Star* was further delayed by the insistence of both crews in wearing their vacsuits in the boarding tubes, despite the tubes being fully aired and secured — and despite the extra anxiety this caused in the passengers to be transferred. It was understandable, of course, that they'd be anxious, as they had no experience in *darkspace* or vacuum at all, and the boarding tubes the ships carried were flimsy things, knocked about by the winds despite being so close to the ships' hulls.

The sight of the crews in vacsuits, despite the passengers having none, must surely have been frightening for those to leave the relative security of their ship and its gravity.

The desire for those vacsuits — and Mister Slott's requisition of hundreds of ship's coveralls from the purser's stores — was explained as the first of those passengers arrived.

Those passengers, having no experience in zero-g, rapidly reduced their own mass, arriving at *Star's* docking port covered in the remains of their last meal aboard *Almorah*.

"Take one and change over there," Gilbertson ordered as the first came through the tube. "Put your clothes in the bag, they'll be cleaned and returned to you, and put this on. Aye, ma'am, I know — do as best you can with your hair, there. Here you are, sir, change behind that screen there and — *bloody hell!* Fergussen! A bucket here — lively now! You there! Yes, you, and all behind you — if you've a need to spew from the transition to gravity, there's buckets for that!"

The mess and stench made Alexis grateful Hodgman had sent Lord Braithwaite and his valet over first, for there was no telling what the herald's reaction might be to being asked to wade through the filth that came to fill the docking tubes.

For nearly a full watch it went on, with half *Star's* crew tossing baggage out one port while passenger after filth-covered passenger came aboard through another. The entire process was paused for the tube to be vented to vacuum and re-aired when its contents became so unbearable that even those who weren't sickened by zero-g, were by the stench of what those before them left behind.

All the while, *Star* and *Almorah* continued to be ground together by the winds, hulls scraped by both the dark matter of the shoal and each other. The winds themselves picked up, becoming strong enough to batter even at the linked tubes between the ships despite the gallenium sails the crew had laid to cover them in order to prevent just that.

Not all of *Almorah's* passengers wished to make the transfer — all had heard the tales of being outside a ship's hull in *darkspace*, well-embellished by the typical spacer's penchant for dramatic flair and a good yarn, spinning even the most mundane tasks into epic sagas of survival and daring. The Dark was dangerous, no doubt, but not nearly so much as those who didn't sail it were led to believe by both those tales and the dramatics of the vidshows seen by all those on-planet.

Some wept at the thought of being exposed to what they believed was almost certain death, while others actively resisted — with both being quickly taken up by *Almorah's* crew and fairly tossed into the tube if necessary, or even bound hand and foot to stop their struggling.

As the first of the latter came onto *Star*, struggling against the bonds *Almorah's* crew had placed around his hands and feet, Alexis knew Captain Hodgman was taking the situation just as seriously as she, for the first words out of the man's mouth after he'd finished spewing were threats to sue.

"You're welcome to, sir," Alexis said, "though I'll be there to testify it's only through Captain Hodgman's action you're alive to do so." She turned to the bosun. "Lay any who come across bound to the side and release them only after all are transferred and we're off this shoal."

"Aye, sir — you heard the captain, lads, stack them like a purser's private stores."

"What — this is outrageous! Release me!"

"I'm sorry, sir," Alexis said, seeing Gilbertson had the situation well in-hand. "I've a ship to attend to."

Chapter Thirty-Four

Alexis made her way aft through the ever more-crowded corridors and spaces aboard the ship. The only space not now crammed with even more humanity than before was that around the repairs being made to the ship's damaged cabling. All else was a standing, jostling crowd, as there was no longer space for the passengers to sit, even with knees drawn in.

The crowd moved like a wave before her, pressing together to make just enough space for her to squeeze by against a bulkhead, then filling in behind her to relieve a bit of the pressure. She reached a ladder down to the hold and paused, grateful for the bit of open space that provided, and pulled out her tablet.

"Delaine?" she asked, connecting to his.

"*Oui, Capitaine?*"

"Be sure everyone has enough space, will you? At least so they're not crushed," she added quietly, wary of the passengers above and below hearing her concern.

"*Oui, Capitaine.*"

If nothing else told the severity of their situation, Alexis was certain Delaine calling her merely "Captain" twice in a row must surely capture it.

He was in the hold itself, tasked with settling passengers there as the incoming wave pushed *Star's* original complement deeper and deeper into the ship.

Alexis nodded, disconnecting the call and continuing into the hold herself, though her destination was the purser's office.

Here there was more space, clear of any passengers for the moment, as Sams' crew set about jettisoning excess supplies through the loading airlocks.

"How goes it, Mister Sams?" Alexis asked.

The purser shook his head, clearly distraught and no less harried than any of *Star's* warrants.

"We've put a whole voyage's profits out the lock already, Captain, and still more to go." He stepped back from her as crewman hefted a heavy panel cut from the side of an empty vat and carried it toward the lock. "Vented all the liquids we can spare already — kept only enough nutrients for the vats and beer to get us to Zariah and a bit of resin for the printers."

Alexis nodded, then, "Food enough for *Star's* complement or —" She trailed off with a significant glance off into the hold where a line of passengers was filing down another ladder and being ushered into newly opened space where there'd once been a vat of some sort.

Sams nodded.

"I've been a'space long enough to know what shoaled with the keel out will do — food enough for ours and theirs, though only barely enough if our position's correct."

"We're almost certain to be in one of three systems, I think," Alexis said. "All much the same distance from Zariah."

"Then we've enough — though it will be a tight passage."

"Thank you, Mister Sams."

Alexis moved on, making her way forward through the much-changed hold. Both vats having to do with the as yet unsolved murders had been dismantled and gone out the lock, the need to gather any further evidence from them being less than the needed space for their new passengers. The wardroom, as well, was dismantled, with the mate's and warrant's cabins reassembled in Alexis' day cabin, to Isom's somewhat tempered dismay, as that left Lord Braithwaite in the same accommodations.

Seeing all was well within the ship, Alexis returned to the quarterdeck to wait out the rest of the transfer, then the air was pumped from the boarding tubes, well-scrubbed before being recirculated into the ship and the interior of the tubes exposed to hard vacuum before the detritus of the transfer was vented to space. The same for those spacers who'd worked inside the tube and their vacsuits — all into a lock and the lock exposed to vacuum, before being re-aired a bit and rapidly vented so that the freeze-dried particles left behind would be expelled.

"It's still not enough, Carew," Captain Hodgman told her as the locks were sealed and the boarding tubes stored. "We're still well and truly stuck — the keel won't budge. I've some lads working at carving it away, but with no keel at all, in-system, with these winds..."

Alexis nodded — removing *Almorah's* keel would leave the other ship in much the same state *Star* was, unable to do much more than sail directly before the winds — and quite possibly damage the ship's hull, as well, hastening the breakup of the ship. Once free of the shoals and with the storm passed, they might be able to print another, or the stub of one, for both ships — enough to sail for Zariah, perhaps — but it would be a last resort.

"*Star* is quite close," Alexis said, "perhaps the mass of both ships is drawing more dark matter in? I'd not suggest we abandon you, but perhaps —"

Hodgman nodded agreement.

"Stand off a bit," he agreed. "If that doesn't allow us to work our way free, we'll blow the keel and —"

Both captains paused and swayed with their ships as a groaning, drawn-out *crack* resounded. They each tensed and paused, as though waiting for word of what had just given way, but none came. The sound, though, served as warning that neither ship should stay within the shoals longer than they must.

Alexis shared another nod with Hodgman, then disconnected the call.

"To Mister Theibaud, if you please, Joyce," Alexis said. "We'll set an admiralty and pay out until we're off the shoals."

"Aye, Captain."

Alexis watched the transition as Delaine led the crew back out onto the hull.

First the admiralty was set, an anchor with broad, wide flukes made to dig into the dark matter and stay in place — Alexis suspected the name had been given to the piece for its rigid inflexibility and refusal to be moved once set, and not, as the official documents stated, that it had been designed and approved by Admiralty itself.

"Cut us loose from *Almorah,* all but three lines, and pay out all," Alexis ordered as soon as the anchor was set and its hold tested.

"Godspeed," Slott muttered.

The effect on *Star* as the lines holding her fast to *Almorah* were released was dramatic.

The ship swung rapidly away from *Almorah,* pushed by the winds to first snub up against the anchor line, then farther away as additional lines to the other ship were paid out. Those lines, still attached to *Almorah* kept *Star* roughly between the other ship and anchor, while also assuring the two ships had some means of coming back together once *Almorah* worked her way free of the shoals.

Once away from the other ship, Alexis could see what effect the shoals had had already and she grimaced. *Almorah's* hull was pitted and cracked from being buffeted by the winds and rocked within the density of the shoal. *Star's* own hull was likely in no better state, she knew, though she'd kept the crew so busy with the transfer of passengers they'd had no time to report on it to her. There was little enough they could do to fight such damage, in any case — no amount of patching would keep up with it, and if the hull did breach, the end would come swiftly as the dark matter worked its way inside and ate at the ship's fusion core.

"Make fast," she ordered as the cessation of the constant grinding vibration told her they were off the shoal. "Set a second admiralty aft and make fast."

"All lines made fast, set a second admiralty aft, aye," Slott repeated.

The second anchor was set and lines drawn taut, giving *Star* three points to stabilize her, but, more importantly, giving *Almorah* lines to draw against as she tried to work her way off the shoal.

"Signal to *Almorah* — *Draw on us as needed.*"

"Aye, Captain."

The quarterdeck lights went out again, replaced by the dimmer emergency lights.

"It weren't me!" Joyce said.

Status calls came rapidly from around the quarterdeck as each station reported.

"No signal from engineering!"

"Transmission loss — all systems on local battery!"

"No signal abaft frame forty-seven!"

"A runner to engineering," Alexis ordered, knowing the engineers would already have someone coming forward to report, but wanting to be certain. "A runner to frame forty-seven starboard to report on the cable conduits. Signal to Mister Gilbertson and I'd admire it did he also make his way to frame forty-seven starboard."

Alexis knew it was starboard, because the first incident of sabotage had been at frame forty-seven port and she was nearly certain this would be their saboteur finishing the job.

The quarterdeck hatch slid open and an engineer, Davies, made his way in.

"What's the status?" Alexis asked.

"The fusion plant is down, Captain — tried a restart, but the capacitors are low."

Alexis' blood chilled — she'd thought the power would only be out due to the lines being sabotaged, but if the plant was completely down, that was a more serious issue.

"What's wrong with the capacitors?" she asked — she could question how the plant had gone down in the first place later, for now the priority was to get it started again.

The ship's capacitors were used to store power — much like batteries, but with the ability to discharge that power much more rapidly. If the fusion plant was shut down for some reason, such as maintenance under normal circumstances, the capacitors were used to give it the sudden and immense jolt of power necessary to restart it.

"Two are dead and one's only holding half charge," Davies said. "We think it was the surges from the cut lines — twice in such a short time, then losing half the ship's draw."

Alexis caught her breath — on a naval ship there'd be six capacitors and four were needed to restart the plant. *Star*, not being subject to battle damage and not having to charge shot for the guns, had a much smaller plant, with only four capacitors to begin with and three being necessary to restart the plant.

"Sweet Dark," Slott whispered.

Alexis felt much the same reaction, but tried to maintain her calm.

"Thank you, Davies — I assume Mister Armstrong is working to repair the capacitors?"

"He is, Captain."

"Very well, then, return and assist him — please keep me updated."

"Aye, Captain."

As Davies left, Slott came to stand next to her at the plot and turned his back to the rest of the quarterdeck occupants to whisper.

"If the capacitors don't have a charge," he said quietly, "they'll not be able to restart the plant."

"Indeed, Mister Slott," Alexis said, much more calmly than she felt.

"Then how —"

"There are options, Mister Slott." She was already running through those in her head, thinking of any options which could breathe life back into what was her ship's heart. "The boats each have a plant and capacitors of their own, though smaller, and a line from *Almorah*, once this storm has passed, would be quite up to the task."

A sharp intake of breath from Joyce alerted her and she looked down at the plot, hazy images from outside the ship displayed there — but clear enough to see chunks of *Almorah's* hull being torn away and ground to dust.

"Signal from *Almorah*, Captain —" Joyce's voice quavered. "*Hull compromised. Godspeed* Star of Tauric."

"Pay out the line to *Almorah*," Alexis ordered, hoping it was not too late.

If they could relieve the stress on that line — leaving it attached, but slack — and the other ship's crew could get to a boat, then they'd have a chance to draw that boat to *Star*, but even as she gave the order, she saw that it was too late.

The line, still under tension, gave way — a piece of *Almorah's* hull still attached to the far end.

"Release the line to *Almorah*," she ordered, shoulders slumping — better to have the now slack line be taken away by the winds rather than whip about and tangle in *Star's* rigging or strike and tangle someone on the hull.

One of *Almorah's* boats detached from the other ship, raising just a bit of sail.

Whoever was aboard tried to slant their course toward *Star*, but the winds took even what little sail they raised and shredded it in an instant. The boat swept past *Star*, quickly blown toward the system's center and almost certain doom — the lines thrown from *Star's* crew on the hull in hopes of snagging the boat and pulling it in torn away as well. Perhaps, if they managed to rig a drift anchor, they might be able to ride out the storm before they were driven upon the system's center shoals, but the winds showed no sign of weakening.

"Pay out on the anchor lines," Alexis ordered. "Give us seven cables on the forward line then make the aft line fast to our bow as well."

"Aye, Captain."

With *Almorah's* crew now off in their boat to meet whatever fate had in store for them, there was no reason to remain close to the other ship and certain danger in doing so. Alexis had no desire to give up the well-set anchor in the shoal, but neither did she want her ship close to the other as its fusion plant was almost certain to be breached soon — assuming *Almorah's* crew hadn't shut it down before abandoning their ship.

Moving the aft line forward would give *Star* two points of anchorage to hold her steady against the continuing storm. Provided the lines held — and Alexis had hopes of that with *Star's* bow now allowed to point directly into the winds — they might make it through the storm themselves.

She pushed thoughts of after from her mind to concentrate on the moment.

All that — their location, the damaged keel, the sabotaged wiring, the saboteur and certain murderer himself, all were of no real matter if *Star* was unable to ride out the storm.

A visible crack appeared in *Almorah's* hull, then another, and finally the ship began to break apart — first chunks of her hull and what was left of her masts, then bits of her interior bulkheads, all to be swept away by the winds or ground to dust against the unknown system's shoals.

Chapter Thirty-Five

"Transition," Alexis said.

And pray we've the power to do so, she added silently.

At the helm, Reynolds' hand hesitated.

"What if we don't have —"

"If we haven't the power," Alexis said, "then we'll find out what happens to such ships. But we know our fate if we don't transition, so push the button, lad."

Reynolds nodded, staring at his console.

Alexis sympathized with his hesitation. There were tales and more tales about ships failing to transition properly to or from *darkspace* and all were both lurid and frightening.

After the storm, *Star of Tauric* seemed too still — deathly still, as though tentative and frightened by the end of *Almorah* and the chance she'd had of suffering the same fate. Now the constant buffeting and shaking from the winds was gone and, with their own fusion plant disabled, even many of the typical sounds and vibrations normal to the ship were missing.

There were power lines from all three ship's boats running

through the companionways to critical systems — all being patrolled by pairs of spacers to discourage more sabotage.

Since the storm ended and *Star* had been able to make what sail she could, searching the system for transition points so that they might enter normal-space and determine their true position, even the crew had been subdued, speaking in low tones and moving slowly, as if to not tempt whatever fates had let them through the storm.

Reynolds closed his eyes and tapped his console.

There was no change for a moment and Alexis held her breath, along with all those on the quarterdeck, entering an oddly complete silence, as there was not even the near-silent rustle of air from the circulation vents or of cooling fans in much of the dark and silent equipment filling the quarterdeck.

Then the space was filled with sighs as the few monitors turned on changed from displaying the black-on-dark images of *darkspace* to fill with stars.

Reynolds' voice broke as he said, "Trans ... transition complete."

Alexis closed her eyes and took a deep breath of relief. While she was as curious as any to find out where ships went when they failed to transition properly ... it wasn't something she wanted to investigate personally.

She tapped at her own console, smaller than the full navigation plot she had turned off to conserve power, to start the computer at its laborious task of determining where they were from the position of the stars.

"Scan for signals, Joyce," she said. It was unlikely there were any ships or stations in a random system, but they could be uncharacteristically lucky for the voyage.

"It will take a moment for the receivers to come on, Captain," Joyce said.

"Very well," Alexis said, then winced, for even the small amount of power needed for the receivers and their system would take away from what the crew and passengers of *Star of Tauric* needed to survive.

They'd discovered, over the course of the storm, that *Star's* batteries were in much the same condition as the rest of the ship, and what should have been measured in several days of power would now supply the ship for less than one. The ship's boats could supply some, but not enough to fully work and sail the ship.

That's what my life is measured in now, she thought. *Mine and everyone aboard's — down to watts and...*

She cut off that line of thought and returned to what she knew she must do. The system was likely empty and, once identified, its position would determine who lived and died.

Her calculations told her *Star* had, at most, eight weeks to live. That was receiving power from the three boats regularly and with no sailing at all, only keeping those aboard alive. The boats, though, couldn't generate enough to power *Star* full time — not with so many aboard. The boats' own batteries were being drained more and more each time *Star* sucked at their systems.

Eight weeks with all three boats, less than that with two, so their hope of rescue stood against one boat being able to reach help and return before *Star's* needs exceeded what the two remaining boats could supply. There'd have to be a decision then, she knew, for those two boats to stand off, refuse to power *Star* any longer, and leave those left aboard to their fate.

A decision Alexis was not willing to put on others.

No, she'd already decided.

If there was no inhabited system near enough for a boat to reach and return in time, she'd simply send all three boats off. There was no point in delaying the doom and putting that weight on Gilbertson, Slott, or Delaine.

She'd send all three of them, each to a boat in command. It was a logical choice.

She'd already prepared and set them to it, putting Delaine, Slott, and Gilbertson each in charge of a boat — ostensibly in preparation for towing *Star* through the system after transition, as the ship had not enough power for her own conventional drive. As well she'd set what women and children she could aboard the boats — to relieve some of the crowding, she'd said.

Slott had argued that there was space aboard the boats for more, but Gilbertson, the old bosun, had given her a look and a nod, then shut Slott down by interrupting with a question of his own.

Alexis thought he knew what she was about.

Once their position was identified, if it was too far for a single boat to go and return with help in time, she'd seal the locks and hatches to the boats.

Delaine would argue and plead, she suspected, but she could have Joyce simply ignore the signals so she'd not be tormented by them in her remaining dreams.

Without power from the boats, *Star* would take, perhaps, three days to die, along with those aboard her. Slott and Gilbertson would likely sail immediately, acceding to her orders and their own desire to live. Delaine would take longer — likely waiting those three days in the hopes Alexis would change her mind.

Alexis closed her eyes and took a deep breath, preparing to give the order as soon as *Star's* systems confirmed there was nothing here to save them.

It's sad, really — I think I rather would have liked to meet the Queen.

She'd not even been able to hug Delaine so tightly as she might before he entered his boat, for fear he'd deduce her plan from it.

"Captain!" Joyce shouted from the signals console. "There's no traffic but there's a beacon!"

Alexis quickly tapped her own console to bring up the signal — it'd been too much to hope that there'd be any signals traffic in the system at all, but a beacon could be nearly as good. A small science outpost, perhaps, or a mining center, where the ship traffic was so little that no other radio signals were broadcast.

"What beacon?" she asked, for Joyce was surely there ahead of her.

Joyce's voice held far less excitement. "It's only an availability announcement."

Alexis sighed.

A bloody for-sale sign.

Whatever the system was, there'd be little of interest here if it was this close to Zariah and still unsold by the survey company who'd initially visited.

The beacon, at least, held the system's name and designation, which would tell them where they were. And how far the trip to Zariah would be.

And how many will stay here with me and perish for want of room in the boats.

She still hadn't thought of a way to convince Delaine to sail on immediately, without her, in one of the boats, but she'd address that when the time came.

She read the system summary — just a number, not worthy of a name — and the navigation plot updated with their true position.

Six weeks' sail to Zariah, she estimated.

Farther than she'd like, which would affect how many more she might put in each boat.

She scanned the surveyor's brochure for the system as she calculated how many passengers could be loaded aboard — then her shoulders slumped in relief so strong she had to pause a moment and scrub at suddenly burning eyes.

"Joyce," she said quietly. "Signal the boats to detach and rig lines. There's bloody atmosphere here."

The three boats, laden with some of the overload of indentures, were set ahead of *Star* — heavy lines strung to the midpoint of each of *Star's* ship-rigged masts and to her bowsprit.

"Ahead easy," Alexis ordered.

"Aye," Joyce answered, "ahead easy."

It was the signals console echoing her and not the helm, for *Star's* own normal-space engines were dark and silent.

The three boats answered Joyce — Delaine, Slott, and Gilbertson, each aboard one of the boats.

Whatever slack had come from them drifting about was taken up as the boats' engines flared briefly and Alexis felt the ship nudged, then the boats took on the slightest bit of constant acceleration and she could feel *Star* begin to move.

The atmosphere, such as it was, was on the fourth planet and they'd entered the system from a Lagrange point with the sixth.

"All report lines taut and stable," Joyce said.

"All ahead full," Alexis said. "Handsomely, mind you."

Star's inertial compensators were offline to save power, and the sense of acceleration increased as the boats increased their thrust to the maximum — well, the least of their maximums, as each had a different ability there.

They'd be days in crossing the gulf between where they'd entered the system and their destination.

Days in which Alexis must find a way to convince the indentures to debark onto a planet which, while its atmosphere was breathable — in the sense that one wouldn't immediately perish — was, on its whole, so unlikable that no one in the last hundred years or more had thought to purchase it, despite its heavily discounted price.

Chapter Thirty-Six

No sooner had *Star* settled into orbit than Alexis sent all three boats down to the surface.

In the course of their journey, she'd had the women and children aboard the boats swapped out for the men most capable of establishing a safe camp.

The boats' holds were filled with what equipment and supplies would be needed — rather, that small collection of what was needed that was also still aboard *Star* and hadn't been dumped over the side to make room for more passengers.

Once unloaded, the boats returned to the ship for the next load of passengers — then again and again.

Star's once crowded companionways slowly emptied until there was only crew aboard.

Once all was unloaded and the site on planet was a beehive of activity, with hundreds of indentures moving supplies and building rough, temporary shelters until something more substantial could be fabricated, Alexis ordered two of the boats back to *Star's* side.

Slott would remain below with the third boat, supervising the production of material through the boat's printer and the building of the shelters — the sailing master, along with three of the ship's larger crewmen, Alexis thought, were best suited to maintaining order amongst the passengers there.

Gilbertson and his boat were needed to keep *Star* powered. With so few still aboard, the boat's fusion plant was almost adequate to power the needs of both the boat and *Star*. They'd have to bring Slott's boat up from the surface periodically to get a bit ahead of *Star's* power needs, but Alexis determined that would be one day in four at the most.

She couldn't count on the third boat, Delaine's, for that purpose, as she had plans for that — provided she could convince Delaine.

"*Mon cœur*," Delaine started as she finished laying out her thoughts.

"If you've a better plan, please voice it," Alexis said. She'd led Delaine back to her cabin, now emptied of the warrants' belongings, if not of the disorder they'd left behind. It was all she could do to get Isom to leave her and Delaine alone for a moment, as the clerk *tut-tutted* about the cabin trying to set things right. Half the sleeping area had been partitioned off for Lord Braithwaite's use now.

"A moment, Delaine," Alexis said, then knocked on the partition. "Lord Braithwaite? Are you in?"

"Good, we're alone," she continued when there was no answer. "Someone must take a boat for help."

"*Monsieur* Gilbertson," Delaine said, "*Monsieur* Slott."

"The bosun is needed to keep order," Alexis said, "and Slott, though sailing master, hasn't the skill to pilot a small boat and work the sails, both. We must send the minimal crew aboard the boat as all hands are needed here to assist the passengers and make what repairs we can to the ship." She laid a hand on his arm. "You and I are the only ones who might command such a journey ... and my responsibility is here with the ship and passengers."

Delaine frowned for a moment.

"I do not like this," he said finally.

"Well, if you were the sort who *liked* being marooned, I doubt we'd have as much in common."

"Marooned, *non*," Delaine said, "but separated from you less."

Alexis nodded. "Nor do I — like it, I mean — but I see no other way. It's unlikely any will come searching for us — perhaps Captain Hodgman will search for his nephew, but do we have a real hope he'll stumble upon us here? And that only if they survived the storm as well, and if damaged they may be some time in making port and even starting a search."

Delaine grunted. "In this boat, it is six weeks sail to the nearest port, ten if the winds are *merde*."

"Less to return with help in a larger ship, if any are willing."

Delaine thought for a moment. "You cannot maintain the ship with only two boats. You need one on planet to support those there and two to power the ship."

"I've done the calculations," Alexis countered. "If I bring the other boat up every fourth day to charge the batteries, two boats can keep *Star* running and support us all while we make repairs."

Delaine smiled. "Ah, if you repair the ship, then there is no need of rescue."

"I'm not sure we can repair the ship," Alexis said. "We'll have to sacrifice some material for a new keel and even fully-repaired, to make such a journey with so many other souls aboard ... no, we make the repairs while we wait for rescue, but we can't rely on it. Even fully repaired we may not be able to start the fusion plant. The engineers tell me it might be possible, were we to tie in the capacitors from all three boats, but we'd just as likely lose one of the boats in the trying. Then there'd be none to send for help." She sighed. "And even fully-powered, we have twice as many passengers as when we started — and the ship was overloaded even then."

"Once repaired, the crew can take the ship itself to Zariah and return with transport."

Alexis shook her head. "I'll not take the ship and leave the passengers behind — they'd feel abandoned and despair. It would be too cruel."

She paused.

"Delaine, we'll be on half-rations for the time you're gone — and even then we'll have barely enough left in the vats and stores to sail to Zariah ourselves ... should you be late in returning..."

"*Merde*," Delaine muttered.

"Indeed. They stood the crowding with a planet in sight — would they for weeks in the Dark? With less food than they'd wish?"

Delaine nodded. "When do you wish me to leave?"

"Never," Alexis said, "and as soon as possible."

"So I may return all the quicker."

Alexis smiled, but it turned sad. "And so our mysterious killer, should he still be with us, cannot sabotage your mission."

Delaine frowned. "You still do not think it was Powell?"

Alexis shook her head — there was still some debate about that amongst the ship's officers, even with the sabotage. Gilbertson, perhaps wishfully, maintained the damage to *Star's* wiring could have been accidental — despite the two events happening in such a small amount of time and in both port and starboard cable runs.

"It's possible," Alexis said. "Perhaps Mister Gilbertson is correct that there was no sabotage, only an accident, but Powell as the killer? To what end? He could have killed Captain Meiggs at any time — why so many others? And then he simply dies in the same way as he did for Meiggs? A bit on the nose, don't you think?"

"Now I have less wish to leave you here."

"Yet you must — now, before the rumor of your leaving has the run of the ship and the killer, if he does exist outside of Powell, takes steps to hinder you." She shook her head. "If that's his plan. I've still no idea why Powell or anyone else would kill these people. Nor why they might sabotage us in such a way."

"It is still possible the mates and *Capitaine* Meiggs were the only ones killed, while the others were the accidents they first seemed."

"It is," Alexis agreed, "yet I can't seem to shake the feeling they're not accidents. This Dixon, the one who went down the ladder ... there's simply a feeling I have that he's the start of it all, even if not the final target. If I could only understand why he was killed, then I'd have the key to it."

"Perhaps you will send the murderer with me and I may discover and deal with him."

"I've had Mister Gilbertson choose two solid men," Alexis said, then paused. "They're, uh, awaiting you at the boat now." She glanced at the partition she'd checked for Lord Braithwaite. "As well as Lord Braithwaite and his valet," she admitted.

Delaine stayed still for a moment, then chuckled. "'As soon as possible,' *mais oui.*"

Alexis flushed. "It's time," she said quietly.

Delaine nodded, then embraced her tightly.

"I shall return as swiftly as I may, *mon amour,*" he said.

Delaine paused at the hatchway, halfway through, and looked back.

"*Alexis ... Je t'aime.*"

"I love you, as well — come back to me."

Alexis didn't follow him; she couldn't bear it.

Instead, she made her way to the quarterdeck, focused one of the ship's optics on the departing boat, and watched it, hardly daring to blink that she might miss an instant, until it reached the nearest Lagrange Point to disappear into *darkspace.*

No telling how long she stood there, still watching the emptiness. She knew Isom had approached her a time or two, but it must have been nothing urgent as he left when she didn't acknowledge him.

Her eye was eventually drawn to the flashing of one of her monitors where the ship's power system was displayed. The batteries were slowly draining now that only one boat was attached to share its fusion plant. The countdown started — four days, twenty hours, two minutes, it read, until *Star's* batteries were depleted completely.

Four days until she'd have to call the second boat up from the surface to recharge for a day.

It was four days later the trouble started.

Chapter Thirty-Seven

"Captain!" a voice called out. "Yer tablet's pinging!"

Alexis muttered words some captains would send a man to the gratings over.

"A bloody moment, will you?" she called back. "I've almost got it!"

She was up to her waist down one of *Star's* wiring conduits, working to pull out the damaged lines.

With so much of the ship's wiring requiring repair, Alexis had stepped in to assist, and they'd found her small stature perfect for crawling into the conduit when some of the wires being replaced hung up in the conduit just shy of the men's reach.

Alexis could crawl straight in if necessary and work it free of tangles with the other cabling or where the short circuits and power surges from the initial cuts had melted a cable's jacket to fuse with the conduit's thermoplastic.

Most she could get fully into, at least.

This one was just out of even her reach, as the conduit's opening was slightly deformed and stopped her progress at her hips.

"It's the quarterdeck, Captain!" the same spacer yelled — she couldn't tell exactly who it was, as the voice was muffled. "They've sent a runner down, as well!"

Alexis waited a moment, then when nothing more was forthcoming, "Well, what is it?"

"Message from Mister Slott on the surface, Captain," a different voice said. "There's trouble with bringing the boat up."

Alexis cursed again.

They had less than twenty-four hours now to bring the other boat up and begin recharging *Star's* batteries.

"What's the hold up?" she called back. "They've had days of notice to schedule any prints to finish!"

"Didn't say, Captain, only as there's trouble and to get you."

Alexis sighed heavily. "Very well, I'll be right there."

She got her elbows under her to scoot backward, but only gained a few centimeters before her movement stopped and no amount of squirming or wriggling could get her going again, her hands and elbows slipping on the slick interior of the conduit.

"Bugger me," she muttered, then louder, "Could someone give my boots a yank? It appears I'm stuck again."

Alexis chose to ignore the muttered comments and chuckles as hands grasped her ankles and pulled her back out of the conduit.

"You're on your own with this for a time, lads," she said.

One of the spacers handed her a rag and she noticed her hands — as well as the upper half of her jumpsuit — were smeared with the thin lubricant used to ease the cables through the conduit.

"Thank you, Williams," she said, taking the cloth and wiping, rather ineffectually, at the stains, while she made her way to the quarterdeck.

"Very well, Joyce," she said as she entered. "Call Mister Slott back if you will."

"Aye, Captain."

A moment later an image of Slott appeared on one of her monitors.

"Whatever is the trouble, Mister Slott?" Alexis asked. "We need your boat alongside instanter to charge the ship."

Slott's face scrunched up in an expression of discomfort.

"Well, Captain, it's like this, see," he said, then went silent and looked at the boat's pilot, then the cockpit's hatch, then back to Alexis. "Ah, well, there's these fellows in the boat, see?"

"Fellows?"

"Near two dozen of them," Slott said. "Won't leave."

Alexis sighed. She'd been a bit afraid of this since their arrival.

There were several hundred people on the planet now, with half of them from *Star* and those transported for some crime or another. They may have been rather docile aboard the ship, all crammed together in an unfamiliar environment, but now they were planetside, in-atmosphere, and, if camping roughly, more in their own element.

She knew she should have sent more men with Slott to guard the boat, but that would have reduced the number she had aboard *Star* to work on repairs, and repairing the ship was of highest importance.

"What is it they want?" she asked. "Have they tried to take the cockpit?"

"No, Captain," Slott said. "They're just ... sitting."

"Sitting?"

"In the seats, Captain. Like they're ready to go somewhere."

"Have you asked them what they want?"

Slott shook his head. "Told them to get out — so as we could lift, but they just ignored me and sat there."

"Very well, ask them what they want, then."

"Aye, Captain."

"*Not* by opening the cockpit hatch," Alexis said quickly as Slott started to rise. "Use the intercom, if you please."

"Oh ... aye, Captain."

Slott keyed the intercom and called back to the boat's main compartment.

"What is it you lads are after?"

He listened for a moment.

"They say they'd like for you to meet with a fellow, Captain," Slott said. "Name of Harben."

"Is he aboard the boat?" Alexis asked.

She thought quickly about how many men she might allow up and still keep the ship safe. This Harben wouldn't agree to come up alone, surely, but neither would she allow him to bring so many men that his equaled or exceeded her remaining crew.

"He's not," Slott said after a further exchange over the intercom. "They say he's outside, wants to meet you down here."

"Of course he does," Alexis muttered.

She thought for a moment.

If *Star* were a navy ship and the indentures crew, this would be mutiny ... as *Star* was not, and these were merely indentures, passengers ... well, no, it was still bloody mutiny when one got down to it, but things could be considered a bit differently. Or piracy, as they weren't properly part of the crew, but still different circumstances when one got down to it. Or perhaps not, as the passengers were, strictly speaking, disembarked — what would their status be upon reentering the ship's boat?

Never mind, she told herself. *The legalities of their position are quite immaterial when the crew and I are outnumbered ten to one.*

"Very well, Mister Slott, tell your unexpected guests to inform their Mister Harben I shall be down shortly."

"Aye, Captain ... do you think that's wise?"

"Clearly not," Alexis said, "but this Harben can't have got the whole of the passengers behind him in so short a time, so it's best I confront him early on. Tell them I'll be down shortly and keep the cockpit hatch sealed."

"Aye, Captain."

"Joyce," Alexis said, "my compliments to Mister Gilbertson and I'd admire him meet me at the boat with a half dozen of his most trusted men. Armed."

"Aye, Captain."

"Isom! I shall want my uniform, I suppose."

Chapter Thirty-Eight

"Circle the field again, Gray," Alexis said to the boat's pilot. "Keep a lookout for anyone on the far side."

The foliage of the field where they'd landed the passengers was still flattened and marked by the multiple landings of the boats and trampling of hundreds of feet crossing it.

Now there was only one boat, landed at the edge nearest the passengers' encampment.

A large crowd gathered near it. Alexis couldn't count them all, but she suspected the crowd was nearly all of the passengers — hundreds of people, at least.

They weren't so near Slott's boat as to seem menacing, nor did they appear angry. They merely stood and watched Alexis' boat as it circled the field once more.

"Land at the far edge," Alexis said.

"Aye, Captain," Gray acknowledged, then set the boat down lightly as far from the crowd and Slott's boat as was possible.

As the boat settled onto its landing struts, Alexis keyed the comms to call Slott.

"Very well, Mister Slott, please inform this Harben that I've arrived and he may come over to have a few words."

"Aye, Captain," Slott said.

There was a pause and Alexis imagined Slott informing the group in his boat of this, then saw a head emerge from his boat's hatch and call out to a group somewhat nearer than the bulk of the crowd. There was a brief exchange before Slott called back.

"He's saying he'd rather you come over and talk to him here, Captain," Slott said.

"Of course he would."

Alexis sighed and thought for a moment.

"Very well. Please inform Mister Harben that I will meet him midway across the field," Alexis said. "Him alone, as I will be, and unarmed."

Another pause for the passing of messages and a man started walking across the field.

Alexis pulled an earpiece from her tablet, inserted it, then tapped it to ensure it was activated and spoke to both Slott and Gray as she left her boat and began striding toward the man.

"Mister Slott, should anything untoward happen here, you are in charge of the ship."

"Aye, Captain."

"If I'm killed this will mean you must act as you see fit, however, if this Harben means to take me captive or some such, you must not, under any circumstances, allow any of his men aboard the boats or ship until I'm released. You are to lift both boats and return to *Star* until I'm free, do you understand?"

"Uh, aye, Captain," Slott said. "But what about the men in the boat already?"

She was nearing Harben now, close enough to see the man was well-dressed and well-groomed — not an easy feat, she thought, after the last bit of their voyage and several days camping rough on the planet's surface.

"Give them a moment to vacate if they will," Alexis said, "then lift. If they've refused to leave, once in orbit ... vent the cabin to vacuum and be done with them. In fact, vent the cabin to vacuum regardless, in case they've left any lingerers behind."

There was a long pause.

"Uh, aye, Captain."

"It's a hard choice, Mister Slott," Alexis said, "but we must not give up the ship, if such is their intent."

She was close enough now that Harben called out to her.

"Captain Carew!" he called, smiling. "Thank you for coming down in such extraordinary times."

"Mister Harben, I presume?" Alexis asked, stopping a couple meters away from the man.

"The very man," Harben said, still smiling and approaching her with a hand outstretched.

Alexis took a moment to look him over. She'd read a bit of his record on the way down.

A petty conman, from his arrests, come aboard *Star* at Norington, a world somewhat fringeward of Dalthus and a few stops before Alexis had come aboard. The world's name sounded familiar to Alexis, though she couldn't recall ever stopping there — perhaps she'd read it in her time aboard HMS *Nightingale* patrolling the area.

Harben did look the part of a conman — wide smile, eyes open and innocent, hand outstretched as though this was simply a friendly meeting.

Alexis took his hand briefly.

"I must ask," Harben said, "is there a navy ship in orbit?" He gestured at her. "It's only the uniform, you understand, and me wondering if we're now rescued."

"I'm afraid not, Mister Harben," Alexis said. "There's only *Star of Tauric* in orbit, still, though I am a naval lieutenant."

Harben nodded. "Though *Star's* a civilian ship, still, yes?"

"She is," Alexis admitted.

Harben nodded again. "And so it's me speaking to Captain

Carew, civilian captain of *Star of Tauric* ... and not Lieutenant Carew of the Royal Navy and all that?"

Alexis regretted, now, wearing her uniform rather than a simple ship's jumpsuit. She'd thought it might lend her some weight with the passengers, but Harben had cut right to the core of its meaning. Without a commission her uniform granted her little in the way of authority above that she held as captain of *Star*.

"You are correct, sir," she said. "I speak only in my role as captain of *Star of Tauric*."

Harben's smile widened. "That's good. To have established who it is I'm speaking to — other than by name, I mean. One's role, so to speak."

"Indeed," Alexis said. "Might I be extended the same courtesy?"

"Indeed," Harben echoed. "Theodore Harben, at your service, Captain — but you'd know that from the ship's records. What you're really asking, as I did, is who I represent here, yes?"

"And what you want, Mister Harben," Alexis said. "Your lads in Mister Slott's boat have got my attention — which I've little of to spare at this point, so please, do, make the most of it."

Harben nodded. "It's your attention I was after, Captain Carew, to discuss our situation." He glanced back at the crowd. "There's more than a little worry in that group ... about our position here and what's to happen. Worry made little better by the thought of that boat lifting."

"The boat is needed in orbit to recharge *Star's* batteries," Alexis said. "It will return tomorrow."

"So you say."

"And so you doubt?"

Alexis felt a bit of relief. Harben didn't seem intent on taking the boat or the ship, at least from his words — which, admittedly, she might be foolish to accept at face value given what the man had been arrested and transported for.

A glib tongue and trustworthy manner is what the records say of him, she thought.

"A bit of doubt keeps one safe," Harben said. "There's some — not myself, mind — who've done a bit of calculating and think, with all us here on the planet's surface your three boats together would just carry you and the ship's crew off to safety."

"They would," Alexis said, "had we not already sent one boat off with only a few aboard to bring back rescue."

Harben nodded. "Again, so you say."

Alexis sighed. "And one might think, Mister Harben, with so many of your men aboard that boat that your intent is to take *Star of Tauric* for yourself."

"I have no designs upon your ship, Captain Carew, nor, to my knowledge, do any of us."

"And I have no intentions toward marooning you and *Star's* other passengers here, as it's my duty to see you safely to port," Alexis said. "So having assured each other that we, neither of us, are so vile as the other might suspect, shall we speak to what will resolve the situation we find ourselves in?"

Harben smiled. "Yes, let us do so." He spread his hands. "Those I represent fear that boat — which provides us all with food, water, and material to build what shelter we may — lifting and not returning. What assurances might be offered to allay their fears?"

"You have my word, Mister Harben," Alexis said. "My goal — my duty — is to see all of us, ship, crew, and passengers, safely to our next port ... or, given the damage to the ship, any safe port."

Harben's eyes narrowed. "Fine words, duty and such. Fine, fine words. Still, see, there're many here who've heard fine words before from those they feared — heard and listened and believed, but now know better and fear the words even more. It's acts these folks are looking for, those speaking so much louder, as they say."

"What acts, exactly, are you looking for, Mister Harben?"

"Leave off on the ship and bring both boats down here," Harben said. "As you've said, there's rescue expected, so what's the point of repairing it?"

"I do expect rescue, Mister Harben, but that's not to say we should give up on the efforts of rescuing ourselves."

Harben shrugged. "The ship'll still be there if we see no rescuers. There's enough here who can count and do maths to know even at its best that ship couldn't get all of us to a safe port. Too many mouths, yes? The printers on that other boat — and the skills of your crew — would be better spent on the settlement down here for a time." He glanced back at the crowd. "It would ease minds and lighten hearts, Captain Carew, were it to look as though we're all in this together."

Alexis sighed. "Mister Harben, we are all in this together, but you and that crowd over there must understand the very real risks we still face." She began ticking them off on her fingers. "It may well be that *Belvedere* and *Swallow* have made port and begun a search for us — that is my great hope. However, *Belvedere* and *Almorah* are sister ships, and we all saw how the latter fared in the storm. *Swallow* is a pinnace, much lighter than either of those or even *Star*. There is a very real possibility of both of them foundering as well — they might well be in straits more dire than our own.

"Further, the boat we've sent for help will be weeks a'space before reaching port. Weeks in which she, too, may encounter difficulties. The risk of such a journey in such a small boat is not to be scoffed at." Alexis paused for a moment, offering up a prayer for Delaine's safety. "Another storm and..."

She trailed off, unwilling to voice such thoughts.

"It is in all of our interests for *Star* to be repaired, rescue or no, and it's part of my duty to see *Star of Tauric* put to rights and delivered to port. Should we pause repairs, it would mean weeks of delay if we then determine rescue is not in the cards."

Harben started to speak but Alexis cut him off.

"This is not so safe a world that either you or the other passengers should want to extend our stay here, Mister Harben. The toxins —"

Now Harben cut her off.

"I've read the reports, Captain, as have others. There's no danger in a few weeks' time, only for those who might think of making a life here."

Alexis nodded. "So the reports say. Reports from the survey company which wishes to sell this world. Reports from a survey team paid, in part, by the value of the worlds they discover. One can quite imagine them leaving a bit off such a survey once they discovered the toxins and their long-term effects." She took a deep breath. "There may well be other, shorter-term, dangers to this world. Were it not for the number of passengers and *Star's* lack of capacity, we'd all be aboard ship right now rather than risk that unknown."

Harben looked back to the crowd. "You'd be surprised, Captain, how some knowns can make the unknown quite appealing, no matter the possible risk." He looked back to Alexis and smiled. "So you've little hope for rescue, then, despite what you've said before?"

"I have high hopes for rescue, Mister Harben. I only don't believe in sitting about idly when there's such a risk. *Star* must be repaired and to do that we need the power of both boats one day in four. Now what will alleviate your concerns, given that requirement?"

Harben paused as though to think, though Alexis was certain he'd already anticipated her refusal to abandon *Star* and had his counter-offer in mind.

"A few lads aboard," Harben suggested. "Say six? We've one here says he can pilot — we'd feel a bit better were he and some friends aboard."

Alexis pondered for a moment. It was one thing to have strangers in the boat's main compartment, but a pilot would be in the cockpit — and six was far too many.

She chewed on her lower lip a bit and thought. A compromise here would give Harben more power with the passengers, but would also allay their fears and reassure them of her own intentions. Yet a pilot and any men were a risk Harben might decide to take the boat by force in any case.

She hadn't got that sense from him, he seemed aboveboard in his concerns — and yet he *was* a transported conman.

"Your pilot," Alexis said finally, "and one other —" She held up a hand to forestall Harben as he started to speak. "— and that will free two of the lads I have aboard to work on the ship."

Harben frowned. "Two and two, then?"

Alexis nodded. "Your pilot and one other; Mister Slott and one other."

"I can sell that to the folk here," Harben said.

"No doubt," Alexis agreed.

Harben nodded. "Your hand on it, then?"

Alexis took the offered hand, certain this would not be the last deal she must strike with the man.

Chapter Thirty-Nine

Back aboard *Star*, both boats nuzzled alongside and connected to the cabling strung from their hatches back to the ship's engineering compartment and the batteries there. Alexis found herself switching her quarterdeck console to the ship's power state so as to watch the battery capacity slowly climb rather than fall.

It was a system she wasn't entirely familiar with, naval ships often forgoing the batteries in favor of increased armoring of the fusion plant and space containing it — the circumstances under which their power going out most often including the entire crew in vacsuits and facing more pressing concerns.

Despite Gilbertson's assurances that the two boats would allow *Star* to recharge, she felt a bit better seeing it happen.

Seeing it work as expected, she switched her monitor back to her previous field of study — Theodore Harben.

There was little else to learn, it seemed, other than what she'd read already.

Conman, come aboard at Norington along with a few other indentures. Transported for being irredeemable under the criteria

Norington applied to such things, which seemed to be taking from the extremely wealthy, a thing appearing to be Harben's preferred object. All the man's victims were the planet's sort of idle, second- or third-generation rich — the sort lacking their parents' and grandparents' ability to generate wealth while still possessing the need to prove themselves able.

Just the sort to fall for the type of get-rich-quick schemes Harben favored.

And Harben just the sort to use his quick wit and talented tongue to improve his own situation now by manipulating the other passengers to some end.

Alexis sighed.

She couldn't see how her agreement with Harben might harm her, but he surely had something in mind. Still, two men on the boat couldn't take the ship and she had them isolated to the boat's cockpit so they couldn't even speak to the crew. Slott and the man kept with him were steady and unlikely to fall for some second-hand scheme Harben might come up with.

Still ... she felt she was missing something and kept coming back to that planet, Norington, as though she should remember something about it — only with so very much for her to worry about, recalling a tenuous thread of memory was only harder.

"Captain?"

Alexis glanced up at the interruption.

Sams and Moore stood by the navigation plot — neither the purser nor carpenter looking particularly happy, which bode ill for their coming to speak to her.

"Yes, gentlemen?" she prompted.

"Ah, Captain, it's about the repairs, see?" Moore said.

"I assumed as much, Mister Moore," Alexis said. "What is it about them?"

"It's the keel, do you see?" Moore asked.

"I do not see the keel," Alexis said, "which is rather the point, as it's missing, all entire — we need you to print a new one, so what is the status on that?"

"We can't," Moore said.

Alexis cocked her head, willing her heart to slow down as Moore's words brought her a chill of fear.

"We need a keel, Mister Moore, else any attempt to sail will set us skidding about at the mercy of the winds."

They needed the keel — a long bit of thermoplastic extending outside the ship's field and lacking gallenium in its construction — to bite into the dark matter of *darkspace* and give the ship a sort of traction to sail into, or even side-to, the winds. Without it, the bulk of the ship would be pushed by those winds, and they'd gain no way at all.

Moore shrugged and looked to the purser. "I can't print what I don't have, Captain, and there's not enough material to print a keel. I can get you two meters, at best."

"Two meters of keel won't get us outside the ship's field, Mister Moore — we need at least ten meters, preferably twenty."

Moore shrugged again. "There's not enough material in the printer vats, Captain."

Alexis looked to the purser, who looked away and licked his lips.

"How do we not have enough material, Mister Sams?" Alexis asked. "I've heard many a carpenter boast they could build a new ship from their stores."

"On a naval ship, maybe, Captain," Sams said. "But this here ain't no naval ship. Captain Meiggs liked it tight — just enough in stores to make the next port for resupply. And then there's what was sent over the side in the storm, see?"

"I see," Alexis said. "So as with the beer, some of the printer vats were empty to start with?"

Sams nodded. "Less mass —"

"A faster sail," Alexis agreed. "No doubt he was right about that."

"And always sailing in convoy," Sams said, "we could —"

"The other ships in convoy would have a full kit of supplies and not wish to slow down to accommodate *Star* were she to receive enough damage as to require so much repair," Alexis muttered.

She rubbed her eyes and saw Sams and Moore staring at her anxiously when she looked at them again.

"Oh, do calm yourselves, gentlemen," she said, "I'm not going to put this on you. I've never met a purser who liked sailing without a full complement of stores, nor a carpenter who'd like to leave port without twice that."

Though she didn't mention that the former would most likely wish it for the opportunity to slice a bit of the purchase for himself, as Sams still struck her as that rarest of breed — an honest purser.

She thought for a moment.

"Have you taken the printer vats on our two boats into account?" she asked.

Moore nodded. "Even with, I can get you perhaps three meters of proper keel."

"Still barely outside the ship's field," Alexis pointed out. "We're tens of meters short still."

Star's original keel had been thirty meters in total — adding only three meters to the broken stub remaining wouldn't be enough.

Alexis looked around the quarterdeck.

There were a few odds and ends which could be returned to the vats and broken down — an extra seat for a console here and there, the entirety of *Star's* never-manned weapons console. She gnawed at her lower lip and began thinking of the rest of the ship — partitions, extraneous bracing, the empty vats themselves, perhaps.

"It'll take all of that and more, Captain," Moore said as though reading her thoughts.

Alexis smiled. "You've been through the exercise yourself, then, I take it?"

Moore nodded. "More than once, Captain." He frowned. "There's a solution, but I'll not say I think you'll like it."

"We cannot sacrifice one of the boats," Alexis warned. "We'll need both of them just to bring the passengers back up once we do have a keel, and likely need their environmental systems with so many packed aboard."

"Not the boats, Captain, no," Moore said.

"What then?" Alexis asked.

Moore looked to Sams, who closed his eyes and spoke. "The masts, Captain."

"Fore and main," Moore added quickly, "not the mizzen."

"Ah, so you'll leave us just the one, gentlemen? To actually sail the ship?"

Moore flushed. "Keel wouldn't be much good if we couldn't."

"No, it wouldn't, Mister Moore."

Alexis thought for a moment.

The ship-rigged fore and mainmasts gave *Star* her speed before the wind — with only the fore-and-aft rig of the mizzen set midway down her hull she'd be slower on the bulk of their journey. If rescue didn't come and they did have to make their own way would that decrease in sail be an issue?

She ran a quick calculation on her tablet — with no data other than her own experience sailing *Star of Tauric* she had little to predict what the ship's best speed might be with only the mizzen sails at work.

"Mister Sams," she asked, "with so many extra mouths to feed..." She trailed off.

"The numbers don't lie, Captain," Moore said.

Alexis sighed. "No, they don't."

Quarter-rations it would be, then, she decided, and earlier than they all might expect.

Chapter Forty

"You lied to us from the start," Harben said, staring at the calculations Alexis sent to his tablet.

They were aboard *Star's* second remaining boat, landed along with Slott's boat after the recharging of the ship's batteries. She'd come down and invited Harben aboard to discuss their latest dilemma and her decision.

"I did not," Alexis said.

"You said half-rations while we await rescue," Harben said. "That's what you said when we all disembarked – never said a thing about quarter-rations." He flicked a finger at his tablet and looked at her, narrowing his eyes. "And this says we'd be on the quarter to reach Zariah."

Alexis nodded. "I said half-rations if we await rescue. I ... simply said nothing about if rescue did not come and we had to sail to Zariah." She took a deep breath. "Things have changed."

"So they have," Harben said. "A lie of omission's still a lie, Carew. I should know, it's my trade, after all."

"You may think that if you like," Alexis said.

"It's no never mind what I think," Harben said, gesturing in the direction of the passengers' camp. "It's those folk out there who'll be doing the thinking."

"Which is why it's so convenient you've been chosen to represent them," Alexis said, "as now it's your task to convince them of the necessity. A simple task, given your trade — as well as the added advantage that you'll be convincing them of the truth."

Harben snorted. "The truth isn't often an advantage in convincing people, I've learned. Most folk aren't particularly fond of it."

Alexis shrugged.

"The truth is what it is. *Star of Tauric* had supplies for fourteen weeks with her original complement of passengers. Taking on the passengers from *Almorah* cut that to seven weeks at normal ration — fourteen at half-rations."

"Barely enough for rescue."

"Indeed," Alexis said. "Ten weeks, at worst, for Mister Theibaud's boat to reach Zariah and three or four more weeks for rescue to arrive."

"Cutting it thin," Harben muttered.

Alexis nodded. "There's some margin of error, but not a great deal. There are some supplies aboard *Star* — those of the other ship's officers — which can be added to the vats to eke out a few more days."

Harben frowned. "Real food not from the vats? Why not share that out and give people a taste?"

"To six hundred mouths? No, there'd be barely a spoonful for each. The vats can grow more beef from the raw materials than that."

Alexis rubbed her forehead.

"If the ship were repaired and rescue didn't come, it would have been three weeks, perhaps, four to Zariah. We could have made that on half-rations or less ... now."

"Aye, now," Harben muttered.

Alexis took a deep breath.

"If we give up the masts to fashion a new keel, we'll be left with only the mizzen, and with so many people, so much mass aboard ...

Star'll be slower than a ship's boat, even. Those three or four weeks of sailing turn to ten or more." She sighed. "Twenty-four weeks from now, when we've food for fourteen at half-rations."

"Why await rescue, then?" Harben asked. "Fix your keel and be on our way."

Alexis nodded. "We will, but a keel isn't as simple as a new run of rigging. It needs time — time to break down the masts in the printer's vats, time to print the thing, time for it to cure and be sturdy enough. It'll be weeks before the ship can sail." She frowned. "I expect we'll be able to sail in twelve weeks, at best — before rescue comes, but close enough we might meet them while still working our way out of the system. And we've yet to restart the fusion plant, so there's that."

"What if we grow some food?" Harben asked. "I've read the survey — the soil here will grow Terran plants, if poorly. There're some of us already doing so — seeds from what fresh and frozen rations came down."

"Yes, I saw the plots while we were landing," Alexis said. "Those doing so are taking a great risk with the planet's toxins."

Harben waved her concerns away. "Folk here are thinking they've more immediate concerns than what price they'll pay forty years hence, would you disagree?"

"I suppose it's their choice," Alexis agreed, "but there are few crops that might come in before we're ready to leave — I suppose what's grown, leaves and all, could contribute to the vats' production once we sail." She frowned. "Separate from others, of course, for those who wish to risk the toxins."

"There, you see?" Harben said. "A few seeds picked from the frozen veg, skip a meal to put the potatoes in the ground instead — it does the folk good to see a bit of growing."

Alexis thought it a bit foolish — time and energy wasted on growing things they'd not have time to enjoy and which could turn out to be poison in the end, no matter how long the poison might take to make its hold.

"I won't try to stop those who wish to, Mister Harben," she said, "but I do discourage it."

"It'll take more than discouragement to stop it once they're on quarter-rations," Harben said. "There'll be foraging, as well, mark my words. There're plants here that're edible — toxins or no — and hungry people won't care."

Alexis wondered if she shouldn't have kept the details of the planet's survey from the passengers to begin with — hungry people, as Harben said, didn't care about the longer term. Only that their bellies were empty now.

There were indeed many plants — and some of the native animals — which were quite edible. And the soil here was amenable to Terran crops with little or no terraforming necessary. The system would have been quite valuable to the survey company that found it ... if the bloody planet hadn't been set on slowly poisoning all who set foot on it.

Chapter Forty-One

Time aboard *Star of Tauric* settled into a rather tedious routine.

With all repaired save the keel, the crew aboard was at loose ends, having already disassembled the masts, as well as nearly anything else that could be spared, and lining the bits up near the printer vats to be tossed in and slowly returned to their constituent parts. The printers worked on segment after segment of a new keel, each set aside to cure as they were completed, and the crew left idle until it was time to install each one.

There'd been no more sabotage, leaving Alexis to wonder if the damaged power and data lines had, indeed, been coincidental accidents as Mister Gilbertson suggested, or, worse, if she'd somehow managed to send the saboteur and murderer off with Delaine.

Alexis could almost wish there'd been more damage to the ship's power and data lines, so that she might return to spending her days stuffed into the conduits for their repair. At least then she'd been active and had purpose, something better than her current idleness.

The quarterdeck hatch slid open and a crewman came in pushing a cart with the quarterdeck crew's lunch trays. They'd taken to eating at their stations, there being so few of them aboard.

It was a stew again, she noted, that being something that could be brought together in a pot from all sorts of odds and ends, with little lost in the cooking.

Alexis recognized him as a landsman, only aboard *Star* for a few weeks, and idly wondered what the man might think of his first voyage into the Dark.

"Thank you —"

Alexis broke off her thanks as the man set a tray in front of her on the navigation plot. The man ducked his head and turned away, but not before Alexis caught a glimpse of his features and a chill ran through her.

He'd done that before, she thought, always in the back of a work party, not the front, always half-turned from her, especially since the storm. She'd thought it nothing more than an inexperienced crewman not wanting the notice of his captain.

Alexis watched the man leave the quarterdeck then pushed her plate of stew aside.

Could it be? Had she truly missed it?

She'd been introduced to the crew verbally and the man pronounced his name so differently, yet still...

She brought up the ship's records.

Crew this time — she'd been so concentrated on the passengers' records, half convinced, since they were all transported criminals, that the killer must be from among them.

But a spacer would have better access, better freedom of movement, and —

Harben, she thought reading the spacer's records. *Bloody Harben no matter how he makes it sound.*

Come aboard at Norington along with all the rest of the trouble.

Landsman — no experience at all, which was *Star of Tauric's* norm.

Perpetually undermanned and underpaying, the ship hemorrhaged able spacers at every opportunity and replaced them with cheaper landsmen.

"Joyce," Alexis said. "My complements to Mister Gilbertson, and I'd admire it if he were to come to the quarterdeck with four of his best."

"Aye, Captain."

An hour later, the quarterdeck was crowded with the addition of the bosun and four hulking spacers.

Alexis hunched over the navigation plot with Gilbertson, ostensibly reviewing the schedule for the ship's repairs.

Harben — the younger Harben, Alexis was certain — entered and began collecting the emptied plates.

Alexis waited until he had them all and was on his way out with hands full before speaking.

"Will it be poison the next time, Harben?" she asked.

The man froze midstep.

"Wh— what?" he asked, not turning.

"The captain's speaking to you!" Gilbertson barked. "Give her your face, not your backside!"

Harben turned as, at Gilbertson's nod, the bosun's four mates closed in on him.

The look on the man's face told Alexis she was correct.

She sighed.

"I'd advise you not enter your father's line of work, Harben," she said, "you've not at all the face for it." She paused. "Or is it brother? He's young enough, I suppose."

Harben's shoulders slumped.

"He's my Da," he said. "Was it the name? Da said it'd be the name what did me in."

One of the bosun's men took the stack of plates from Harben

while two others grasped his arms. The fourth stood by behind the man, ready for any attempt at flight or attack.

"It was the resemblance first," Alexis said, "and then the name. Had I never met your father in such circumstance, I'd not have seen it."

Harben nodded.

"Da called me a fool, but there weren't time between his trial and the ship's leaving for me to get new papers — none of Da's old crew'd talk to me." He shrugged. "Didn't know anyone myself who could do it."

"So you came aboard *Star* to help your father somehow?" Alexis asked. The man seemed resigned and talkative now he was caught — she thought it best to get as much of the story from him now before he could recover and think it better to deny everything.

Harben nodded again.

"By killing eight people," Alexis said.

Harben's shoulders slumped further, and his face scrunched up.

"Wasn't the plan," he whispered.

"And yet they're dead — why?"

Harben's voice was so low Alexis could barely hear him.

"He recognized me," Harben said. "Saw me visiting Da at the prison and then here on the ship — said he'd ... wanted money, but I don't have so much as to give him none!"

"Dixon, you mean," Alexis said.

Harben glanced up. "Was that his name? I never knew."

"So you shoved him down a ladder?" Alexis asked.

Harben nodded. "Had to shut him up — you can see that, can't you?"

"Why put Sals out the lock?"

Harben's face screwed up as though he were horribly frustrated. "Saw me do it for the first one, didn't he? Lord, didn't Da let me have it after? 'Can't just run from witness to witness, boy!' he said. Well, what were I supposed to do, then?"

"Edwards and Baxter?" Alexis asked.

Harben looked confused.

"The two in the hold," Alexis clarified.

Harben nodded and Alexis wondered how many other people the man had killed without even knowing their names.

"Aye," Harben said. "I found those ... those little spaces between the vats. Knew I'd need a place to plan things, a base you might say. Then I found the vat was empty and it seemed so perfect." He took a deep breath. "Those two saw me. Didn't think on it at first, but they kept coming back. Couldn't let them see me there so often."

"So you rigged the cargo to shift on them," Alexis said.

"Had to push it — stuck up there, in the stacks, waiting for them. Seemed like days. Then when they finally did come again, I had to wait until they were well into their rut so they'd not move out of the way." He nodded. "Da says you have to have patience in things."

"No doubt," Alexis said, a bit chilled by how easily the man described waiting to ensure the murder of two innocents who'd done him no wrong.

"Da was angry about it," Harben said. "Said I shouldn't be killing people a'tall — always said that. 'Killing's wrong, Dain,' he'd say. Every time. 'Don't do it again,' he'd say. Ever since that first boy, he'd say that." His eyes widened as though in a plea. "You can't blame Da for it, he was always telling me not to."

Alexis frowned. Since the first boy? Dixon had been older than Harben.

"Boy?" she asked. "Daniel Dixon was older than you."

Harben frowned. "Dixon?"

"The man you pushed down the ladder."

"Oh, not him — he wasn't a boy," Harben said. "The boy back at school, I meant ... I forget his name. Sorry. I suppose you could look it up if it's important."

"Bloody hell," Gilbertson muttered.

"Indeed," Alexis agreed, feeling her blood chill. Just how many people had this Harben killed?

"Evens was next?" Alexis asked, then clarified: "The first mate?"

Harben nodded. "Had a plan by then."

"We'll return to your plan in a moment," Alexis said, but she felt she had to ask something first. Evens had family she knew of — Meiggs' daughter would want to know how her husband had died. Perhaps they could recover the body if they were so inclined. "What happened to Evens?"

Harben shrugged. "Kilt him."

"Yes, I see — could you tell us how? And where he is now?"

Harben laughed. "Now? In a dozen or more guts, I'd wager. He was rutting in some alley with a whore — stood her up against the wall and took her from behind." Harben giggled. "Took him from behind, I did." He closed his eyes and smiled. "Knife slid in easy. It always does." He opened his eyes. "I like the knife best, I think." He raised his right hand a bit and clenched it as though holding one. "You can feel ... things through it."

The two bosun's mates grasping his arms edged away but tightened their grip and the spacer behind Harben clenched his fists.

"What..." Alexis found her mouth dry and had to pause to lick her lips and swallow.

"What then?" she asked finally, truly not wanting to hear it, but needing to get everything she could from Harben before he gained the sense to shut up — if he ever would, the man seemed to have no guilt or remorse whatsoever for his crimes.

Harben shrugged. "Killed the girl, of course, then ... I forget the name of the world, but they had a lot of pigs. Alley smelled of 'em, so I knew the pens were near." He shrugged again and smiled. "I like pigs. In you go and all's taken care of nicely. A good pig's a proper partner to have."

Alexis took a deep breath.

No, she thought, *there's not a bit of that Mistress Evens, or any of the man's other family, needs to hear.*

She glanced around at the quarterdeck crew and saw anger on their faces — Evens had been well-liked by *Star of Tauric's* crew.

"You said you had a plan by then," Alexis prompted. "What was it?"

Harben shrugged. "Take the ship, of course."

Alexis raised an eyebrow. "Take the ship?"

Harben nodded. "With the mates and captain gone, sure. Who'd there be to stop me?"

"Me for one," Gilbertson said, taking an angry step forward.

"Belay that, Mister Gilbertson," Alexis said.

Harben chuckled at Gilbertson's glare.

"What could you possibly think to do with this ship?" Alexis asked. "Piracy or some such? With three hundred passengers aboard, none of whom know a thing about *darkspace*?"

"Find a world where we'd be better off," Harben said. "One where we'd not be sold as cattle."

Alexis paused in her initial reaction. It wasn't so far-fetched a plan as one might think at first hearing it. Yes, there were severe penalties for a world that allowed indentures to run from their ship — yet would those same apply to a group appearing with their own ship? Who was to say, on some extreme Fringe world in need of colonists, that such a group was indentures at all?

"Ah, you see," Harben said. "Not so bad a plan after all, was it then?"

"So you and your father sought to take —"

"Not Da," Harben interrupted. "Da said I should've stayed back on Norington."

Alexis considered that. It was possibly true — the elder Harben's records contained no history of violence, only confidence games. His son, it seemed, had enough penchant for killing to satisfy both generations.

"What about disabling the ship during the storm?" Alexis asked.

Harben shrugged. "Figured that'd be as good a time as any. Since I hadn't managed to get rid of you — if we could get the ship separated from the others during the storm, figured we could take the ship after." He sighed. "Then with the ship so broken ... and now Da's down on planet."

Alexis nodded. If it hadn't been for the collision with *Almorah* and the subsequent loss of *Star's* keel, it might have worked. Damaged and separated from the rest of the convoy, the crew might not have stood up to any concerted effort at taking the ship.

"Well, your plan's shite now, boyo," Gilbertson said.

Harben smiled.

"That's alright," he said, smiling as though he had no cares at all. "Da's got his own plan now."

Chapter Forty-Two

"It was the name, wasn't it?" Harben — the elder Harben — asked.

Alexis nodded. "It was the name that clinched it, but his resemblance to you that sparked the thought — and he confessed rather quickly once confronted."

She was back on the surface, returning the second boat after recharging *Star's* batteries again.

"Told the boy that'd be the end of him aboard ship," Harben said. "I'd have made him get a new identity, but he didn't come to me with his damn fool scheme before the ship sailed. Nothing to do then." He sighed. "What will you do with him? Try to hang him, I suppose?" He shook his head. "I'll not allow it."

Alexis tapped her boat's console, clearing the screen of the paused image at the end of the younger Harben's talk on *Star's* quarterdeck. She'd said nothing to confront the father, merely played the quarterdeck log's recording of his son's confession and watched his reaction.

She shook her head to answer Harben's question. "A magistrate on Zariah will decide, once we're there, but he's confessed to eight killings and attempting three others. I can't imagine a good outcome for him."

"I'll not allow it," Harben repeated.

"We'll see, Mister Harben," Alexis said. "For now, I'll not tell the other passengers it was your son who got them into this — or made our situation so dire, at least."

Better, she thought, both the devil she knew and the one she had some leverage over.

"And you'll be wanting?" Harben asked, eyes narrowing.

"We'll see, Mister Harben."

Alexis watched as the ship's largest printer came to a stop.

The printhead, nearly as large as she was, repeatedly zipped back and forth, then to and fro, about half a meter in each direction, pulled by the cabling strung from its corners to large pylons now attached to *Star's* hull. It did this for a moment, as though trying to determine where its next work lie, then zipped off to its home position nearest the pylon set in the aft, port section of the ship's hull.

"That's all there is," Gilbertson said over her suit's radio.

Alexis looked around.

The ship looked nearly naked without her fore- and mainmasts.

Even here in normal-space where those masts would normally be unstepped and lain back against the hull, their absence made a visible void that felt wrong to anyone who knew what ships should look like.

Even the newly completed keel looked out of place — the endcap of gallenium laced thermoplastic being far too large for the end.

"Less than I'd like, but it'll have to do," Gilbertson added.

Alexis nodded, though she knew the bosun couldn't see her inside her suit's polarized helmet.

They'd gotten twenty-three meters of keel after throwing in the masts, spars, and every bit of spare partitioning, empty crates and vats, and every bit of loose ends they could find aboard ship. All that had gone into the telescoping sections of the new keel now retracted into the hull so that the printer could print the endcap.

Extended, only the first and last sections were the normal, gallenium-laced thermoplastic of the ship's hull, the rest contained none of the metal that helped the ship slide through the dark matter of *darkspace* without resistance — those were thermoplastic laced with other metals to increase their mass and interact with the dark matter to bite into it even more and resist the push of dark energy winds.

"It will have to do," Alexis reluctantly agreed.

That resistance was what would allow *Star* to sail against those winds, and the less there was of it, the longer *Star* would have to tack side-to-side to make headway.

Less keel will make for an even longer journey, Alexis thought to herself, already doing what calculations she could to estimate how much longer and how that would affect their food supply.

"There's the material in the other boat," Gilbertson said, "and on-planet. Add that and we might get one more section."

"Yes, but the passengers do need shelter," Alexis said, "until we've completed the other repairs and managed to restart the fusion plant. Once that's done, we'll have to sail instanter to have any chance of reaching Zariah before our food runs out, so there'll be no time to print another section and allow it to cure properly."

She'd already calculated that — while she hated to leave the material of the passengers' shelters behind, by the time they were to bring it all up from the planet's surface and run it through the printer's vats to recycle it, *Star* would be in *darkspace*, and the printer wouldn't work outside the ship's hull there.

Chapter Forty-Three

Alexis tapped her quarterdeck console as though the thing might be stuck and the date it displayed incorrect. She could wish the thing would spin backwards, admitting it had skipped several in its display.

Delaine was overdue.

Not yet out of the window for what time it might take to sail a small boat to Zariah and return with rescue, but far enough into that window that she'd begun to worry — for both him and herself.

Repairs on *Star* were almost complete, and the ship would be ready to sail in a week's time.

Ready to sail, that is, in all respects save the fusion plant.

She'd put off the decision to try restarting it with the remaining boats in the hope Delaine would return and make the issue moot.

Now she couldn't delay any longer.

She had a feeling, nothing concrete she could put her finger on, that Harben would try something when *Star's* repairs were complete. She knew he was against the attempt to start the plant, having deluded himself into thinking he and the passengers who followed him could somehow make a go of it on this planet.

Now was the one day in four when what she'd begun thinking of as the passengers' boat was docked alongside *Star* to recharge the ship's batteries.

The next time, or at the latest the time after, would be when Harben would expect her to try restarting the plant.

Waiting until the last minute was wisest, since failure to restart *Star's* plant might well damage that of one or both of the boats. Likely, even.

Waiting until the last minute would give Harben time to act.

"Joyce," Alexis said finally, her deliberations at an end. "My compliments to Mister Gilbertson and I'd admire it did he and four of his most trusted men meet me at the port boat hatch."

"Aye, Captain," Joyce said.

The port boat hatch was unguarded and, as so many of those aboard *Star*, the log camera pointed at the hatch and supposed to be sharing its feed with the boat itself was inoperative.

Alexis met the bosun and his four men in the companionway.

Gilbertson cracked his knuckles.

"Been waiting for this, Captain," he muttered.

"No doubt," Alexis agreed.

In truth, she relished the thought of retaking the boat as well.

The boat was a part of *Star of Tauric*, and *Star of Tauric* was hers. To have strangers, not crew, in the cockpit, to be denied access, to not have the boat under her control — well, it irked her to no end. Perhaps unreasonably so, but their presence put her real duty — the safety of the ship and all aboard her — at some risk.

Harben was relying on his two men — the young pilot and another — to be able to control the elderly sailing master, Slott, and the single spacer from *Star* in the locked cockpit. He wasn't wrong — Slott was neither young nor spry and the pilot, though a bit spindly, would easily overpower him. As for the other two, well, Alexis had made sure the spacer assigned to accompany Slott didn't appear overly strong.

What Harben hadn't taken into account was that Alexis was *Star's* registered captain now — and there was not a lock aboard the ship, or its boats, which wouldn't yield to her.

"They may have some plan," Alexis told the others. "So restrain them quickly. Give them, especially the pilot, no chance to touch the controls."

"Aye, Captain," the men murmured.

Alexis rushed through the open airlock and directly to the cockpit hatch.

She keyed the hatch quickly and it slid open, but the way was still blocked.

They, Harben's two men, had opened the cabinets just inside the cockpit, blocking the middle of the hatchway — there was space near the floor and above the cabinet doors, but most of the hatch's opening was blocked.

They'd set something to keep the cabinet doors from being closed, as well, as the first shove at the blockage showed.

Alexis saw Harben's pilot, after a first, shocked glance at the hatchway, turn to the control board.

Slott reached across the board from his position, but the pilot shoved his hands away.

"Heave, lads!" Gilbertson called as they set their shoulders to the blockage.

Alexis dropped to hands and knees as the cabinet doors sagged inward against the weight of the bosun's men but didn't give way.

She scurried under the blockage into the tangle of legs that was now Harben's other man and the spacer she'd sent with Slott grappling in the narrow, constrained space of the cockpit.

A knee caught her in the side of the head, a foot stamped on her left hand, and a mass fell atop her back as one of the two, she couldn't tell which, gained the upper hand over the other.

"At 'em, lads!" Gilbertson called again.

There was a sharp crack as something broke under their efforts.

Alexis scrambled out from under whoever was atop her and clawed her way up the pilot's seat, and in some cases up Harben's pilot himself, as that fellow struggled with Slott.

She got hold of one of the man's arms and yanked it sharply behind both him and his seat, causing him to cry out, but he maintained his struggle with Slott, still trying to reach the boat's controls.

There were thuds and cries behind her as the bosun and his men subdued Harben's other man, but the cockpit itself was so tight a space and so crowded with bodies now that it was only Alexis and Slott who could reach the pilot.

Slott bent forward to use both his hands to restrain the pilot's remaining one, but the younger man was able to break free, shoving Slott away and reaching forward.

Alexis grasped the wrist she held and yanked upward with all her strength, bringing a cry, a *pop*, and finally a scream from the pilot as she brought his arm upward then grasped his elbow and pulled it away from his back with all her might.

The pilot cried out again, leaving off all thought of the boat's console, reaching behind him with his free hand and leaning forward to try and take the pressure off his other arm.

Slott leapt at him, grasping and restraining his free arm while placing his whole body between the pilot and the boat's controls.

It was then two of the bosun's men got their way cleared and reached past Alexis to grasp the pilot's upper arms and shoulders themselves, causing another cry of pain.

"Drag him out of here, lads," Alexis said, breathing heavily.

The spacers did, along with Harben's other man.

"Put them in the compartment we prepared," Alexis said, then sat in the boat's pilot seat to regain her breath.

With the ship so crowded, she'd not kept up with her conditioning, much less her martial arts training, aboard *Star*, and she was shocked at what a few weeks of missing such things did to her.

"About time we took our boat back," Slott murmured.

"Gentle with them," Alexis ordered as Gilbertson shook Harben's pilot roughly. "We've no particular quarrel with them."

"'No particular quarrel —'" Slott began.

"None," Alexis interrupted him. "The passengers' fears are real, and while I despise their tactics, there's been no real harm done."

Alexis went to the engineering space deep in *Star of Tauric's* aft hold.

The compartment was normally quiet and still with an engineer or two monitoring the ship's systems.

Now it was all a-bustle.

Every console was manned, and spacers hurried to and fro.

Long lines of heavily insulated cables were strung from the cold, dark, silent fusion plant that was the ship's heart through the empty companionways to the remaining two ship's boats.

The newly printed capacitors stood in a row, looking oddly out of place as they were smaller than the damaged ones which had once filled that space.

With nothing to do but watch until the time came to give the order, Alexis stepped to the side and simply waited.

Slott entered the compartment and made his way to her side.

"Begging your pardon, Captain," he said, "but what's to be done with those on the surface now we have control of our own boats again?"

"Nothing has changed there, Mister Slott," Alexis said.

"Nothing changed?" His face grew red. "But they ... that was mutiny, pure and simple. Coming aboard our boat? Forcing us to take their pilot aboard? Mutiny."

Alexis nodded. "No doubt."

"And you'll do nothing to them?"

"There are six hundred men, women, and children planetside, Mister Slott," Alexis said, keeping her eyes on the cables as they were attached to the plant. "None of them spacers and all of them frightened to be on a world like that — and all not knowing if we'd abandon them to save ourselves."

"But —"

"You may deem it mutiny — I prefer to call it a reasonable easing of their fears."

Slott shook his head. "Nothing reasonable about that Harben fellow."

"No?" Alexis chuckled. "I've found him quite reasonable — once one begins to understand him."

"I'd not allow that one back aboard ship," Slott said. "He'll be more trouble, just you mark my words."

"No doubt Mister Harben has his own plans, Mister Slott, but I don't think you'll be much disturbed by them."

Slott's brow furrowed. "You know what he's up to then?"

"I have my suspicions," Alexis said, then sighed. "I think he, and those who follow him, are being foolish and will come to regret it, but if I'm right, their plans present no danger to the ship, the crew, or the passengers not a part of his plans — given our circumstances, I'll wish them all the best of it, if I'm correct."

"And if you're not?"

Alexis glanced at Slott and then to the fusion plant where the engineers seemed nearly done with their work. "If Mister Harben's plans do present a danger to us, then I'll deal with him appropriately."

Slott snorted.

"Mister Slott," Alexis said, "you've had quite an ordeal, being stuck aboard the boat these last many weeks. Why don't you avail yourself of the privacy and comforts of the wardroom — before *Star* is so crowded with passengers again that we cannot have a bit of space to ourselves?"

Slott scowled and hurried off.

Alexis could understand his concerns — he'd been, effectively, a hostage aboard that boat for weeks on end, with little respite. He was surely angry at Harben and the passengers aligned with him for that.

Alexis, on the other hand, knew she'd need Harben's cooperation when she started bringing those passengers back aboard *Star*, and she had no wish to antagonize the man further.

As it was, if her suspicions about Harben's plan were correct, she'd have to do something with the man's son that would anger Slott, and all of *Star's* crew, even more.

The engineers had nearly made all the necessary connections, and she watched as they made the last of them. They all stood back to wait while the fusion plants on the two boats cycled up to full power as they charged the ship's new capacitors.

"Likely be an hour or more for full charge, Captain," the chief engineer told her, coming to stand by her side.

"Will it, Mister Armstrong?" Alexis asked, finding herself unable to take her eyes from the capacitors, despite their just sitting there.

"Aye," Armstrong said, staring at the capacitors as well.

"Time enough for a bit of luncheon in my cabin," Alexis said.

"Would be," Armstrong said.

"Would you join me?" Alexis asked. "Isom says there's a bit of mustard left in my stores."

Armstrong raised his eyebrows. "That'd be welcome. A bit of good mustard's just the thing to cover the taste of the vats," he agreed.

They stood for a bit in silence, eyes on the capacitors.

"We're not, either of us, likely to move from this spot for some time, are we?" Alexis asked.

Armstrong shook his head. "Seems unlikely, Captain."

Alexis sighed. She knew there was really nothing she could do to speed things along, nor to assist if something went wrong — Armstrong, at least, was in his element and might have something to do if things went wrong.

"I could have Isom bring our meal to us here," she suggested.

Armstrong nodded. "Could," he said. "A bit of mustard beef'd right hit the spot."

They stood for a bit in silence, eyes on the capacitors.

"I do find my stomach oddly a-dance, Mister Armstrong," Alexis said, finally.

"Aye, Captain, that's the way of engineering at times such as this."

Alexis nodded. "So, perhaps, *after* we've successfully lit the plant?"

Armstrong sighed. "Likely best, Captain," he said. "There's some things an empty stomach's best for, I've found."

"Very well, then."

They stood for a time in silence, eyes on the capacitors, until, finally, Armstrong took a deep breath.

"Ready for your order, Captain," he said.

"They're ready then?" Alexis asked.

Armstrong nodded to the monitors along the wall, which were partially blocked by his engineers who were all still and looking at Alexis. The compartment's hatch was crowded with bodies, as it seemed every spacer aboard *Star of Tauric* had gathered there to see into the space.

"They don't look any different," Alexis said.

"They're full," Armstrong assured her. "Our plant's ready to pull on them, all the boats' capacitors and their plants, plus the ship's and boats' batteries."

"And that'll be enough?"

Armstrong shrugged. "Calculations say yes, if barely."

Alexis considered that. Barely. Barely enough power available to light the plant, according to the original specifications and Armstrong's best guesses as to what decades of wear might have added.

"Very well," Alexis said. "The order's given."

Armstrong nodded to one of his men. "Light the plant."

The man nodded and tapped a console.

Everything went dark.

Chapter Forty-Four

"Will you have the last of the mustard, Mister Armstrong?" Alexis asked.

They were gathered about the table in Alexis' dining cabin — Armstrong, Gilbertson, Sams, and Slott — the closest things to officers she had aboard *Star*.

The lights shone brightly — in fact, the lights everywhere on the ship shone brightly, whether someone was in the compartment or not. It was as though the crew, after so long conserving power, felt the need, now the fusion plant was restarted, to use what they had with some profligacy.

"Wouldn't you like it, Captain?" Armstrong asked. "It is yours after all."

"This was Mister Theibaud's," Alexis said, "he left his stores behind when he sailed."

She paused a moment, offering up a silent prayer for Delaine. That he was overdue could simply mean that he'd been delayed, not that he'd met some fate she couldn't bear to think on.

Armstrong cleared his throat. "Thank you, Captain, I'll relish the last bit of that."

The engineer took the offered jar and scraped the last remnants from it onto his plate.

"That French lad's a good ship handler," Slott said into the continuing silence. "We'll likely find him coming for us on our own way to Zariah."

"No doubt," Gilbertson agreed.

"Yes," Alexis said, shaking herself out of her worries — she had no time for that.

"I must say," Slott said, "that sudden darkness had us all a bit on edge."

Gilbertson nodded.

"Aye," Armstrong said, "myself as well, though I'd admit it to few. *Star's* plant's so old it took a bit more than we thought to restart. Pulled all the batteries could give, as well, and none left for the rest of the ship. I'm only glad it was enough.

"What would have happened if it hadn't been?" Gilbertson asked.

Armstrong shrugged. "Depends on whether it was the reactor or the containment field that failed first. For the one we'd have been in the dark with nothing left in the batteries at all — not a pleasant outcome."

"And for the other?"

"It'd have got pretty light ... for a moment."

There was another pause as the group reflected on how very close they'd been to becoming part of that light.

"More wine?" Isom asked, breaking the silence. "I'm afraid it's the last of it, sir."

Alexis nodded. "Pour it out for us, Isom, and you've saved a bit for yourself, haven't you?"

Isom flushed. "Ah, yes, sir."

"Enjoy it in your own time, Isom," Alexis said. "We'll all be on vat beef, and small rations of that, for the journey to Zariah."

"There's still some canned and frozen stores," Sams said. "Not enough to divide amongst so many indentures, but enough for the crew and officers to enjoy with a few meals along the way."

Alexis shook her head. "I'm afraid I have plans for those, Mister Sams."

"Plans?"

"I'll enlighten you on the morrow, before we take the boats down to begin loading the passengers."

"What will you do about that Harben fellow?" Slott asked. "I'd not recommend bringing him back aboard ship."

"And his son," Gilbertson said. "No need to feed that one all the way back to Zariah. Hang him as soon as we're in *darkspace*, I say."

"I believe we'll find," Alexis assured them, "that neither Harben shall be much of our concern after tomorrow, gentlemen."

"Planning to hang them both together?" Gilbertson asked.

Alexis pursed her lips. She could well understand Gilbertson's — and Slott's, and the rest of the crew's — desire to see the Harbens hang. The younger one responsible for so many murders and the elder, in their eyes, a queer sort of mutineer who'd endangered them all with his demands.

"I believe I know what will happen with the Harbens on the morrow — I only ask that you trust my actions will be best for the ship, crew, and other passengers."

Gilbertson nodded, looking satisfied.

Alexis glanced around at the others — Slott and Sams had furrowed brows, while Armstrong appeared entirely disinterested in the fate of the Harbens, but all seemed satisfied to trust her decision.

She only hoped they would remain so when they found out what that was — and that she was right about the elder Harben's intent.

Alexis lay in her bunk, lights out and trying to sleep.

She could hear Isom in the dining cabin, just beyond the light bulkhead, quietly clearing away the last remains of dinner before making his way to the pantry and his own rest.

Despite her confident words to the sailing master and bosun, Alexis was not at all sure what the morrow would bring — nor was she certain of where her own duty lay.

She *was* certain that it was time for *Star* to leave this system — as certain as she was that Harben and his fellows would resist that.

But what must she do about Harben, his followers, and their intent?

If *Star* were a naval vessel and Alexis under commission, that would be clear — bring the crew back aboard, enforce discipline, and set sail. Yet Harben and the passengers were not crew, and *Star* was not under Admiralty command.

She'd come aboard as first mate, making it her duty to follow Captain Meiggs' orders. In his absence, that duty fell to preserving the ship for Meiggs' heirs, and, as *Star* was a commercial enterprise, that included preserving for those heirs the value of *Star's* ... cargo.

Alexis ground her teeth — despite the regulations, she couldn't bear to think of the passengers as simply cargo. They were *people* — no matter their crimes, which, when one got right down to it, were mostly of the venal sort. Were the passengers all cut from the same cloth as the younger Harben, she'd have no qualms at all — but many of *Star's* original complement weren't even the criminals themselves. They were the wives, children, sometimes husbands, of those transported for debt, a drunken brawl gone bad, theft, yes, but the sort to feed one's family, not enrich oneself.

Could she, in good conscience, use force against them?

Could she, in fact, use force at all?

Aye, there's the rub, isn't it? She thought.

Star's crew, even if she stripped the ship bare of men, numbered barely three dozen, and that only if she pressed even the engineers and Isom to the task.

The passengers numbered in the hundreds.

Sure, not all of them would stand with Harben — those who'd

voluntarily indentured themselves, come from *Almorah,* would eagerly reboard for the chance to continue on to their new lives, but *Star's* original complement was very different, wasn't it? True, not all of those, even, would stand with Harben and what she was certain was his rather mad scheme, but enough, she suspected, would — and he'd had time to convince many, hadn't he?

No, she was certain she wouldn't be able to get Harben and his fellows to board willingly — not without a show of force she didn't have at her disposal.

Or a use *of force I'm quite unwilling to undertake*, she told the dark silence of her cabin.

Her duty to the ship, Meiggs' heirs, *Star's* crew, and her passengers — *cargo* be damned — were all at odds.

Sighing and knowing she'd not sleep until she'd found her answer, Alexis rolled out of bed and made her way back to her dining cabin.

"Something else, sir?" Isom asked as she slid the hatch open.

He'd cleared the table, set the room to rights, and was certainly preparing to seek out his own bed, which made Alexis feel a bit guilty, but she needed a certain answer before morning.

Alexis set her tablet on the table and sat.

"I'm afraid I've need of your skills to research a thing or two, Isom."

"Of course, sir, I'll just retrieve my tablet and we'll get to it."

"Thank you, Isom."

"Not at all, sir."

"Oh, and Isom?" Alexis called as her clerk and steward turned to retrieve his tablet from her pantry.

"Sir?"

"You've a bit of mustard on your chin."

Chapter Forty-Five

The elder Harben was neither pleased, nor shy about showing it.

"What are you about, Carew?" he asked, scowling at the two boats landed in the middle of the field they'd been using.

Alexis had landed and exited her boat, making her way toward the passengers' encampment, Gilbertson and two of his men escorting Harben's pilot and other man behind her. Isom was with her, as well, stumbling a bit on the uneven terrain as he made some last-minute notes on his tablet.

When he'd seen the change in their routine of returning the boat which had been supporting the indentures, Harben stalked across the field to meet her, along with four others.

"It's time to load the passengers aboard *Star of Tauric*, Mister Harben," Alexis said, "and sail for Zariah." She turned her head. "Mister Gilbertson, release those two and return to the boats with your men while I have a word with Mister Harben, if you please."

"Captain —"

"I'll be fine, Mister Gilbertson. I'm just off to have a final chat with Mister Harben and whatever others have become the leaders of the passengers."

Harben narrowed his eyes. "Sail? You've started the fusion plant, then?"

Alexis nodded, starting to walk toward the crowd of indentures who'd come up from the makeshift settlement. She noted it was nearly all of them, responding to the change in what they surely thought should have been a single boat's return.

"You said you'd give us notice!" Harben scowled at her. "If it had failed — you've put us all at risk!"

Alexis continued walking.

"It's done, Mister Harben," she said, "and successfully. The ship is ready to sail. Since you have other plans, I thought it best to protect the interests of my crew and those who'll wish to return to Zariah with us." She raised her voice a bit — she'd not be able to reach all of the crowd, numbering in the hundreds, but suspected her words would be whispered amongst those nearest to those in the back. "I assume you will not be?"

"What —"

"That is your plan, Mister Harben, is it not? To remain here?"

"I — what do you mean?"

Alexis shook her head. "Come now, Mister Harben. It's a foolish plan, I think, but let's have it out in the open. I'll not stop you or any who wish to remain here, but I *will* see to it that any who wish to return to Zariah are able to board the ship."

There was a stirring and muttering in the crowd as her words were passed.

Harben's brow furrowed. "You'd let us stay?"

Alexis sighed. "I've not much choice unless I resort to violence to load you aboard ship against your will, and I'll not do that." She raised her voice more. "It's a foolish plan, as I said — this planet has any number of ways in which it wishes to kill you."

Harben nodded. "That's the way of it, then?" He raised his own voice. "I've read the reports. The toxins here'll take a few years off a full life — perhaps ten out of a hundred? Is that not a fair trade to breathe free, walk where you will, and not be sold about like cattle?"

"The toxins do more than that and you know it," Alexis said. "Your children —"

Harben cut her off. "Aye, the birth defects — but the report says these toxins of yours need time to build up. We'll have children young, many of them, and build from there."

"You've little in the way of supplies," Alexis said. "Nothing to alter the soil for terrestrial crops, no grains to plant, no animals to breed for work or food."

"We have some things we can plant," Harben said, "and this world has plants and animals we can eat. Yes," he hurried on before Alexis could speak, "there's not the nutrition those from home would bring. We may have to eat more of them to get what we need." He narrowed his eyes. "And we'd have had the vat aboard that boat if you'd not stolen it from us — it could've grown us beef from the native material here. Could've fed us well for years!"

There was an angry grumbling from some of the crowd, but Alexis merely smiled.

"I'll be leaving you the boat, Mister Harben," she said. "Both, in fact."

That stilled the muttering and left Harben speechless for a moment.

"We are not at odds, Mister Harben," Alexis said. "I think this is foolish of you and you'll likely regret the decision, but my duty lies with the safety and health of all who came here aboard *Star*, and those from *Almorah*, as well. I may not be able to see you safely back aboard if you refuse to come, but I'll do my utmost to see you safe here. Those who truly wish to stay."

Harben stared at her a moment. "That is ... unexpected."

Alexis smiled. "Given your chosen profession, Mister Harben, I'd have thought you better at reading a person's heart."

Harben nodded. "So had I."

Alexis raised her voice further. "*Star* sails when the last of you who wish to leave is aboard — please go, gather your belongings, and then form a queue to board the boats. It will be a long trip, with crowded conditions and little food, but I do swear I'll do my utmost to get you there." She sighed. "For those of you who wish to stay, I do wish you the best of luck."

"There's a thing you've forgot, Carew," Harben said quietly.

Alexis raised an eyebrow.

"My son," Harben said.

"He killed eight people aboard *Star of Tauric*, Mister Harben," Alexis said, "and attempted three more — not to speak of however many he killed back on your home of Norington."

"He's my son, Carew. I'll not let you hang him."

Alexis pursed her lips as though considering the matter, despite having already decided. She turned back to the waiting boats and waved.

Gilbertson exited the boat, his face visibly red and creased with anger.

Beside him, hands bound behind his back, walked the younger Harben.

"I'll not hang him, Mister Harben," Alexis said.

Harben watched his son and *Star's* bosun approach until the pair stood beside Alexis.

Gilbertson gave the younger Harben a sharp shove, sending him to stand beside his father.

The elder Harben's shoulders slumped. "Thank you," he said.

"No, I'll not hang him, though I expect you will," Alexis said louder.

"What —"

"Eight murders aboard ship," Alexis said loudly and nodded to Isom who tapped his tablet. "And untold others back on Norington. I've sent his confession to all here who have a tablet." She raised her voice further. "If you're staying, I understand the reason. Most of you aboard *Star* were transported for debt, or theft, or some other minor, petty crime — the most of you because you were poor, and that's a hard life, aye."

She shook her head.

"Some few of you were transported for violence, aye, even murder ... but a mistimed blow in a drunken brawl, even a killing in anger — well, it's naught compared to what this man's confessed to. And he'll do it again, here — he's a taste for it."

Alexis returned her gaze to the elder Harben, who was staring at her, mouth slack and face white.

"You who've chosen to stay — well, I can only assume it's to have the chance to build yourselves a life here. Build a world that's yours and hasn't ... what was it you said, Mister Harben? Sold you off like cattle? Part of building that world will be deciding what to do with the likes of Dain Harben here."

"Da?" the younger Harben asked, face puzzled.

"Shut up, boy," Harben said.

"But, Da —"

"I said be quiet, boy, and let me think." Harben took a deep breath, eyes closed, then glared at Alexis. "You're a hard woman, Carew."

"You've chosen a hard path here, Mister Harben." She shrugged. "I'd have taken care of things aboard *Star* once we sailed, but you demanded him."

"Aye," Harben shook his head and closed his eyes. "I'll be careful in what I ask for, if ever we deal again." He turned to the four men who'd initially accompanied him to meet Alexis. "Take him to my tent and keep him there." He sighed. "Don't untie him."

"Da?" Harben's son asked again as the men grasped his arms and pulled him away. "Da? What's happening? What's she mean? Da!"

Harben closed his eyes, face pained, but didn't turn to watch.

"I might still talk him free of this," Harben said after a time, though softly so only those nearest could hear.

"You might," Alexis agreed equally softly. "I'll not wish you luck with that."

Harben sighed. "If that's all, Carew, I think I'm done bargaining with you — it's not often a man gets all he asks for and can't find joy in it."

"One more thing, Mister Harben," Alexis said. "Well, two. For the first, when the boats return, they'll have the last of the frozen and canned stores aboard *Star*. We'll do well enough on the vats until we reach Zariah, and you'll get more use out of them. Perhaps some will have seeds that might sprout as well."

Harben raised his eyebrows. "That's unexpected, but we'll be grateful — and the second?"

"I had my clerk, Isom, do a bit of research and he found a thing you might have interest in. Isom?"

Isom stepped up beside Alexis, tablet raised.

"I've sent it to all your tablets, as well, Mister Harben," Isom said. "It's the Royal Charter of Planetary Survey Companies, if you see, and I'll draw your attention to Section Twelve — On Good Faith and Forfeiture."

Isom cleared his throat and began reading from his tablet.

"'Whereas, the interest of the Crown in this Charter is the settling and development of Worlds within the Realm," he read, "and, Whereas, the Companies may, to their Own Interests, rightly spend their Time and Monies toward the sale of those Worlds Most Profitable to Them, and, Whereas, this Interest lies in Direct Opposition to the Crown's, be it known that any System, Unsettled and Undeveloped for the term of Five Years after Registration in the Survey, shall be declared In Jeopardy.'"

Isom raised his eyes and looked at Harben.

"It's of note, Mister Harben, sir," Isom said, "that this world was first surveyed one hundred thirty-seven years ago — which is quite a bit more than the required five, and I'll then draw your attention to paragraph eighteen of the section twelve, sir, where it says, ah..."

Isom cleared his throat again.

"'Should a System, having been declared In Jeopardy due to a Chartered Company's failure to settle or develop said System, or failure to sell said System to any who do settle or develop it to the Benefit of the Crown, be thereafter settled or developed by any Group of persons, said group numbering One Hundred or more, in Opposition to the Chartered Company's desires and interests, said Group to maintain a Presence and Settle or Develop said World for a period of Seven Years and a Day...'"

Isom paused to lick his lips.

"'Said Group shall, upon registration of proof of their Presence, Settlement or Development, of said System for said Seven Years and a Day with any Royal Magistrate, shall, upon acceptance, be granted Sole and Exclusive Rights and Ownership of said System in Perpetuity, to the entire detriment of the Chartered Company's previously held Rights.'"

Isom took a breath.

"There's a bit more, sir, about the proper forms and such, but that's the gist."

Harben was staring at the clerk, open mouthed, and the nearby crowd, those who'd not gone off to gather their belongings and board the boats, were muttering excitedly.

"That means..." Harben trailed off.

"It does, Mister Harben," Alexis said.

"Seven years and a day," Harben whispered.

Alexis nodded. "Seven years and a day, Mister Harben, and this world is yours with no need to hide. A fully vested Crown Colony, to do with as you will. Your previous status of indenture will hold no weight since, as government of a sovereign world, you may release yourselves from it."

Harben's eyes glistened, then he frowned. "But if others come to settle..." He cocked his head. "They'll know we're here when you return to Zariah."

Alexis smiled. "This world's gone unsold for over a hundred years, I very much doubt it will find a buyer in the next seven."

Isom cleared his throat. "Seven years and a day, sir, if you don't mind me saying." He paused. "And there's some question of whether the clock'd start its ticking from the time we arrived or when the ship leaves."

"Indeed," Alexis agreed. "I'd start counting days from when *Star* makes transition to *darkspace*, Mister Harben — as that's when you'll truly be in full possession."

She took a deep breath.

"As for your other concern," she said, "I'd suggest you move your settlement from here to some other part of the planet — there is a rather lot of it for anyone searching to cover." She smiled. "But as for knowing you're here ... I have some thoughts on that and will ask you to trust me."

Chapter Forty-Six

"'Lost due to damage from storm and sabotage,'" Delaine read from his tablet.

Alexis laid her hand on his bare chest, her head already there, and snuggled closer.

They were in her cabin aboard *Star of Tauric*, and propriety be damned.

After she'd sailed for Zariah, four weeks out, they'd spotted the distant light of another ship's sails, shaped their course for it, and encountered their own rescue fleet — the remainder of their convoy, *Swallow* and *Belvedere*, along with two other Marchant ships brought in by the elder Hodgman.

Those ships had been in port at Zariah when Delaine arrived — late from an encounter with yet another, though thankfully milder, storm on his own journey.

Now *Star's* compartments and companionways fairly echoed with emptiness, the indentures from *Almorah* having been quickly transferred to the Marchant ships, leaving her with only the thirty or so of her original complement who'd chosen not to remain behind with Harben.

"You'll find I use that phrase quite often," Alexis murmured.

She closed her eyes and listened to Delaine's heartbeat.

After transferring the Marchant indentures off of *Star*, she'd been able to reclaim her full cabin, settling Lord Braithwaite in the wardroom with what space would have gone to *Star's* first and second mates combined.

With the end of their voyage in sight — and spurred by no little relief at finding Delaine still lived — she'd voided her own rule about sharing the cabin with him.

If the crew balked at all about it, well they could just bugger off for all she cared. She was captain of *Star* for the few more weeks of their travel to Zariah and if she chose to make it a "family ship" then she would.

"So, I see," Delaine said. "Do you truly think, with so many others returning, that this report will do what you wish?"

Alexis nodded, liking the feel of her cheek rubbing against his chest.

"I believe so," she said. "I report that the missing passengers from *Star* and the ship's boats were all lost to damage from the storm and sabotage. This is nothing but the truth — without those two things, we'd not have been separated from the convoy and we'd have reached Zariah without incident. Everything after stems from the storm."

She sighed.

"The magistrate on Zariah will be most interested in the murders and sabotage, but with Dain Harben's confession and him also being lost — for those same reasons — I doubt the courts will wish to pursue the matter further.

"As for those returning with us, the Marchant passengers will likely never set foot on Zariah — I foresee the elder Captain Hodgman sailing immediately, with *Swallow* in tow, perhaps not even transitioning out of *darkspace*.

"With Captain Meiggs gone, *Star's* crew will seek other berths as soon as they may, as the ship will almost certainly be put up for sale. *Star's* passengers will have their indentures sold as quick as may be, as well, though my forgiveness of their prior debt should make their next lives a bit easier. In either case, the Zariahn officials won't wish them to stay overlong, having been transported once already."

She shrugged.

"I doubt the magistrate will even seek to question any of them and by the time *Star's* insurance company might look into things, all whom they might question will be long gone and virtually unreachable."

Delaine frowned.

"It is not, I think, the whole truth," he said.

Alexis shrugged again. "If I commanded *Star* under a naval commission, I'd agree — that would present a higher duty. As it is, my duty is to the ship, the crew, the passengers, and, with Captain Meiggs' passing, his heirs. I think this solution best protects the interests of all."

She frowned.

"Perhaps the company insuring *Star's* passengers would disagree — they'll have to pay Captain Meiggs' heirs for those 'lost' — but what else would I do? Force the passengers who didn't wish to board *Star*? The crew was outnumbered by them nearly forty-fold — any force would result in deaths on both sides. Isom did some calculations on Meiggs' policy, and it would only take a few of those deaths to cost them more than simply paying for those 'lost' passengers."

Delaine chuckled.

"You have been thorough, *ma petite*," he said.

"I've tried. Now I can only hope." She snuggled closer and closed her eyes. "With luck, now, we might take passenger carriage to New London, be done with this bloody knighthood business, and return home as quickly as may be."

Chapter Forty-Seven

Things went much as Alexis predicted for their arrival on Zariah. The Marchant ships, along with *Swallow*, didn't even bother to transition to normal space, they simply waited until *Star* had done so and went on their way. The Zariahn officials wasted no time at all in placing *Star's* remaining passengers into waiting for the next indenture convoy, scheduled to arrive in less than a fortnight. As for the long list of murders attributed to Dain Harben, the Zariahn magistrates informed Alexis that, there being no one to prosecute at this time, the matter would be taken up in some months when they had time.

Captain Meiggs' agent took charge of *Star of Tauric*, as well as the filing of insurance claims — something Alexis expected to only happen once she was well away from Zariah.

Lord Braithwaite, nearly in tears at the sight of a departures board filled with passenger ships, booked them passage on a line leaving in a week's time and traveling almost directly for New London, leaving Alexis time to deal with another matter.

The Zariahn Prize Court's offices, at least on the outside, were as disappointingly bland as Alexis remembered them.

Set three levels up from the quay on the system's main station, there were frosted glass panels set to conceal the open vacuum hatch, with a small door etched with the Royal Seal and simply the words "Prize Court."

Alexis sighed and straightened her shoulders, glancing at those with her as she gathered her thoughts.

Delaine, Isom, and, oddly, Lord Braithwaite had all chosen to accompany her.

She had the ready coin to simply pay what the prize court was demanding and she did not, when one came down to it, begrudge its redistribution to the crew of *Merlin* — that, after all, had been what she'd wished to do when the court had made its original mistake in awarding her and her small prize crew the full value of the pirate ship *Grapple.*

It was only the overbearing tone of the court's demand that grated on her.

Oh, paying out that much coin would sting a bit, but she'd received far more than that in prize money since. Even with her expenditures and investments, and she'd gone over those in detail with Isom before deciding to simply pay what the court wished, including what they sought to recover from the other members of her prize crew, and be done with it.

Most of her funds were still invested back on Dalthus in the form of either reinvestment in her families' lands or put out as loans to those she'd brought there — the families of *Hermione's* crew who'd come to settle there, those of her boat crew who'd brought their families or started new ones and wished to start a bit of a business on the side, and — to her surprise, though Isom assured her she'd approved it, a rather profitable venture into the system's gallenium mines.

Much had been spent on getting those families to Dalthus at all, as she'd not wished them to make a fresh start as indentures and had paid their passage herself — including, most recently, the Islikis — and shipping Nabb and her boat crew back and forth from her commissions so as not to lose any of them.

There'd be some belt tightening after this, for, as her investments might be profitable, they weren't very liquid, and the prize court would be taking nearly three-quarters of her ready coin — though, that she did have, in ready coin, the prize value of an entire ship gave her some pause.

She'd not considered before that she'd become quite wealthy by many standards. While she knew her family was one of the wealthiest on Dalthus, that was in lands, which were very different than coin. One couldn't very well pop into the chandlery and exchange a bag of dirt for ... well, anything, really. The lands were wealth in the future, not the now.

"You may still choose to fight them, *ma petite*," Delaine said, laying a hand on her arm.

"I say fight," Isom said. "I've a list of proper barristers who'll relish a row with the prize court."

Alexis shook her head. "No, it's only their demands on the other members of *Merlin's* crew that angered me — to tell the truth, I feel I should have sent the *Merlins* all their proper share long ago. They were so kind to me, and doubly-so when the prize court made this mistake — I have so much now that it's only right."

She turned to Lord Braithwaite.

"Are you certain you wouldn't prefer to wait at our lodgings, my lord?" she asked. "This is only a bit of an errand."

Braithwaite shook his head. "No, I think not. I have but the one task at the moment, that being to see you safely to New London and through your investiture — having very nearly lost you once, I feel it's best to keep you within arm's reach for the duration." He nodded at the doorway. "Perhaps my presence might even help with the court here."

Alexis took a deep breath and squared her shoulders again before entering.

Inside was more banality.

A medium sized waiting room with benches occupied by two

ship's captains and a few spacers. At the far side was a reception desk occupied by a woman and flanked by two armed guards.

Alexis didn't recall the guards being there on previous visits, but given the near-universal hatred spacers had for the prize courts, she could understand their presence.

The queuing area was empty, so Alexis moved to the reception desk, the others following along behind her.

The receptionist looked up, then looked down at her desk again.

Alexis waited.

The receptionist glanced up and Alexis tried to make eye contact, but the woman bent over her desk again.

"Ahem," Alexis said.

"A moment," the receptionist said, not looking up.

"Ma'am?" Alexis said after another pause. "I've only to speak to a Mister Edric Bramley and —"

"*Sshh!*" the receptionist said without looking up.

Lord Braithwaite stepped forward. "Madam, perhaps if you —"

The receptionist's finger pointed at him. "*Ssshhtt!*"

She looked up and glared at Braithwaite.

"Do you not understand *ssshhtt*?" she asked. "Do any of you understand —"

Her eyes widened as she looked at Alexis.

She glanced at her desktop screen, eyes widening further, then back to Alexis and her face paled.

The receptionist's pointed finger moved from Braithwaite to Alexis.

"*It's her!*" she screamed. "*Her!* She's one of *them!*"

Chapter Forty-Eight

"What —" Alexis asked, bewildered by the receptionist's screaming, but the two guards were already moving.

Each had one hand on the butt of their sidearm and the other outstretched toward Alexis' group, while they moved forward.

"You!" one ordered. "All of you! Out of the offices immediately!"

Alexis blinked.

"If you'd only tell Mister Bramley that I've come to settle things," Alexis said. "I've brought a great deal of coin and —"

"*She's going to do it!*" the receptionist screamed, rising from her desk and fleeing through the door into the inner offices.

"What in the Dark is she —" Alexis began.

"*Out!* The lot of you!" the guards said, advancing in unison.

Lord Braithwaite let out a heavy sigh and looked at Alexis.

"Whatever is it about you that has this effect on people?" he asked her.

"I assure you I have no idea what this is all about, my lord," she said.

Braithwaite shook his head. "Well, we simply haven't the time for this nonsense."

He turned to the guards.

"Now, see here, gentlemen," he said, stepping toward them. "I am — *urk!*"

One of the guards drew a baton, shoved it into Braithwaite's gut, and pressed a stud on the handle.

Braithwaite's body jerked and he fell to the deck.

"Sweet Dark," Alexis whispered after the silence that followed. "Is he..."

Braithwaite groaned, but didn't open his eyes.

Alexis breathed a sigh of relief.

"Right," the guard who'd stunned Braithwaite said, "now you lot —"

"Do — do you have any idea who that is?" Alexis interrupted him.

"He's the bugger what the rest of you lot're gonna drag on out after you," the guard said.

"No, you fool," Alexis said, "he's a Queen's Herald!"

Silence filled the prize court waiting room.

"I'll, uh, reschedule my appointment for another time, shall I?" one of the waiting captains said, hurrying toward the exit.

He was closely followed by the rest of those waiting.

"Really?" one of the guards asked.

"*Oui,*" Delaine said.

"A Queen's Herald," Isom said, "and a bloody Lord from New London itself, he is."

The two guards shared a look.

Alexis knelt. "M'lord, are you all right?"

Braithwaite shuddered, but managed to speak — albeit with a bit of drooling. "Cah ... fer ... magistrape..."

The guards shared another look. Queen's Herald or not, muffled by a slack-jawed mouth full of drool or not, those they could legitimately stun did not generally, upon recovery, call for a magistrate themselves — quite the opposite in fact.

"Bugger it," the guard who'd stunned Braithwaite muttered and dashed from the room, quickly followed by his partner.

"Schtop ... t'ose ... meh..." Braithwaite muttered raising a weaving arm to point.

"I'm sure we can find them, m'lord," Alexis told him, grasping his upper arm as he tried to rise. "But first let's get you off the floor and into a chair?"

Braithwaite nodded, flinging drool about. "Schtit," he said.

"Do you need the head, m'lord?" Isom asked. "I've heard a stunning often —"

Braithwaite shook his head, flinging streams of drool. "*Schtit!*" he said, pointing, somewhat, at a chair.

"Sorry, m'lord," Isom said, grasping his other arm and helping Alexis to pull him from the floor. "It's only that a stunning sometimes has ... effects. Didn't want no embarrassments."

"Schtit," Braithwaite muttered as they eased him into a chair.

"Exactly, m'lord," Isom said.

Alexis released Braithwaite's arm as he sat, and she crouched in front of him.

"Are you feeling better, m'lord?" she asked. "A stunning lasts only a few minutes — would you like some water?"

Braithwaite nodded. "Ahter. Ink ahter."

"Isom," Alexis said, "would you see if there's any water about for Lord Braithwaite?"

"Aye, sir."

Alexis set Braithwaite's forearms firmly on the chair's arms. "Now, m'lord, if you'll just sit still for a few minutes, you'll feel quite a bit better. Just give the stunner's effects a bit of time to wear off."

"*Schtit,*" Braithwaite agreed.

"And perhaps not attempt to speak, m'lord," Alexis added. "There's already a great deal of liquid about."

Braithwaite's head lolled forward.

"*Out!*" a voice called, and Alexis turned to see Isom returning to the reception area backwards from the inner office. He stumbled a bit on the threshold, then turned and hurried back to Alexis.

"No water to be had in there, sir," he muttered.

"*Get them out!*" the voice called, louder, and the doorway was filled with a presence Alexis remembered well from her time aboard the revenue cutter *Nightingale.*

Alexis remembered Edric Bramley, prize court agent, as fat and florid, with little hair and narrow, hooded eyes. If her memory had elaborated on the man's poorer qualities over the years — well, his body had kept apace with her memory and he looked exactly as she expected.

"*Get* —" Bramley's gaze took in the nearly empty reception area. "Where are my guards?"

"Run like rabbits after they stunned a Queen's Herald," Isom said.

"A what?" Bramley asked, then his eyes settled on Alexis. "*You!* Get —"

Alexis had had enough. She'd come to the prize court offices simply to pay Bramley off and save those she cared for from further troubles. Such a simple errand to be met with such screaming, threats, and violence, even to the reduction of Lord Braithwaite to ... well, his current state. Then shutting their offices to them and demanding they leave? No, she'd not have it — this would be settled today.

"*Belay that this instant!*" she bellowed, standing and advancing on Bramley. "*You* took action against me, sir! *You* demanded coin!"

Bramley's face went pale, and he took a step back as Alexis continued.

"Your guards are not here — whatever their purpose might have been — and you've only me to deal with, so if it's coin you want, sir, then you'll bloody well open up, take what I have to give you, and let me be on my way!"

Alexis' brow furrowed.

While she'd been speaking, Bramley's face had gone dead white, he'd lowered his pointing hands, grasped his own buttocks, and backed himself against the frosted glass enclosing the offices.

Alexis frowned – it was not, in her experience, the norm for others to hide their buttocks when she spoke to them.

"Are you unwell, Mister Bramley?" she asked. "I mean, I do believe there are a great many things quite wrong with you, but are you *particularly* unwell in this specific instance?"

Bramley clenched his eyes shut.

"Please ... not the coin," he whispered.

Chapter Forty-Nine

"I do not understand spacers," Bramley muttered. "They complain when we don't award them coin —" He winced at the word and his hands darted toward his buttocks. "— and then we offer it to them..."

Bramley swiped at his tablet and a monitor at the room's end lit up.

It had taken some time, and a recovered Lord Braithwaite, to assure Bramley that whatever he so feared was not what Alexis intended. That brought them to a conference room where Bramley said, he hoped, to explain and settle the matter.

"I don't know what ... what *witchery* you practice, Carew," Bramley muttered, "but what sane man has ever responded to an offer of payment with *that?*"

Alexis read the response on the screen, presumably to the prize court's notice of their action on the *Grapple* award.

"Well, yes," she said, "but —"

"And then *this*," Bramley said, swiping.

"Oh, dear," Alexis murmured.

"And *this!*"

"Well," Alexis said, seeing who the message was from, an older *Merlin* who'd taken delight in regaling others with decades of curses learned in a hundred foreign ports. "I do remember him as being rather coarse."

"To a man," Bramley said, "they refused *money*." His finger trembled as he swiped his tablet. "And then, after they'd thought things over, it seems, they started sending these..."

Alexis read.

"Oh, my," Isom said.

"What does that say?" Lord Braithwaite asked. "My vision still isn't quite ... 'If you send me a single shilling you' ... what's that?"

"'Arse-faced, bollox-swallowing, banker's son,' m'lord," Isom said.

"Ah."

Isom whispered to Delaine. "Do like how he makes the banker-bit seem like the worst, building up to it and all."

Alexis cleared her throat while Braithwaite squinted at the screen.

"'A single shilling', ahem, etc. 'I'll fly to Zariah, change them all to farthings, and ...'," Braithwaite sat back in his chair, frowning. "I can see where that might be quite uncomfortable."

"They're all the same!" Bramley said, trembling. "From all over, from multiple ships they're on! It's a coordinated attack, I tell you!" He pointed at Alexis. "And all your doing, I've no doubt!"

Alexis sighed. "It's not anything coordinated, Mister Bramley, they're spacers. They threaten to shove ... all manner of things ... well, there, when they're angry at someone."

"It's a threat!" Bramley insisted. "It's why we had the guards!" He closed his eyes. "Do you have any idea how many farthings there are to the pound?"

Chapter Fifty

Alexis and Delaine took a final look around their room — Isom had already packed and made his own inspection to ensure they'd left nothing behind, but she liked to assure herself as well.

They went downstairs to find the others — Lord Braithwaite, his valet, and Isom — already waiting, luggage piled atop a rented anti-grav cart.

"Ah, excellent," Braithwaite said as they exited the lift. "Come along, then."

Alexis sighed. She expected she'd be listening to the Queen's Herald tell her "Come along, then," for the entirety of their trip to New London. It would almost certainly be, "Come along to dinner, then," and "Come along to tea, then," and "Come along so I might impart some new tidbit of utterly useless propriety to you, then."

"We've hours before the ship sails, m'lord," she said. "No need to hurry so."

"Of course," Braithwaite said, "but the sooner aboard, the sooner I might stop worrying about what you've got yourself into next."

Alexis sighed. "Very well, lead on."

The others started away, but Alexis paused.

Braithwaite had taken only a step or two before turning to watch her. "Lieutenant?" he said, quite a bit more slowly and carefully than she felt warranted.

"I ... I feel I've forgot something," Alexis said.

"No, no," Braithwaite said. "Your man assured me it's all packed. Every bit. Assured me twice, in fact, and I've come to believe he's quite a reliable fellow."

"It's only —"

"Lieutenant."

Alexis looked around the hotel's lobby, eyes landing on the concierge desk. She smiled, then held her hands up, palms toward Braithwaite.

"I've only one simple errand to complete," she said, starting for the desk.

"No!" Braithwaite cried. "No more errands. You've left ample funds on deposit with the prize court so that your fellows will owe nothing, regardless of the final decision. Our ship leaves today, and I will see you on it."

"A moment," Alexis assured him. "I'll be done before our luggage can make it through the door, I assure you."

Braithwaite sighed. "Very well," he said and started after her.

"I'll only be just there," she said, pointing. "Well within sight, m'lord, I assure you."

Braithwaite took a deep breath. "Very well," he said, but made no move to follow her again.

Alexis moved off, then stopped again. "You two, neither," she snapped at Delaine and Isom who'd both moved to follow her. "It's not a dozen strides, and I'll return straightaway."

"Well, sir —"

"But, *ma* —"

"*Stay!*" she said as they both spoke. "Gentlemen! I do not, I assure you, cause some sort of trouble whenever I am left unsupervised. I am quite capable of completing a simple, innocent errand without your presence."

Eyes narrowed in warning, she backed away, then turned and made her way to the desk.

"Yes, mum?" the concierge said. "May I help you?"

"Have you an envelope?" Alexis asked. "And something to write with?"

"Of course, mum."

The requested items were produced, and Alexis scribbled a note on the envelope — then she fished in her pocket and withdrew what coin she had on her. She placed two shillings on the counter to cover the tip to have her note delivered, then slid a third coin across to the concierge.

"Do you suppose you might change this for me?" she asked.

The concierge raised an eyebrow. "Change for tuppence, mum?"

Alexis nodded, reading what she'd written.

To: The Zariahn Prize Court
Into the hands of Edric Bramley

"Indeed," she said, "in farthings, if you please."

Author's Note

Back in the late 80s and early 90s — which, by the way, was ten years ago, not thirty, and I'm sticking to that — some friends and I would go to the Walt Disney World resorts to see a singer/songwriter who performed there, named John Charles — first at the Tambu Lounge in the Polynesian Resort and then aboard the Empress Lilly, a steamboat at the then Disney Village (which later became Downtown Disney). He did fantastic covers, but I always liked his original works best, and played one of his songs, *Forever in this Moment*, for the dance with my daughter at her wedding.

We nagged him for *years* to release an album of his original songs — this was in the time of the CD, so it wasn't as easy to release music as it is today — and when he finally did, he titled the album *This Took Forever!*

This story, of course, has absolutely nothing to do with the release of this book.

Yeah.

I'm going to address the multi-year hiatus between *The Queen's Pardon* and *A Brief, Interminable Peace*. I've done so before, on both my blog at darkspace.press and on Patreon, and I'm doing so again here for two reasons: 1) as readers who've waited forever for the next bit of Alexis' story, you deserve to know; and, B) ... I went through some stuff. It wasn't the worst stuff someone could go through, not by any means, but it happened and, aside from explaining to long-time readers of the series, I also hope that if there's one person out there reading this who's experiencing the same sort of thing and resisting getting help — dude, go get some bloody help.

So in 2020 the pandemic hit, and my employer went to remote work. That aspect I was excited about — with no commute to eat up time and wear me down, I thought the writing I'd been doing consistently since 2013 would ramp up. I fully expected to end 2020 with Carew 7 released, the first in my Dark Frontiers series released, possibly the next in the Dark Artifice series I publish as Richard Grantham, and a decent start on Carew 8. This was all achievable at the rate I'd been writing, with some additional from the extra time.

And nothing happened.

The writing shut off like someone had flipped a switch, as did a lot of other things in my life. As time progressed, even when we came out of lockdown, I found myself having less and less energy and enthusiasm about ... anything.

People started telling me I was depressed — but that couldn't be, could it? I looked around at my life — I had a good job I mostly enjoyed at the time, a wonderful wife whom I love dearly, my parents were healthy and doing well, my daughter was happily married to a great guy and I got both a dude I like a lot and a grandbaby out of the deal, and I was a moderately successful author with a growing audience. There was literally nothing in my life that gave me any right whatsoever to be depressed.

Apparently, that's not how it works.

Things started getting really bad the summer of 2022 when my day job got much, much worse. No details, but in the course of six months, they utterly destroyed any sense of loyalty or enthusiasm I had for the work I'd been doing for them for twenty-five years. It had always been a dysfunctional sort of place, but they quickly went full-Simple Jack.

Summer 2022 to summer 2023 things continued to get much worse until I finally agreed to see someone about it in October 2023 — at the urging of my wife, daughter, and best friend, all of whom saw that there was something wrong.

I went on the drugs. I didn't want to go on the drugs, but I was being an asshole to my wife, who is the kindest, gentlest person I've ever met. Seriously, if we find an ant in the car, I have to pull over and find it a good home.

And the switch got flipped back.

Within a couple weeks, I felt better, I acted better, and I started writing again. A lot. Not Carew, but I was at least writing.

That lasted until January 2024, when things started to trail off and get bad again, so we upped my meds (to the typical dosage, as I'd started as low as possible), but I couldn't get Carew going and even the other writing stayed trailed off.

Now, back in 2023, three doctors — medical, psychiatrist, and therapist — all identified the work nonsense that started in 2022 as a proximate cause for how bad things had gotten, and told me I needed to take a leave of absence if I wanted to truly get back to being myself.

I'm stubborn and didn't want to do that, because I'm also a bit of an idiot.

So, I went to my employer and told them that my doctors recommended a leave of absence, but I didn't think that would benefit anyone, and instead requested an ADA accommodation instead. They denied that with the reason of "you're too important to the company to allow for that accommodation."

Dude ... I said there's Option A and Option B and you said Option B ain't happening, so where do you think we're going from here?

I tried to make it work, but things stayed ridiculous and in August 2024 I put in for short-term leave.

I felt so much better. Not because I wasn't working — I was working. I put more hours in writing (writing, editing, plotting, etc.) than I ever had at the day job. I had to force myself to take a 'day off' from the writing now and then, with the largest streak being writing on nineteen consecutive days, and one day writing twelve thousand words.

So, the moral of this story is: A) If the people in your life are telling you there's something wrong and you need help, believe them; and, 2) if there's something unbearably toxic in your life, find a way to get rid of it.

And that's what it took for me to finish this damn book and get a good handle on what will become Carew 8.

In addition, I wrote and released a new book — a different pen name and a very different genre, which I will not share here, because it has some spicy-times scenes and I'm a bit embarrassed over it, but what it did do was meet with commercial success. Between that and Carew, having two successful series, I decided to quit the day-job and become a full-time writer.

My wife, during that time, was incredibly supportive of the decision. She worked so hard on editing and designing covers to ensure we would be successful — and it is a 'we,' I owe much of the success of that other book to her cover and editing, in addition to her support.

I owe much of the fact that I'm still writing at all to the Patreon supporters who stuck with me for *years* without a new release and with very little in the way of my posting on Patreon. I cannot count the number of "are you dead?" messages I received there, but still they kept their pledges going and the knowledge of their support kept me at least *trying* to write when I could very easily have just given up at it.

And a very special 'thank you' to the couple who, when the original preorder of this book was canceled in October 2023, actually tracked down my phone number to call and ask if I was okay ... I call that 'creepily sweet' in only the most positive ways. That memory is truly something I'll treasure the rest of my days.

J.A. Sutherland
Orlando, FL
October 17, 2024

www.ingramcontent.com/pod-product-compliance
Lightning Source LLC
Chambersburg PA
CBHW020257030826
48979CB00026B/1378/J

* 9 7 8 1 9 4 8 5 0 0 6 4 7 *